REPLACED
Replaced
Book 1

NOLON KING
LAUREN STREET

STERLING & STONE

Chapter One

TRAFFIC WAS the nightmare of modern life, and living in New York for her entire life, Jessica was plenty used to it. The difference right now was that she felt trapped behind the wheel, frozen in time and reminded of her mortality.

Jessica kept wanting to punch the steering wheel, not that it would accomplish anything. Even while gridlocked, the line of glowing brake lights laid out before her like an endless stream of lava. With the hours growing more stagnant than the traffic itself, she understood that the hell of this trip in a U-Haul had little to do with all the vehicles in her way.

She and David had picked a terrible time to move states. The traffic leaving NYC had been bad, cars moving at the speed of blood through clogged arteries. And then, as she left the iconic skyline behind her, she was presented with a different challenge, thanks to the convoluted maze of cars weaving through highways that curved and coiled like a slumbering dragon through Pennsylvania. Then she'd hit an angry storm in Ohio and legitimately feared for her life. A raging tempest with gnarled black clouds swirling high overhead. Lightning slashed the sky and rain pelted the U-Haul in sheets, the thunder like rolling drums while a violent wind whipped the rain sideways as it battered the vehicle.

Or had that been Indiana?

Thinking about it now, Jessica wasn't sure. But she could still feel the gripping fear from endless buckets of rain splashing onto her windshield. She couldn't even see a foot in front of her.

It was definitely in Indiana where the roads had flooded. She remembered the mile marker, leaning lazily to the side as she inched by it, twenty miles past the state border, where traffic slowed to a belligerent crawl.

For too many miles now, Jessica had not even been able to see an exit. So she stayed in line, slowly drifting forward with the rest of the traffic, adding hours to the trip while waiting for the next time she could call home.

The rented U-Haul was painted a dull white, with thick metal sides and a low roof. Small, tinted windows and oversized tires made the vehicle a beast to maneuver on even the clearest road, and the conditions on her trip across the states had been terrible. Jessica had been hoping to make the journey in two days, but she was now still too far from Dallas on day number three.

She hoped this trek wasn't some kind of omen of days to come.

She shrugged off that thought. Anxiety was a killer.

Time kept ticking while she steered herself away from glances at the clock.

She got snagged in another ugly snarl of traffic and eased her foot off of the gas as the vehicle in front of her came to a stop. Then she looked up at the rearview mirror instead of over at the clock to check the time. It had only been five minutes since she'd last checked.

The driver of the U-Haul behind her honked his horn, acting like the asshole he had been ever since the grid-locked had started and he found himself trapped behind her.

Jessica barely recognized her reflection. Her eyes were fatigued from relentless hours of concentration. Her hair was a tangled mess. Did she even brush it this morning?

She looked back at the road, then finally lost her battle of resistance just seconds later with a glance at the dashboard as the time flickered to 11:57 a.m.

Only ten minutes past the last time she looked, and still three minutes away from the noon that Jessica swore it had to be.

Thirty-three minutes until she could call David again.

At least she was (finally, and only ever so slightly) ahead of the new schedule that had been forced upon her after a bleary-eyed departure at four in the morning.

David had argued strongly against Jessica hitting the road so early, his voice coated with a thick mix of concern and frustration.

"I don't care how much time we've lost so far! You need sleep. And it isn't worth risking your well-being just to save a few hours. Gwen will still be here, no matter what time you arrive."

But the desperation in her heart conquered any argument he might have for her safety. She needed to see David. He was her rock. And she needed to hold Gwen again.

Gwen was far too new to be this far away from her mommy. The adoption agency had said next month. Then the timeline shifted. To the week of their move. They already had the plans in place, and neither of them was going to suggest a delay. Not after they had waited so long for their baby to get here.

Seeing Gwen and David is what drove her to rise before the sun while the world around her was still swathed in darkness. Coffee in her system, her foot on the gas pedal, heading west.

She kept one hand on the worn steering wheel as the other reached out for her phone, needing to hear David's soothing baritone and Gwen's innocent cooing. That would be enough to settle her emotions for the last leg of the trip.

It was all her fault it had played out like this. Jessica was only alone on the road because that was exactly where she had decided to be. Against all logic, she had volunteered to navigate the interstate with all of their worldly possessions. Not that a small apartment in New York had the space to hold much. The cargo was light — a collection of boxes filled with fragments of her and David's shared lives. Or at least what little they had to show for it.

David was almost monastically minimalist, and she loved it. He was the only person she had ever been with who cared enough to leave their shared living space consistently uncluttered. Her boxes were full of sentimentality. Old photos, favorite books (even though she only read on her phone or tablet these days), and the occasional knick-knacks that she simply could not bear to part with.

David was more than ready to brave the trip and navigate the U-Haul through whatever terrain and weather might come their way, but her stubborn fear of flying had landed them on the runway of this predicament. She almost changed her mind when Gwen arrived, but David wasn't able to transfer his ticket and the flight was sold out. She told him she didn't mind keeping their plans the same, even though she would miss a few days with Gwen.

Turns out, Jessica minded more than she thought.

And because Gwen was barely a week old, Jessica

couldn't fathom strapping her fragile little body into a car seat and subjecting her to the unpredictable tribulations of the three-day journey.

And thank God she hadn't. Trying to navigate this traffic with a wee baby? She couldn't imagine it. But still, the painful choice to send her daughter ahead had left a mommy-shaped void in Gwen's life that Jessica was now racing to fill.

Despite the traffic jams and intermittent storms outside the vehicle, there was a certain tranquility to the solitary journey. Amid the hum of the engine and the endless stretches of road, she found pockets of solitude that were perfect for introspection. Which was a rare element in the dizzying busyness of her everyday life.

Doubts were like annoying backseat drivers, lodging themselves in the nooks of Jessica's mind. Questions about motherhood and her ability to be a good parent (though great would be better) gnawed at her insides with a relentless persistence.

Fear of turning into her own mother hung above her like an ominous cloud.

It was absurd to keep thinking that an infant wouldn't like her, but Jessica was born and raised to fear and expect rejection.

Memories danced like dust motes in sunlight as she followed the vehicle in front of her.

From the moment the phone call came letting her and David know Gwen was on her way, Jessica vowed that things would be different than they had been with her own mother. She repeated that mantra from New York to Texas, unblinking in her resolve not to repeat the icy cold woman's mistakes.

Come hell or high water, she would shower Gwen with

the nurturing warmth that Jessica had craved for all of her life.

The promise of therapy was yet another anchor she couldn't wait to experience. The thought of unpacking her personal baggage to dissect the shadows of her past, and disarming those triggers that could potentially impact her relationship with Gwen, was as daunting as it was an undeniable comfort.

"You can have therapy five days a week if you want!" David had said with a big grin as they planned their reboot in Dallas. She'd laughed. Not that Jessica wanted five days a week. One would be plenty, and more than she had ever had before.

The sign for the I-30 was a needed reminder that her long drive was almost over. Six more hours, and then she would finally be in her new home.

Jessica smiled as the time clicked over to 12:29. One minute to go. Their calls never lasted long, but it was to stay connected. And Jessica always had plenty of things to say on account of all those minutes to kill. This time she wanted him to know that she was still wearing his old Coldplay shirt, even though it had been three days. She needed the smell of him.

She held the phone in her right hand, finger tracing over the entry marked *Whiskerface*, smiling as she remembered their silly little argument about shaving that had led to the nickname (David hated scraping that razor down his cheeks, but Jessica loved the feel of his freshly smooth skin). He changed the contact name on her phone as a joke, but Jessica had liked the new one so much that she never changed it back.

They checked in with each other once every hour. That was his way of making sure that she was doing okay while crossing the country to meet him.

He answered on the first ring.

Jessica heard Gwen's gurgling coo in the background, barely even a sound. Maybe she imagined it? But it was still loud enough to soften the harsh road beneath her.

"Hey there," David said.

"Is something wrong with the phone? I can barely hear you."

"Sorry…" He was only slightly louder, most of the noise in their call coming from the sound of him moving around and jostling the phone in his hand.

"Is everything okay?"

"Of course. Sorry, just distracted. I'm about to put Gwen down for a nap." Gwen now sounded further away than ever. "You just surprised me when you called."

"I call every hour … we agreed."

"Yeah, I didn't realize the time. Because of your early start this morning."

Jessica heard another voice. Softer and coming from the background. It was a woman's voice, and it flooded her system with illogical panic.

Then she heard the sound of canned laughter from the TV. A feeling of relief washed over her.

"Can I talk to her?" Jessica asked.

"Sure thing … here she is." Silence after the sound of the jostling phone. "Go ahead."

"I love you, my little Gwen. Mommy can't wait to see you again. I'll be snuggling you up in just six more hours. And I'm counting down the minutes, each and every one!"

More silence, then David was back on the phone. " Where are you now?"

"I'm crossing the border into Arkansas. I-30 is just ahead."

"You're making good time."

"See. It's a good thing I left so early this morning!"

"But you also sound exhausted, and you definitely need some sleep. I can't wait to hear you snoring tonight."

"I don't snore." Jessica laughed because they both knew she sounded like a chainsaw once she got going. He had recorded her more than once. "I'm fine, David. I promise."

"Your last break was three hours ago. Please, rest."

"I promise to—"

"Sorry. I have a call coming in from work. We'll talk again in an hour, okay?"

"Okay, David. I love you." The sound of a woman's laughter echoed in the background. Bright and cheerful and full of too much life for it to have come from the TV. "Is there someone—"

"I love you too. Just remember, you're almost here. And your new home is waiting."

Then the call disconnected, and Jessica was left with the echo of David's voice, the humming highway, and the unsettling echo of a woman who had not sounded like she was coming from the TV.

She followed the car ahead of her, the trill of laughter still ringing in her ear.

Chapter Two

THE NEXT HOUR was going to be excruciating.

Of course she had only heard the TV, and calling David back now after he just hung up to ask him about the laughter (and the voice, there had been that voice earlier) would not go a long way in letting her husband know that she trusted him more than anyone else in her life. More than she had ever trusted anyone before. It could have been a neighbor who stopped by to welcome them to the area. Or a colleague from work.

What was wrong with her? They had only been apart for a few days, and she was already suspecting David of betrayal. Therapy could not come soon enough.

Jessica focused on his last words: "Just remember, you're almost here. And your new home is waiting."

That's all she needed to hear. At least until 1:30.

A new home, a different city, a fresh start. Not only for their marriage, but for the rest of Jessica's entire life. In another six hours, the endless drive across all of those desolate highways would finally be worth it. Then she could start on building the rest of her forever with David and Gwen. The three of them making up the family she had almost stopped believing she could have.

Jessica glanced into her rearview mirror again, but this time she was not daunted by her own weary expression, so much as bothered by yet another look at that faded U-Haul behind her. It looked just like the one she was driving, down to the Montana mountains on the side of the box.

Regardless of the slow traffic, he insisted on kissing her tailgate.

She moved her foot from the accelerator to the brake.

The U-Haul neared her rear bumper, honked, then backed off, blasting his horn for the second time.

Jessica finally lost her temper and flipped him the bird. Then she caught sight of a sign. Rest stop in five miles.

The internal debate began.

Should she stop or continue on?

As much as she wanted to stay the course, David would be delighted to know that she had pulled off for a short rest. It was the commonsense thing to do.

Plus, she really needed to pee. She had been holding it in far too long already, neglecting to hydrate for fear of overfilling her bladder.

But best of all, once she'd emptied her bladder, Jessica could get some coffee.

And get away from the dickhead behind her.

She flipped on the blinker and slowed as she neared the turnoff.

The driver blared his horn again and gunned it past her, almost hitting Jessica.

Fucker.

He was long gone, but she flipped him the bird anyway. It made her feel better.

She got out of the U-Haul and stretched her legs, doing a little downward dog on the grass when she was sure that no one was looking.

Then, she stretched her arms wide while walking to a small red brick building with restrooms, vending machines, and a scattering of tables adjacent to a pay-as-you-go coffee station run by a group of local Shriners.

After she peed and washed up (there was no hot water, but the cold water served its purpose and woke her up), Jessica bought a cup of joe and an apple fritter on her way back to the truck. The coffee was strong enough to stand a spoon in, but the donut was more delicious than it had any right to be: crunchy on the outside, doughy on the inside, and every bite full of a greasy sweetness that made her momentarily forget her fatigue.

The rest stop was surrounded by open fields that sprawled out for miles, with dusty roads snaking around them. Bright sun drenched the area in a golden hue. A few trees were clustered about the area and threw off a small amount of shade.

More than anything else, Jessica noticed how much warmer the air was.

She was hit with a blast of excitement. She was getting closer. It was the energetic lift she needed. She returned to the U-Haul and started the engine, cranking the AC before going for another round of yoga on the grass.

And then she was back on the road.

She had spent her entire life in the throbbing heart of New York, where concrete towers kissed the sky and a symphony of honking horns had always served as an evening lullaby. Resilient, tough, and constantly caught in the crossfire of city life, being a New Yorker was all that she knew.

But Jessica had always yearned for something different. Or quieter. And that made David a godsend. Constant travel made him a wanderer by profession, living in an ocean of hotel rooms and time zones. That intercontinental schedule had helped him to land him several top awards, which he'd taken obvious pride in showing her.

She was working as a barista at the Peony Hotel when fate had David checking in there. Jessica was drawn to the man like a bee to a flower, adoring his meandering yet consistently colorful stories. He was like a novel she could never put down.

She was surprised that David had noticed her at all. And after they had been seeing each other awhile, she finally asked. Why would a guy like him ever want to date the girl who made a marginal latte at best?

David had laughed, saying he didn't actually know anything about lattes before trying hers. He had simply noticed her because she reminded him of an ex.

The words had only stung for a blink, because seconds later he was bringing a subtle blush to her cheeks.

"But you're so much kinder than my ex ever was. And she could never smile like you smile every time you're making my latte."

An instant spark soon became a flame that loudly crackled as they shared their dreams and secrets.

Thanks to his father's career in the Air Force, and a childhood of getting dragged across the glove, David had grown up to embrace that nomadic lifestyle into adulthood. The thought of switching hotels whenever boredom struck him kept life intriguing, and the kind of indulgence that Jessica could only fantasize about in the quiet of her tiny yet overpriced apartment.

David's undeniable charisma, unbridled sense of

adventure, and touching sensitivity converged into a tempest that swept Jessica off her feet. Within a year of his first latte, they were married.

And then the shared dream of parenthood came to a crushing halt. David was infertile. They began the adoption process and turned the dream of family into an absolute reality.

Then Prairie Corporation offered to relocate David to Dallas.

Jessica had never considered living outside of New York, but she found herself drawn to the promise of open spaces and a slower pace of life. Dallas was somewhere they could put down some roots, create a home, and become a family.

So they said farewell to Jessica's tiny apartment in the city, where they had relocated after their wedding, and set their sights on a new life in the Lone Star State.

While Jessica gingerly wrapped the only childhood memories she wished to keep, David packed the U-Haul, loading the truck with a gentle care that belied his great strength.

And now she was almost there. Six more hours.

No way was she going to fuck this up.

Life had never been better for her, and that was exactly how she planned to keep it. Six more hours. And then she wouldn't get in the car for a week.

She kept counting down as the minutes dwindled, leaving more and more mile markers behind her as she closed the distance between herself and Dallas.

The next time she spoke to David, the TV was off. She heard no other voices in the background. He was delighted to hear from her, teasing her now about hurrying up and putting the pedal to the metal.

She had been so foolish earlier. No reason to ask about the woman's voice.

But just as the outline of Dallas came into view, a long line of vehicles unfolded before her, and once again Jessica was riding the brakes.

Chapter Three

JESSICA'S U-HAUL had barely moved by the time the sun started its descent. The Dallas skyline was still too far away for comfort. She'd been hoping to plan her arrival in daylight. Now she would have to look for their new home in the dark, down unfamiliar streets.

She had expected a forest of skyscrapers, a mirror of the steel and glass giants she was used to seeing in Manhattan. But the horizon held only a loose bundle of buildings, and a cityscape that sprawled across prairie more than it stacked into the sky.

Still, in the honey-glow of her first Texas sunset, every glinting window felt like it was welcoming her home.

Except she really didn't want to be sitting here, contemplating sunsets. A lethargic sloth doing yoga would go faster than this traffic. She inched forward again. Siri finally announced that her exit was now just two away.

And then the flow came to an absolute standstill.

Jessica sighed, her grip on the steering wheel tightening as the car in front of her killed its engine.

The faint wailing of sirens cut through the quiet with a mix of high-pitched wails and low rumbles.

She tried calling David but got no answer.

She frowned, trying not to worry. Then she checked the time. Almost seven. He was probably just getting Gwen to bed.

Fatigue crept into her bones. She felt grimy and sweaty after a full day of driving. Her stomach growled. She was still paying for the coffee and fritter with acid and bloat. David had accidentally packed her wallet in Gwen's diaper bag and taken it with him. But thankfully, she had just gotten a new credit card. She would have stopped for food had she known the drive was going to take this long.

She tried peering around the vehicle in front of her. She could see nothing. Other vehicles switched off and she finally relented and shut down the U-Haul.

She leaned back, waiting, trying to avoid looking at the clock. When she finally did, she saw that it was already nine.

She called David again. No answer.

Drivers had started to get out of their vehicles and mill about on the highway. Enough that she wondered why she was keeping herself trapped inside the stuffy cabin.

It was the heat, Jessica realized once outside the truck. But she was getting low on gas. She couldn't just sit inside, AC fired up, until it was time to drive again. Yeah, Siri said less than 30 minutes. But what if she got lost on the unfamiliar roads? It was probably not the place for another round of downward dog, but she still needed to stretch her muscles.

She traded a glance with the woman from the car in front. She shrugged, as though Jessica had asked about the cause of the gridlock.

"I'll check it out," Jessica said and waved at the woman with an impromptu sense of camaraderie.

She walked down a half-mile gauntlet of disgruntled drivers and crying children, vehicles parked like this was the set of some apocalyptic movie. She kept an ear out for the start of any engine, which she knew would send her dashing back to the U-Haul, full throttle.

But the cacophony of honking horns from earlier had surrendered to the eerie quiet of twilight.

And then Jessica reached the scene of the accident. Or at least as close as she was willing to get.

Spectators stood alone or in huddled gossiping groups of two or three. Lights from the emergency vehicles spun a red and blue kaleidoscope of colors over the concerned faces of curious onlookers.

Fire trucks, ambulances, and police cruisers commanded the highway ahead.

Jessica conquered her hesitance and slowly made her way forward, drawn by the spectacle as much as a need to know.

As she neared the nucleus of the commotion, a man detached himself from a group and approached her.

"U-Haul got creamed by a semi," he said, his tone holding a disturbing nonchalance that somehow frayed her nerves even further. "Other driver didn't even stop. Probably drunk."

A shiver of unease rippled down Jessica's spine. She could see the U-Haul now. Or what was left of it. The box had twisted and folded and somehow now seemed to read *Moan*. The cab was almost flattened, the windshield shattered. Two tires lay on the opposite side of the road.

And there was something on the asphalt hidden beneath a white sheet. It seemed too small to be a body, unless it too had been reduced to a mangled mess.

Had to have been the same asshole that had been riding her bumper earlier.

"Any idea how much longer we'll be stuck?" Her voice was barely above a whisper.

A woman snorted behind her. Jessica turned to see her leaning against a Nissan Altima, arms crossed with boredom.

"Brains all over the highway, honey." The woman's lips turned up in a grimace that highlighted rather than hid her morbid satisfaction. "They'll be scraping him off the road for another couple of hours."

Jessica's stomach lurched and whatever was left of the fritter turned acrid. "Thanks."

She headed back to the U-Haul, grateful that she hadn't had to witness the other driver's misfortune. She caught the other driver's eye as she returned. Jessica could tell she was eager for information.

"Going to be another couple of hours," Jessica said with an apologetic shrug. No reason to spread the news about all of those brains.

She climbed back into the truck, leaving the driver's door open.

She dialed David again. Still no answer. She thought about leaving a voicemail, but she didn't like leaving voice messages and would rather text.

So she typed out a quick message, her thumbs moving rote against the screen: *Go to bed. Stuck in traffic, might be a couple more hours.*

? he texted back.

Car accident. I'm okay but the road's blocked.

It seemed like he was going to respond because she spotted the three dots indicating he was typing. But then it stopped.

And no message came.

Ten minutes later, David still hadn't responded.

Must have been Gwen.

Or maybe he was in bed and had fallen asleep.

Either way, Jessica was jealous.

A burst of laughter erupted from Jessica's mouth, startling her. God, she was getting giddy. From exhaustion. Dehydration. Lack of food. Probably all three.

She rummaged through her purse until she finally found an old and forgotten granola bar. She pulled it out and ripped it open. Who cared how long it had been stuffed in there.

The oats and honey had a slightly stale taste, but in the lonely cavern of her growling stomach, the granola was a delicacy.

She washed it down with a mouthful of warm water from a half-empty bottle. She almost spat it out. Not thinking it would have warmed up in the hot Texas air.

And then she realized how parched she was and swallowed it all, even though drinking it might mean she'd have to pee on the side of the road.

She closed the door and locked it, shutting her eyes, and trying to mute the cruel narration reminding her that if she hadn't stopped for that fritter and coffee, she would already be miles away from this macabre scene. Or would have been smack dab in the middle of it. Maybe it would have been her U-Haul tangoing with the semi. Which would mean—

She broke off. Nope. She wasn't going to get lost in a whirlpool of anxious thoughts. New state, new life, new habits. That was something David had taught her. How to interrupt a negative thought with a positive one.

So instead she began imagining her first Costco run as a new mother, with Gwen sleeping in the cart as she pushed her through the store. Or maybe not. Maybe

Jessica should go shopping on the weekend, while David stayed with their daughter.

Were babies even allowed in Costco? Jessica had no idea. She had only gone to Costco a few times, back when her roommate had a card.

After some fast math, she realized that had been nearly ten years ago. A long time before she had given a shit about babies.

But now she was looking forward to all the new things she'd get to do as a mother. Once Dallas finally became home and—

A blaring horn snapped Jessica upright. She wiped a hint of drool from her chin. She'd obviously fallen asleep in the dark and the warmth. The line of cars to her left had sprung to life. She turned on the ignition, blasted the AC, and hit the car lights. The vehicle in front had already progressed a couple of hundred feet.

She rolled down the window and waved to the car behind her. And then she started driving. Traffic was slow but polite. As though they had all bonded during the long wait.

Driving past the scene of the accident, Jessica saw the crushed U-Haul had been placed on the back of a flatbed, its crumpled body barely recognizable in the dark.

She was flooded with gratitude.

"*Thank you*," she whispered to the night.

Thank you for making her stop, for the many delays, and for that rest area where she was smart enough to stop for a potty break and the opportunity to refuel herself with coffee and a donut. Thank you for her own life, for Gwen's, and for David's when another had so tragically ended.

Maybe that driver hadn't been an asshole.

Maybe he'd been trying to get home to his family, same as her.

Maybe somewhere out there in the dark right now, someone was already grieving his loss.

Or maybe she needed to stop entertaining dark thoughts. Because according to Siri, Jessica was minutes away from her family.

Chapter Four

JESSICA FOLLOWED SIRI'S INSTRUCTIONS, turning onto the street as instructed.

The road was lined with houses that were just as unfamiliar to Jessica as the city itself. All new sights she would have to get used to. And boy, did Jessica wish she was looking for her new home in the daylight.

The neighborhood appeared to be a mix of single-story ranches, two-story colonials, split-level homes, and townhouses, though styles blended from one to the next. The darkness was cut by softly glowing streetlights that lined both sides of the boulevard.

She drove slowly, searching for the street number. And then she hit 2095. And knew the next one would be it. And it was. Number 2097.

Her heart beat faster when she finally laid eyes on the house. An old-fashioned brick exterior. Bright white shutters fronting large windows. A wide porch ran the entire length of the front of the house. Two wicker rocking chairs sat at one end, beckoning to her tired soul.

Jessica had imagined living in the home ever since

David had first shown her a photo. There had been no chairs in that picture. So he must have bought them as a surprise. She could almost feel herself sitting in one of the rockers now, gently moving back and forth as she cradled Gwen in her arms.

She gave herself a mental shake. Imagining could come later. Now, all she wanted to do was get out of the truck. Have a shower. Kiss her baby. Cuddle with David. Those were the most important things in her life at the moment.

Even though she was the only vehicle on the road, she flicked the indicator and pulled up to the curb in front of the house. Then she cut the engine.

She was finally here. This beautiful brick house was really her home.

She smiled and slid out of the truck, taking a look around, recording every detail of the place in her mind. The manicured lawn, the tended flowerbeds, the neatly trimmed hedges on both sides of the stone walkway that led right to the front door.

It felt like home already.

Not at all like a place that had only recently been moved into.

The house was also dark. David had forgotten to leave the porch light on. She wasn't surprised. She was supposed to get here hours earlier.

She opened the flashlight app on her phone, but she was down to ten percent battery. It had been working overtime on the GPS. She stuffed it back into her purse, then grabbed her overnight bag from the passenger seat and got out. She was hit with another wave of hot air. She closed the door and locked the U-Haul. Unpacking could wait until tomorrow. Right now she needed a shower and her face on a pillow.

She walked up to the front porch, excited to see the place in daylight. It looked like a mansion compared to their small apartment in New York, which was cramped and dim, with a single window that barely allowed for any natural light. Thin drywall so all the neighbors' conversations (and a whole lot more) were easily heard. The bathroom was basically a shower stall with no windows, a sink, and a toilet. A worn-out couch and coffee table for her furniture, and both of them looked like a joke.

"Leave all the crap behind," David had said. "Just pack the memories."

They were going to buy all new furniture together, but they had picked out their bed online, and Jessica couldn't stop picturing herself in it.

It felt weird to knock, but she didn't want to just walk right in and risk startling David. So she pulled out her phone and sent him a text: *I'm here.*

But he still wasn't answering his phone. That meant David was probably asleep.

She fumbled for the house key he had given her, then guided it toward the lock, her fingers tracing the contours of the keyhole before she pushed it in.

But the key refused to turn.

She extracted it and examined it before trying again.

It still fit in the lock. It just wouldn't turn. Like it was a puzzle piece from the wrong box. She pulled it out again, her finger hovering above the doorbell, then she dropped her hand. She didn't want to wake Gwen.

She eyed the key with a frown.

Maybe David had given her a key to the back door? Weird, but possible.

The frail light of her phone lit up a path along the side of the house. As soon as she reached it, she turned the flashlight off. Now she was down to eight percent.

She navigated her way around the side of the house. Thank God for the moon. It at least provided a little light. She eventually reached a quaint garage at the back of the house.

She tried the key. It didn't work.

"*Fuck*," she said. Frustration simmered under layers of exhaustion. Either some idiot had made a mistake while cutting her key, or David had accidentally given her the wrong one.

Either way, *FUCK*!

She glanced down the short driveway and spotted a silver sedan glinting in the dark. Obviously his rental. She peered in through the garage window. What looked like a hunter green Volvo hunkered in the shadows.

Odd. They had planned to shop for a vehicle together, same as the furniture.

And even if he had rented a car for her too, that didn't look like a rental.

Not that the silver BMW looked like one other. It had the air of a well-used car. Slight dent in the door. Dust and bugs splattered on the windshield. A bent wiper.

She texted David again: *I can't get in.*

And still, infuriatingly, there was no response.

What was she supposed to do, break a window in her brand-new house? That was a hell of a way to start a new life.

Unless … what if she had the wrong house? Jesus, why hadn't she double checked?

Maybe he'd given her the wrong address or transposed the digit. It's possible that more than one house looked alike in the dark. She felt relieved. That accounted for there being no rocking chairs in the photo he'd shown her. She was simply at the wrong location.

Jessica walked back to the front of the house and

studied the address. Then she scrolled through David's old texts. Number 2097. She got the address from her purse to double-triple confirm. Sure enough, the numbers still matched. Maybe she got the street wrong?

She walked up to the corner to double check the street sign. It matched as well.

Okay, what if David had made a mistake when giving her the address in the first place, and she repeated it ever since, without either one of them ever bothering to double check?

She gave herself a shake. This was ridiculous. She needed to do something other than stand in front of the house, giving the neighbors a reason to call the cops. Because she looked like a burglar. Albeit one with a U-Haul. Or maybe that made it worse.

She walked back to the front porch and stared at the doorbell. She hated the thought of using it. So she knocked instead. Waiting in the dark. And, of course, now that she was here, the urge to pee had kicked in. She knocked again. This time a lot harder.

Still nothing. She knocked again. This time the loudest. Still no answer. She grumbled, then marched back to the U-Haul in defeat.

She unlocked the vehicle and climbed inside the cabin, slamming the door behind her.

She tried to get comfortable. Then realized she was being stupid. David wouldn't want her to sleep in the U-Haul just to avoid waking Gwen. It had been a long three days, and she needed to see him. Surely, he needed to see her just as much. Yes, she could get a hotel room. But he'd probably panic upon waking to find she wasn't there. After all, he was expecting her.

And she was not going to spend the night in the truck. Not after the long hours she'd already done. And especially not after seeing its sibling smashed to smithereens on the highway. She was planning on returning the truck tomorrow morning and never looking at another U-Haul for the rest of her life.

She'd be more than happy to take care of Gwen if she woke up. It would be like a blanket on her soul. And David could get back to sleep.

So she returned to the house and rang the doorbell.

Then she waited. And waited.

And waited some more.

She stepped back onto the front path, watching the house. And was just about to head back onto the porch and ring it for the second time when a light went bright upstairs.

David looked out the window.

Or at least Jessica thought it was him. She couldn't really see anything more than a fast-moving shadow appearing in the window, but he shared her husband's general shape and size.

Who else could it be?

Assuming she had the right address.

Jessica squinted, but that didn't help.

She gave the shape a wave, but it disappeared without returning the gesture.

And the house stayed dark.

Jessica waited. Still, David didn't come to the door.

She grumbled and stepped forward to ring the doorbell again.

But then the lights inside the house turned on, and Jessica exhaled with relief.

It was hot. And late. She was tired. And hungry. She had dragged herself across the interstate highways from New York to Texas, and unreasonable notions had just been about to pick at the fraying edges of her mind.

A shadow moved behind the frosted glass panel on the other side of the door. The light over her head went on, flooding the porch with a warm glow.

From behind the door came the sound of a baby's cries. Shit. She had woken Gwen. She immediately felt like a bad mother. Not that Gwen would ever remember this moment.

The door parted a crack, the safety chain still in place.

A woman peered out at her.

"May I help you?" she asked, as the unmistakable sound of Jessica's screaming daughter grew louder in the background.

Chapter Five

JESSICA STARED at the unfamiliar silhouette of the woman standing on the threshold of the house. For a moment, she was struck dumb. Trapped in amber. The world moving around her while she remained frozen.

It didn't help that the woman looked like she could have been Jessica's sister. Long and wavy chestnut hair framed a heart-shaped face. Her hazel eyes were rimmed with thick dark lashes. Her full lips were curved down in apprehension.

"I'm sorry," Jessica finally managed to stutter, the words feeling thick and clumsy in her mouth. "There must be some mistake. I'm looking for 2097 Longhorn Drive."

The woman looked at her with confusion. "Yes," she said slowly, her voice surprisingly soft against the clamor of Gwen's cries. "This is 2097 Longhorn Drive."

A pit opened in Jessica's stomach. Her hands were suddenly clammy, and she balled them into fists.

Was there another Longhorn Drive in Dallas?

Had the real estate agent put the wrong address on the contract?

Or was her sleep deprived mind somehow responsible for this stupid confusion?

"I'm sorry," she said. "David must have given me the wrong address."

"David?" The woman wrinkled her brow, and the next question came like a bucket of cold water. "David Clarke?"

Jessica could only nod, her brain struggling to keep pace with the surreality of this scenario. "Yes. My husband, David Clarke."

Disbelief flashed across the woman's face in a haunting mirror of her own emotions. "One moment," she said. And then she closed the door in Jessica's face. What the actual fuck was happening here?

Another shadow joined the woman behind the glass. Jessica pressed her ear to the door but heard only the vague rumblings of conservation.

She stepped back again, sweating in the oppressive Texan night. What the hell was keeping this woman? And how did she know David?

Then the door opened again. But this time, the safety chain was removed. And David stood there, his familiar form clad in a pair of pajamas she had never seen before. Silk instead of the usual flannel. His face was pinched with sleep, his hair tousled and unkempt.

The woman stood next to him, still looking like a doppelgänger of Jessica herself, even more so now that her long and lean frame was fully visible. Gwen wailed in her arms, wearing an old Wilco tee that Jessica had seen before.

Something was terribly wrong. Jessica's heart slammed against her ribs as she stared at David and the woman. A deeply unsettling feeling dropped over her. She felt like she was looking at a distorted image of her life in a carnival mirror.

Shouldn't she be the one holding Gwen and standing next to David, looking out into the dark?

A single word escaped her lips. "David."

"Yes?" He replied like a stranger. There was no sign of recognition in his eyes.

"Can I come in?"

"No."

"Why not? It's our house."

David looked taken aback. "What do you mean, 'our house'?"

She glanced at the woman, who just looked confused. So she turned her attention back to David. "I'm tired. No, I'm beyond tired. I'm fucking exhausted. I've been on the road for three days now and—"

"And what?"

Jessica tried to enter the house, but David stepped forward, blocking her way. Turning his body into an immovable object. "This isn't your house."

She stared at him. "What?"

His face hardened with an unfamiliar coldness. "I don't even know who you are."

"This is stupid," Jessica countered with a nervous laugh, because again, *what the actual fuck?* But her laughter fell flat, swallowed by the thick Texas night and the pregnant pause from both David and the woman holding Gwen. Jessica felt small and fragile under their scrutiny. And then it hit her. "Is this supposed to be some kind of joke?"

The air crackled with tension.

"Who are you?" the woman asked.

Jessica turned to her. "Jessica Clarke, David's wife, and that" — she pointed to her daughter — "is our daughter Gwen."

"No, this is our house." The woman spoke in a calm

and measured voice. "I'm Jessica Clarke, married to David, and this is our daughter, Bella."

Jessica felt like she'd been hit by a two by four. *What?*

She was having trouble processing the words.

The woman continued, "It's time for you to go home now, whoever you—"

Jessica lunged forward, desperate to enter the home she had driven across the country for.

But David's arm shot out, barring her entry. "I don't know who you are or why you're here, but you need to leave right now before I call the police."

"David, stop! Why are you being so cruel? It isn't funny!" She hated the desperation in her voice. Why was he doing this? If it was a trick, it had gone too far. "Please."

But David gently but firmly pushed her out the door, punctuating his dismissal with a curt, "Goodnight."

And then he closed the door in her face. Jessica remained where she was. Despite the heat, she felt cold. Either from exhaustion or shock. Or maybe both. Her new life in Texas had officially been turned upside down.

She could still see their shadows on the other side of the door. They were close together. Probably taking about her. And that knowledge seeped into her veins like poison.

After what felt like an eternity of waiting for them to open the door and laugh at her, Jessica finally moved. But she didn't leave, instead reaching out for the door handle.

But the door (her door) was locked again. And then the lights went out, shrouding her once more in darkness.

She rapped on the door.

Silence.

She banged louder, each strike hitting harder than the last. Her vision blurring as tears filled her eyes, biting her cheek to keep them at bay.

Finally, the door swung open again, but this time only David was there, his eyes filled with annoyance, uncertainty, and something else that Jessica could not identify.

"What the hell is going on, David?" she demanded.

David sighed, raking a hand through his mess of unkempt hair. "I don't know who you are, but move along. It's late. Go home."

"Home?" she sputtered. "*This* is my home!"

"No, it's not." David shook his head with another hardened gaze. "My wife and I have lived here for years."

"What the hell are you talking about?" Her hands were balled into fists, and she was dangerously close to using one of them to break his nose. "This joke has gone on long enough. It's not funny anymore."

"Joke?"

"We've lived together for three years!"

"How is that possible if we've never met?" David asked, his bafflement unwavering.

"But we have met! How else would I know your name? And where you live? Jesus Christ, we're married."

He laughed then. But it was hard like New York ice. "Married? I have a wife. You just met her. And I have no idea how you know my name. But if you don't leave right now, I will call the police."

And he slammed the door in her face.

The unmistakable sound of a lock clicking into place confirmed this was no longer a joke. But some kind of twisted nightmare.

She stood frozen on the porch. Then the porch light went out again, plunging her into darkness, and it was like the last flicker of her hope was extinguished.

Jessica had been prepared for many challenges in this move, but nothing could have braced her for this unanticipated … whatever it was. She was laden with new weight, unable to pick up her feet, so she shuffled back to the U-Haul.

She climbed into the driver's seat and clung to the steering wheel, as though it were some kind of lifeline. She felt the edges of a panic attack creeping up on her. And she breathed deep.

Take an action. Take an action.

So she slid the truck key into the ignition and started it up. Then she flipped on the heat. Trying to chase away the chill.

Finally, she pulled away from the curb, accelerating until the house was swallowed by the black abyss of night.

She drove through the unfamiliar streets until she spotted a swath of trees and a weathered sign proclaiming the space was a public reserve, open from dawn to dusk.

She eased the U-Haul into the parking lot. Gravel crunched beneath the tires as she made her way to the farthest corner of the lot and parked under the shadow of a gnarled oak, its twisted limbs stretching out like a skeletal hand against the night sky.

She killed the engine. The silence was jarring.

Then she collapsed. Like she was a balloon, stuck with a pin, and all the air had spilled out. She hunched over the steering wheel, leaning her forehead against the plastic. And cried.

Not just for herself. And her predicament. But for Gwen, for the love she felt for David, for the life she thought they had been building together.

She cried long and hard. Thinking it sounded as though there was an animal in pain nearby. Then realized it was her. She cried until her eyes were swollen and her head pounded. Until she was dehydrated and there was nothing left to give.

Then she glanced outside the window and spotted the lights of a plane. That surprised her. Surely, the world had stopped? Or maybe it was just hers.

And then she wondered what David and the other Jessica were thinking inside the house.

Chapter Six

JESS STOOD in the shadowed entryway, looking at the closed door as though it were a fortress between her and the insane woman who looked remarkably similar to Jess.

A heavy silence filled the room until she finally broke it despite her reluctance, now that Bella's crying had settled into a series of sweet little snores.

"David?" Her voice was a low murmur as her husband walked toward the living room, his body language restless. "What just happened? Is that woman trying to steal my life?"

He shook his head, his broad shoulders rigid, eyes still on the window, peeking through the blinds as the U-Haul's taillights disappeared down the street.

"She's leaving." He released the blind. "And now she's gone."

Jess shifted Bella to her other arm and opened the door, peering out. The U-Haul was no longer parked in front of their home. Instead, an empty spot yawned in the dark.

She sighed, feeling an odd blend of unease and relief as she closed the door and locked it.

A part of Jess empathized with the poor woman, though a much larger part recoiled at the thought of her mirror image claiming her life, home, and husband.

"I'm going to put her down," Jess said, gesturing to Bella. David nodded, drawn back to the window. She didn't blame him. What a strange evening this was turning into.

She went back upstairs to the nursery.

And laid Bella down in the crib.

Her tiny eyelashes fluttered against her rosy cheeks as she wiggled into a comfortable position and started snoring again.

Jess leaned down and pressed a light kiss against Bella's forehead. Then she exited the room, closing the nursery door only part way. And headed back downstairs.

Her mind circled back to the last time their tranquil night had been shattered by the sudden peal of the doorbell. That time it was Patsy. Their next-door neighbor. And she was still irritated by her interruption. Mainly because the woman had an uncanny knack of popping up at the most inconvenient of times.

When they first moved in three years ago, Jess appreciated that her neighbor was a well-meaning guardian of the neighborhood. But now she recognized Patsy was meddlesome, and her misguided attempts at "helping her neighbors out" had been the bane of many an evening.

Last week while she and David were watching "The Bachelor," Patsy had come and rang the doorbell because David left his phone in the car. She seemed hard pressed to explain why she had been snooping in their driveway, instead pinning her late-night intrusion on a platform of moral duty.

"I wouldn't want to feel responsible for the temptation of any soulless thieves on our street if I could have done something to stop someone from breaking into your car," Patsy said, as though their sleepy suburban neighborhood was a hotbed for criminals trafficking in stolen phones.

Jess had thought it was Patsy ringing again. She'd told David to ignore it; that was their new plan in dealing with the woman. Ignore her and maybe she'll go away (although she never did). But it was why Jess had taken so long to answer the door.

But tonight's interruption was nothing compared to the usual nonsense Patsy delivered to their door.

She stopped in the doorway of the living room. David was still where she had left him, staring out the window and watching the street. But, at the same time, he felt a million miles away from her.

Had David betrayed her again?

The thought kept worming its way to the front of her mind.

She hated thinking he would hurt their marriage again, especially now that Bella was here. But there was nothing she could do to keep the idea out of her mind.

Once planted, always rooted. No matter how hard she tried to forgive his indiscretion, it lingered like a fog, ready to cast its pall as the cause of any stumble their marriage might take.

It was settling in now. No matter how hard she tried to stifle the thought. And she was trying hard. But the question that David had cheated with that woman crept deeper into her brain. She shook off the apprehension.

She had to stay away from that downward spiral, no matter what.

Even one step onto the slippery slope of questioning his loyalty could threaten to unravel all the work they had done over the past few years.

"What the hell was that all about?" Jess asked.

He started, obviously lost in his own thoughts.

David scrubbed his hands over his face, and his usually bright eyes were now clouded with confusion. Or was that apprehension? "I don't know, Jess. You have to believe me, I've never seen that woman before in my life."

"Well, you've kind of seen her." She tried for a laugh, but it didn't work out.

He stared at her, his whole body tightening. "What do you mean?"

"Are you kidding me?" She gestured to her face. "She looked more like me than my own sister. If I had one. Which I don't."

His shoulders sagged as he realized she was making a joke. "I guess."

"You don't think so?"

David shook his head. "You're the only one who looks like you."

She walked over and kissed his cheek. For some reason, that answer went a long way toward reassuring her.

He glanced at her. "Do you think we should call the cops?"

Jess shrank back in an instinctive retreat. The very thought of law enforcement sent a shiver of unease through her entire body.

He noted her reaction. "Sorry."

"It's all right," she said. "No, we're not calling the cops. The poor woman is just suffering from some mental health issues."

His eyes softened, and the empathy she loved so much about him made her heart warm. "Okay, but I'm just gonna check the back door again. Make sure it's locked."

Jess nodded, watching him head down the hall and into

the kitchen. He returned a moment later and they stared at each other. There was a long beat of silence, and then they burst out laughing in unison.

The sound obliterated the tension that had been a drag on the room.

"Jesus." Jess leaned against the wall, absently rubbing the spot over her heart. "My heart's still pounding."

"Me too," David said, wiping his eyes. "Whisky?"

"Yes." She longed for something narcotic. But the legal kind would have to do. "That sounds great."

David made his way to the kitchen. Jess went over to the window. The blinds were still parted. The parking spot in front of the house was still vacant.

They lived in a safe neighborhood, and Patsy was the only Peeping Tom she ever had to worry about. But tonight seemed different.

She pulled the blinds closed, then sank into the plush sofa, resting her head back against the cushion until David returned. He carried a crystal glass of whisky in each hand.

Handing one to Jess before sitting down beside her, David leaned back, resting his head against her shoulder.

Jess took a drink. The liquid burned as it trickled down her throat, igniting a warmth that spread through her body.

"That woman said she was me. That Bella was her baby."

"Yeah." David nodded. "Do you know her from some-where? The adoptive moms' group? Your work, maybe?"

She shook her head. "No."

"You sure?"

"Do you think I wouldn't remember someone who looks like my deepfake?"

David laughed. "That's not what a deepfake is."

No, she supposed not. But despite the woman's similar face (and height and body), no connections came to mind. She didn't have a single thread of familiarity to sew herself a clue.

"So nowhere?" David asked, as though Jess was the one who should have a better clue as to what the hell happened.

"No." She shook her head again to make it perfectly clear. "I've never seen that woman before in my life."

"I thought maybe she was an employee at Prairie Corp." God, she was grateful he brought it up, so she didn't have to ask if he knew her. "But I know almost everyone there."

"Maybe she's a new hire."

"Maybe. But most of the people there know you, and don't you think they'd say, 'Hey David, your wife's doppelgänger is now working in the mail room.'"

Jess laughed. "Yeah, I suppose they would." And then before she could help herself, she added, "But she knew your name, David."

She braced herself in case he was offended. But he seemed as perplexed by that as her.

"Yeah." He ran a hand through his hair again. "But how?"

"Maybe you met her on a work trip?"

He swirled the whisky in his glass, meditating on the suggestion. "I just feel like I would have remembered her. But then I meet a lot of people—"

Jess gasped.

David looked at her. "What?"

She set her whisky glass down on the coffee table and got to her feet. "I'll be back."

"Where are you going?"

"I think I might know where she's from." Jess headed

to the kitchen, where life was tracked on the refrigerator with a series of colorful magnets.

She sorted through coupons, a torn calendar page, and a list of groceries to find the clipping. A public relations puff piece featuring Prairie Corp. David was prominent in the photo as he presented a check to a charity group that helped rehabilitate convicts after their release.

Jess returned to the living room and handed the paper to David. "Maybe she was here this night."

He glanced at the clipping, studying the black-and-white photo. "You think?"

She shrugged. "I have no idea. But there were hundreds of people there." She tried for a smile. "I would definitely remember you if I saw that picture."

"But how did she know where we live?"

The attempted smile dissolved. "Yeah…" Jess didn't finish her thought. No need; David was obviously just as uncomfortable with tonight as she was. She'd been so distracted by the woman's look, she hadn't even stopped to question how she knew where they lived. "Maybe I was wrong. Maybe we should call the police."

"And say what?" David asked. "It doesn't make much sense to call them now that she's gone."

"What if she comes back?"

"Then we'll call them." David attempted a reassuring smile. It was bright enough to dim her worry by a watt or two. Then he stood, yawning. "I've gotta be up in five hours. I'm going to bed."

"I'll be up in a just a minute."

"Gonna finish your whisky?"

"Does a one-legged duck swim in circles?"

"I don't know?" David laughed. "I've never heard that one."

"Is whisky wet?" Jess asked.

He smiled, kissed her cheek. She heard him walk down to the kitchen and deposit his glass. Moments later, his footsteps sounded on the stairs.

And then she was alone. Jess walked to the front door and checked that it was locked. Again. And then did the same for the back door. But she still couldn't go back to bed.

She returned to the living room and stood by the window. Parting the blinds, staring out at the street as though expecting the U-Haul to suddenly reappear at any second.

She couldn't shake the image of that strange yet too familiar woman standing on her porch, insisting that her name was Jessica Clarke, she was married to David, and Bella was her child.

Chapter Seven

HEADLIGHTS SWEPT across the window of the U-Haul as a car inched down the road toward the park.

When the vehicle slowed even more, Jessica realized it was a police cruiser. Her heart clenched. Had David sent them after her? She hadn't thought about that as she'd driven away from 2097 Longhorn Drive.

She wiped the tears from her face.

Jessica wasn't sure if an encounter with a cop right now would be good, bad, or downright terrible. She watched the cruiser with bated breath. Maybe they would pass on by. Leave her to the turmoil chewing right through her.

But no. The vehicle parked.

Moments later, a figure emerged from the vehicle, flashlight in hand, and began their approach to the U-Haul. The beam of light sliced through the darkness as Jessica rolled down the driver's side window.

She glanced out. "Evening."

"Ma'am." The officer had short brown hair, a strong jawline, and a stern gaze. She gave Jessica a cordial nod. Her name tag read, *Carlson*. "How are you doing tonight?"

Jessica shrugged.

"You lost?"

Jessica almost laughed. "No." It was only one word. But her voice sounded thin, almost hysterical.

"I'm going to need to see some identification."

Jessica chewed on her lip. All she had was her credit card. She pulled that out and showed it to the officer.

"Anything else?"

Jessica shook her head. "It's at home." It was a lie. But easier to explain than the truth. There was plenty of that coming, she anticipated, and it was strange and convoluted enough.

"And where is home? New York?" the officer asked. She'd obviously noted the U-Haul's license plates.

"No." Jessica shook her head. "Not anymore. I just moved here."

"To Dallas?"

"Uh huh."

"So what are you doing in the park?"

Jessica didn't answer. Not because she was trying to be deceptive. She literally didn't know what to say. She didn't even understand what the hell she was doing in the park.

"Do you know your address?"

"Of course I know my address." That might have been a lie.

"Well?" Officer Carlson looked at her. "Would you like to tell me what it is?"

"2097 Longhorn Drive."

"You're in the right neighborhood." Carlson nodded. "So I ask again: what are you doing in the park when it's closed?"

"My husband won't let me into the house." Her eyes filled with tears again. She cleared her throat. She would not cry again.

Office Carlson softened like butter under a lamp. "The two of you have an argument?"

"I'm not sure," Jessica said. "I just want to see my baby."

The officer tensed. "He's keeping you from the baby?"

Jessica nodded.

"How about I escort you home?"

A tear fell from Jessica's eye. She nodded, relief flooding over her. Someone was going to help her make sense of tonight.

"I think I'd like to have a chat with him."

"Thank you." Jessica turned the key in the ignition.

"Follow me," Carlson said.

Jessica nodded, waiting for her to return to her vehicle. It took a few minutes, and she wondered if the cop was calling her in. Just when she started to lose hope, she flashed her headlights.

Jessica pulled out of the parking lot, then followed the cruiser along the street and back to 2097 Longhorn Drive. Seconds later, she was parked in the spot she had occupied earlier.

She turned off the ignition and was about to get out when Officer Carlson walked over. "I'll have you wait in the vehicle, Jessica."

"Okay."

"Your husband's name?"

"David. David Clarke."

"Alright, I'll have a short conversation with him. See if we can't get you back in your bed with your baby."

"Thank you."

She watched Carlson headed up the walk to the front porch. Jessica wanted to launch herself out of the truck and follow. But instead, she climbed across the gear shift and rolled down the passenger window.

Carlson stepped onto the front porch and rang the doorbell. The house stayed dark.

She rapped her knuckles on the door.

A light turned on upstairs.

A figure appeared in the window.

Jessica held her breath, counting nine Mississippis before the porch light went on, bathing the rocking chairs in a warm glow.

Then the door opened, and David appeared. He seemed fairly relaxed, studying the cop on his porch as if flummoxed by her presence.

Like she had been his only disturbance tonight.

They started talking, but Jessica couldn't make out any words. Just the low rumblings of each of their voices.

Then the female cop gestured to the U-Haul.

David looked up. Then froze. And shook his head.

Jessica had no idea how she was supposed to hold on to her shit after that.

She would have been perfectly happy to follow orders and stay in the U-Haul if David hadn't started lying. She'd had enough.

She should have told Officer Carlson everything that had happened in the first place.

So she might as well tell her now.

She kicked the truck door open, then stalked across the yard.

Neither David nor Officer Carlson seemed happy to see her.

"Ma'am, Jessica—"

"He's lying!"

"I believe I asked you to stay in the truck."

"I NEED TO EXPLAIN."

David folded his arms across his chest, a look of irritation on his face.

"You need to calm down," Officer Carlson said. Her eyes had hardened, and it was enough to make Jessica shrink back.

But not enough to shut her up. "I don't know why he's lying and pretending that he doesn't know me. But it's not funny." A new thought occurred to Jessica. "Maybe the woman who lives here has done something to him."

"The woman who lives here?" David said. "You mean my wife?"

Jessica stamped her foot. "She's not your wife. I'm your wife."

And then the woman appeared. The once who'd answered the door earlier. This time without Bella, and her brows pinched in apparent worry.

Officer Carlson turned to her. Then glanced at Jessica, obviously comparing the two. "And you are?"

"Jessica Clarke."

"She's not," Jessica said. "I'm Jessica Clarke."

"I don't suppose you have any identification?"

"Of course," said the woman masquerading as Jessica. She disappeared for a moment, then reappeared with a wallet.

Plucked out her license and handed it over.

Officer Carlson looked from the driver's license to its owner and back. Twice. Then she handed it back.

Jessica lurched forward, snatching it from her doppel-gänger's hand. She recoiled, and Officer Carlson stepped forward.

"Ma'am."

But Jessie ignored her. Staring in shock at the ID. It read *JESSICA CLARKE*. None of this was making any sense.

Officer Carlson plucked the license from her hand and delivered it back to the woman inside the house.

"He's replaced me," Jessica said.

"Pardon?" Carlson said.

"David's replaced me with this woman." She turned to look at David. "Why?"

"Jesus," David said, "I haven't replaced anyone." He turned and plucked a framed photo from the wall. Held it out. "Our wedding, eight years ago."

Jessica snatched the photo. In it, David wore a suit, the other woman a wedding dress. There was a light-box sign with the date: *July 18, 2015.*

"It's time to leave these folks in peace." Officer Carlson took the framed photo from Jessica and gave it back to David. "My apologies for disturbing you."

"Wait!" Jessica said. All three turned to look at her. "If I'm not Jessica Clarke, why do I have a credit card in that name?"

The woman stiffened. "You have my credit card?"

Carlson looked at her. "You're missing a credit card?"

The woman nodded. "I lost it last month. American Express. They were going to send a new card, but I never received it."

The cop held out her hand. "Card."

Jessica pulled it out of her wallet. "That one's mine."

The other woman fingered it. "I don't know. It could be the replacement card."

"It's not," Jessica said.

David looked it over. "It seems fairly new."

"Because we ordered it last month," Jessica said. "Due to my name change."

Carlson tucked the card in her breast pocket. "I'll hang onto this until we can determine ownership."

"But it's my card," Jessica said.

"Then you can get it back when you bring a statement to the station."

"This is ridiculous," Jessica said. "I'm Jessica Clarke. And if I'm not, how do I have his phone number?"

Carlson looked like she had plenty of ways to answer that question, but she simply held out her hand. "Let's see it."

God, she hoped she had enough power left. Less than six percent. She opened her contacts and pointed to David's number.

"Whiskerface?" Officer Carlson said. "That doesn't tell me anything."

"It was a joke between me and David," Jessica said.

Officer Carlson held the phone up to David.

He shook his head. "That's not my number."

Officer Carlson showed Jessica's phone to the imposter.

"Definitely not." She also shook her head. "David's number has 69 in it. He likes to joke about it. Even though it's not funny."

"It's a little funny," he muttered.

"I can prove it!" Jessica said. "I'll call him."

Officer Carlson sighed.

"Please," Jessica said.

The cop turned to David. "Get your phone?"

"It's upstairs."

Carlson nodded. "I'll wait."

David gave her an uncertain nod. Then he disappeared from the doorway, leaving them all to a lingering and uncomfortable silence. What was probably a minute, felt like a hundred.

Jessica couldn't look at either woman. She kept her eyes on her feet. Willing this nightmare to be over.

David returned.

Officer Carlson hit the number for Whiskerface. Then she put the phone on speaker.

"Hello?" Whiskerface answered on the third ring. It was a man's voice. But Jessica didn't recognize it.

"Amber. Where are you?" said the voice.

Carlson looked at her.

Jessica shook her head. "Who is this?"

"Is this some kind of joke?" Whiskerface sounded genuinely confused. "What's going on, Amber?"

"This isn't Amber. It's Jessica."

"Jesus, not this again," the man said.

Carlson plucked the phone from her hand. "Can you tell me who just called you?"

"Who the hell are you?" the man asked.

"Officer Carlson, Dallas PD."

"Oh." He sounded immediately conciliatory. "That's my wife, Amber. Amber Brown. We had a fight yesterday. She packed up the house and left. I've been frantically trying to get a hold of her."

"Describe her for me." Officer Carlson stared at Jessica while awaiting his answer.

"I don't know … slender, I guess, with dark hair. She's pretty tall, and—"

Carlson cut him off. "Can you tell me what she's wearing?"

"I know what she was wearing the last time I saw her, if that helps," said the man. "She had on my Coldplay T-shirt. Plus her favorite pair of jeans. There's a hole in the right knee. When she gets anxious, she picks at it."

Jessica glanced down at the hole on the right knee. That's exactly what she did. WHAT THE FUCK WAS HAPPENING HERE?

"And where do you live?" Officer Carlson asked.

"Just outside of Houston."

"And how long have you lived there?"

"Eleven years," said the man. "Is she there? Can I talk to her? The kids are freaking out."

"I don't have any kids!" Jessica said. "I don't know who that man is! And we sure as hell don't have any children together!"

"Any reason she'd be calling herself Jessica?"

"It's her middle name," the man said. Jessica felt a chill go down her back. How did he know that? "She stops answering to Amber when she gets pissy sometimes."

"I don't suppose you know a Jessica or David Clarke?"

"Nope."

"Thank you for your time." Carlson disconnected and handed the phone back to Jessica.

"He's lying," Jessica said.

"So Amber isn't your name?"

"It used to be my name … before…" Jessica hesitated, unsure of how to continue. Or how it was going to make her sound.

"Before what?" Carlson asked.

"Before I got married. Which is when I changed it. Officially. My full name is Amber Jessica, but David liked Jessica better, and a fresh start felt nice, so I started going by Jessica a few years ago."

"We're not married." David was still looking at her like she was a stranger. "You need to stop saying that."

"Is there someone else who can prove your identity?" Carlson asked. "Parent? Sibling? Friend?"

Jessica shook her head.

"Then it's time to leave." The officer reached out a hand.

But Jessica shrank away. "Wait. I'll call a friend."

"Jesus," David snapped. "This is starting to feel like a goddamn reality show."

The other woman — Jessica Clarke, if that really was her name — placed a hand on David's arm. Gave him a pat as though she was trying to reassure him.

Jessica scrolled through her contacts, stopping when she came across Beth. Then she hit dial and put the phone on speaker.

Beth answer on the third ring. "What do you want, Amber? Do you know what time it is?"

"I'm so sorry, Beth. But I need your help. You're on speaker phone right now, and I need you to tell some people who I am."

"What's this about?"

"Please."

"Okay." Beth still sounded unsure. "You're Amber Brown."

"No, my married name."

There was a moment of silence. "I don't know your married name. You didn't let us meet him."

"It's important."

"Is it important that you skipped out and left Glenda and I with the rest of your lease?"

"I told you I was getting married."

"Yeah, to the guy we didn't get to meet because we what, weren't good enough?"

"I didn't say that." This was so uncomfortable with everyone watching her.

"You didn't have to. We got the picture."

"Beth." But she'd already hung up. "Fuck."

"She called you Amber," Officer Carlson said. And even she looked done with Jessica.

"I told you. That was my name before. When I lived with Glenda and Beth."

"Come on, Amber." Carlson nodded at David and

Jessica's replacement. "We're leaving these poor folks in peace."

"Wait." She had to try one more time. "If I don't live here, then how do I have a key to the house?"

"She has a key to our house?" Jessica's doppelgänger stepped back, looking alarmed.

"Bullshit." David curled his lip.

"You gave it to me yourself," Jessica said.

"Jesus Christ." He turned to Carlson. "I swear to God, I have never met this woman before."

"Give me the key." Carlson held her hand out.

Jessica handed it to her.

Carlson turned toward David and gestured at the lock. "You mind if I give it a try?"

He stepped out onto the porch while Replacement Jessica stayed inside. Then he closed the door.

Officer Carlson tried the key, but to no one's surprise, including Jessica, it refused to turn.

"I know what it looks like," Jessica said, hearing the futility of her words. "But that's the key that he gave me for this house."

"I'm gonna let you folks get back to bed now," Carlson said before returning the dummy key to Jessica. "Come on, we're—"

"NO!" Jessica felt frantic. Her entire nervous system suddenly flooded with adrenaline. She was starting to feel crazy, despite never having any cause to question her sanity before tonight. "Please, David! Why are you doing this to me?"

Carlson stepped forward and took her arm. "Ma'am, if you don't calm down right now, I'm going to arrest you for—"

"YOU CAN'T DO THIS TO ME! I'M—"

That's all she managed to get out. In seconds, Officer

Carlson had both of Jessica's arms behind her back and had snapped on the handcuffs.

"Amber Brown, I'm arresting you for causing a disturbance. You have the right to remain silent. Anything you say can and will be used against you in a court of law. You have the right to an attorney. If you cannot afford one, one will be appointed to you. Do you understand these rights as they have been read to you?"

"No!"

"You don't understand what I just said?"

"No, I do. But I'm not causing a disturbance. I'm trying to get in the house. You don't understand."

"Good night," Carlson said, nodding at David. "I'll send a tow truck to impound the vehicle. It'll be out of your way by the morning."

Then she applied a little pressure to Jessica's wrist, and she relented, allowing the officer to guide her down the stairs onto the front path.

"I'm going to jail?" Jessica asked.

"For tonight," Carlson said.

"But I haven't done anything wrong."

They stopped before the cruiser. Carlson opened the back door. Jessica didn't want to get in. She watched the officer's hand drop to her taser.

She climbed in and sat.

Carlson slammed the door behind her.

Then she walked to the U-Haul and rolled up the windows. She pulled out Jessica's purse and overnight bag, then locked the vehicle and put Jessica's belongings in the trunk.

Then she got in the driver's seat. And started typing on her data terminal.

Jessica looked out the window. David still stood on the

porch, watching them. The door opened behind him, and the replacement Jessica stepped out.

She took David's hand. Held it tight in her own.

Jessica turned away. Hot tears pricked her eyes.

Then Carlson turned on the ignition. And a moment later, they drove away into the dark of the Dallas night.

Chapter Eight

Jess tugged David's hand, leading him back into the house. Then he closed and locked the front door while Jess tucked her license back into the wallet, then set it on the cabinet in the hallway.

He was pale, his eyes weary. But there was something else she couldn't quite put her finger on. Fear?

"You look exhausted," Jess said.

"My heart hit the floor when Madam Batshit said she had a key," David said.

Jess pulled him into an embrace. "Mine too."

He held her close, the silence of the night creating a comforting bubble of normalcy around them.

Then Jess gave him a shake. "Bed."

He nodded, and they separated.

David flicked off the living room light, then they quietly climbed the stairs to the second floor.

"I'm going to check on Bella," Jess said.

David nodded and headed to the bedroom.

Bella was still fast asleep in her crib. But Jessica needed

to touch her. She placed a hand gently on her daughter's back for comfort. Not Bella's. But her own.

Then she made her way across the hall to her and David's bedroom.

He was already in bed with the covers pulled up to his chest.

He glanced over as she entered but said nothing.

Jess paused in front of the dresser mirror and studied her reflection. "Don't you think it's strange how much Amber and I look alike?"

"You're on a first-name basis with the crazy woman now?"

"What else am I supposed to call her?"

"I don't see what's wrong with Madam Batshit."

"It's not as catchy as you think." Jess kept staring at her reflection. "She had the same eyes, the same hair … we could be twins. Maybe I should call her Jessica. Or Jess."

David looked horrified. "Absolutely not. There might be similarities, but you, my love, are truly one of a kind."

"Apparently not," Jess said, deliberately keeping her voice light. "I obviously have a doppelgänger out there."

David's eyebrows knitted.

"What is it?" she asked.

"Maybe it's not me she knows. Maybe it's you."

"Me?" Jess said.

"Yeah. What if that Amber woman saw you somewhere and then had a psychotic breakdown, and now she legitimately thinks that she's you?"

"I think I liked it better when you were calling her Madam Batshit."

David laughed. But it had an edge.

"This is starting to sound like one of those stupid Netflix movies."

"Can you think of a better explanation?"

"Definitely not." Jess shook her head. "That was seriously the strangest shit ever."

"You've got that right."

Jessica climbed into bed beside him and switched off the bedside lamp. He slid his arm under her shoulders, and she snuggled in next to him.

But suddenly she didn't feel tired. She felt wired. As though she had drunk a gallon of coffee. "Could she be Bella's biological mother?" The thought only occurred to Jess as she said it, but now that it was out of her mouth, it sounded like a legitimate theory. "That would at least make sense."

David shook his head. "No."

"How do you know? You said that you never met her mother." At least, that's what he told her. Had he been lying about it? "Did you meet her?"

"No." David dismissed her concern with a laugh. "Of course I never met her! I have no idea who she is. But Bella was a closed adoption. So there is zero chance that they would have passed along our details to the mother."

"Maybe she has a contact on the inside."

"You thought the previous idea sounded like a Netflix movie?"

"I know," Jessica said. "But can you call to check in the morning? Just to make sure?"

"Of course I can."

"Promise that you will."

He pressed a kiss on the corner of her brow. "I promise to call the adoption agency in the morning and make sure that they didn't pass on any of our information to Bella's birth mother."

Jess nodded, but she didn't feel satisfied.

"What is it?" David asked, picking up on it.

"If she is Bella's mother, why claim her name is Jessica Clarke? That part still doesn't make any sense to me."

"Nothing about this makes sense." He shrugged. "Maybe she was high. Or drunk. Or bipolar or something."

"Maybe."

David yawned. "Can we finish this obviously and necessarily long conversation tomorrow? I need to be up in a few hours."

But Jess was still too wired. "Did Amber's husband say his name when they were on the phone?"

Another long yawn, then David shook his head. "I don't think so, but I'm not exactly thinking straight. Maybe he did and I've already forgotten. What are you thinking?"

"That she's the wife of one of your colleagues at Prairie."

He was silent for a while, as though cataloguing everyone he worked with. "There's only one person at Prairie with the last name Brown, and that's Gloria."

"What about Fresh Start? Maybe Amber is married to one of them."

No answer.

Jess nudged him. "David."

He jerked, yawning. "What?"

"Amber. Could she be the wife of someone from the Fresh Start Foundation?"

"Yes." He gave a slow nod. "Maybe. I don't know, Jess. I need to finish this conversation in the morning. My bones feel like they've been hollowed out, and I need to get up for work in a few hours."

"You're right. I'm so sorry!" She snuggled down next to him. "Go to sleep."

He mumbled something unintelligible.

She rolled onto her side so that her back was to him,

wondering how long she had until Bella started crying again. A few hours at most, because as tired as David was, Jess would stir when he left the bed and probably not get back to any real sleep before Bella needed her.

How could a person be so deeply fatigued and so incredibly wired at the same time? She didn't need to worry about Amber coming back, because she had been arrested.

Madam Batshit, as David had called her, would be spending the night in jail.

But Jess's brain kept wanting to put the word *poor* in front of the woman's name. Instead of, or perhaps in addition to, *crazy*. Even though she felt the woman was a clear and present danger to her family, the obvious desperation in her eyes was something Jess felt deep in her soul.

She'd been in that place of despair before. It wasn't fun.

She closed her eyes and tried to clear her mind. Everything would be better in the morning. But sleep still eluded her.

She counted backward from a hundred, or tried to, but distracting thoughts kept popping up when she hit the seventies. Each and every time.

She mentally went through the items on her to-do list for the following day. That didn't work either. So she tried to slip out of bed without a sound.

But David rolled over when her feet hit the floor.

"Where are you going?" Even half asleep, he still sounded worried.

"Going to get some work done."

"Is that really a good idea?"

"I can't sleep. At least this way I won't keep you up all night with all my tossing and turning. Besides, MotionMosaic needs my T-shirt graphic by the end of the week."

"You're not keeping me up."

She laughed and leaned over him. "I love you. Good night." Then she kissed him on the head and headed for the door. She heard him snoring by the time she got there.

She walked down the hall to her office and turned on the light. Then she sat behind her desk and woke the computer. She needed to design a new graphic tee every two weeks. But had been running behind on the last one, because Bella had been so occupying. Jess wasn't about to gain any new free time, so she might as well work on the shirt design now.

But an hour later, she had made barely a dent in the work, her concentration like leaves in a late autumn gust.

Besides, it was hard to focus on anything with that window right in front of her.

She kept glancing outside into the dark, wondering when (not if) Amber Brown's U-Haul would come driving back to the house.

Chapter Nine

JESSICA SAT in the back of the police cruiser, angry and more than a little scared. The streets seemed empty, but probably only because the homes were so dark and the trees were so still. The only audible sound was the engine and the hushed sounds of static on Carlson's radio (she had turned it down so any conversation was intelligible).

Jessica balled her hands into fists, pulling against the handcuffs. It hurt. But somehow it felt good. And at least she was no longer crying. Her earlier despair was now a burning hot rage.

"I'm not Amber Brown anymore. I changed my name to Jessica Clarke when I got married."

No response from up front.

"That was on July 7, 2023. The day I married David Clarke, the man who lives at 2097 Longhorn and is pretending to not know me."

Still nothing.

"And in addition to stealing my house, they've stolen my baby."

"I remember all of this from that little fit you threw on

the front porch," Officer Carlson said. "You remember, the one that got you in the back seat?"

"Because you didn't listen to me."

"Ma'am, I've listened to you plenty, and I can assure you that by now you're not telling me anything new. You're lucky I don't—"

"She's done something to David."

"What?"

"That woman. She's done something to make David forget about me! That's the only thing that makes any sense."

"Right." The officer nodded. "Hypnotism is the only thing that could possibly make any sense here."

"I never said anything about hypnotism."

"What else does 'doing something to make him forget you' mean? Do you think she hit him on the head with a giant hammer, like in an old Bugs Bunny cartoon?"

"This isn't funny."

"We agree on that."

"I swear I'm not lying," Jessica said.

"Maybe not. Have you had anything to drink tonight?"

"No. Of course not. I was driving the U-Haul until all of this happened."

"Any drugs?" Officer Carlson met her eyes in the rearview mirror.

"No. Obviously. Same answer."

"Then enjoy the ride." Officer Carlson was done with her.

Jessica screamed. Her legs flailing, kicking the back of Carlson's seat.

Carlson slammed on the brakes and looked in the rearview mirror again. "Do that again, and I will hit you with an assault charge in addition to causing a disturbance. You understand me, Amber?"

Of course she understood. Jessica had no other choice except to nod. Carlson's face finally relaxed.

"I just need for someone to hear me," she said. "For someone to believe me."

"Then I suggest you work on your story," Carlson said. "Or tell me the truth."

Jessica said nothing.

So Carlson continued to drive.

Jessica remained silent, watching as the officer pulled into the back of a cream-colored brick building with steel framed windows. She pulled into a garage. Moments later, the door closed behind them. She got out of the car and opened the back door.

Jessica got out. Carlson guided her through a metal door and into a clean, modern building. Overly bright fluorescent lights illuminated tan walls and polished tile floors.

Jessica was guided to a waiting area. Metal chairs lined the wall behind her. An officer sat behind a long wooden counter. On the wall opposite him was a flat screen TV that rolled through a variety of police statistics (*auto crime down by eight percent!*). He looked up when she and Carlson stopped before him.

His name tag read *Barton*. He had a thick build and a square face that framed an almost comically stern expression. He looked like he hadn't laughed since his hair was black. It was now salt and pepper.

"Name?" he said with no emotion.

"Amber Brown," Officer Carlson said.

"Jessica Clarke," Jessica said.

Barton wrote *Amber Brown*, then he looked back up at Jessica. "Birthdate?"

"August 19, 1994."

Barton nodded to the wall where he obviously wanted Jessica to stand.

Carlson walked her over. She stood straight and still, facing Barton.

He pulled a digital camera out from behind the bench and took several photos.

Then Carlson turned her to the right, and then the left, Barton snapping photos each time.

Then Carlson removed the handcuffs, clipping them back to her waist. Jessica rubbed her wrists.

"Fingerprints." Barton expected his lone word to do all the heavy lifting.

Carlson walked her back to the bench.

"Right hand first." He set a form on the counter. It had little boxes for each fingertip, then larger spaces for a palm print. He took her hand, then he inked each finger, rolling them one at a time onto the ink pad, pressing them firmly onto the white form.

Only after her personal smudges were done did she brighten. "You're going to run my fingerprints, right?"

"I'm sorry?" Barton didn't really mean that. He was just obviously not used to talking to perps. If that's what she was.

"If you run my prints, you'll be able to prove I'm the real Jessica."

Carlson sighed. "You've been arrested before?"

"No." She looked around the room. "This isn't really my usual thing."

"So if you've never been arrested, what the hell are we supposed to compare your prints to?"

Jessica frowned. "I don't know. Getting arrested is a totally new and unwelcome experience for me."

"You should keep it that way."

Barton pushed the intake paperwork in front of her. "Sign here."

Jessica picked up the pen and dramatically scrawled

her signature on the form. *JESSICA CLARKE*. It was the name she had proudly written countless times since she first said *I do*.

Carlson sighed.

Officer Barton pursed his lips but clearly determined that she wasn't worth arguing with.

He took the paperwork and turned his back on her, waking up his computer. Then he started typing.

A jail guard appeared and took hold of her, marching Jessica down a sterile, brightly lit hallway.

She stalled, turning back to Carlson. "You're leaving me?"

"Get some sleep."

"How am I supposed to do that when another woman is sleeping in my bed?"

Both the jail guard and Barton looked at Carlson. "Christ, I am not paid enough for this." Then she turned and walked out.

The guard tugged Jessica. She walked with her down to the cells. She unlocked a door, and they reached another counter.

"Shoes off," the guard said.

Jessica kicked them off her feet. Retrieved them and set them on the counter.

"Any jewelry, sharps, drugs?" the guard asked.

Jessica clutched the delicate locket around her neck. David had given it to her on their second anniversary. And then she caught the sparkle of the diamond on her engagement ring, still twinkling with the same brilliance it did on the day he had proposed. Now she wondered if the diamond was a fake.

And why hadn't she shown the ring to Officer Carlson while still standing on the porch? Make David deny that he had proposed to her on that magical evening in Central

Park, halfway across the placid lake when he stopped rowing and presented her ring, with only the distant skyline of New York as their witness.

Their only witness.

"I don't want to," she said.

"Now," said the guard. "You'll get them back in the morning."

She plucked it from her finger and dropped it into a plastic tray with a quiet clink. Her necklace followed. And then her phone.

"What about my purse and bag? Officer Carlson had them."

"They'll be waiting for you as well."

Jessica nodded. The guard put her items into a plastic bag and sealed it. Then she led her further down the corridor and opened a cell.

"In you go."

Jessica stared in at the cinderblock room. The heavy metal door. The security camera — its green light blinking like an all-seeing eye — in the corner of the ceiling.

The guard gave her a nudge.

She stepped inside. The door closed behind her. And then she was alone.

Inside, a metal cot was pushed against the far wall. A thin, uninviting blanket lay folded at one end. She walked over and sat. It was cold. Or maybe she was just goddamn tired. Or in shock. Or all of it. Shivering, she picked it up, shaking it out and wrapped it around her shoulders. The rough material scratched her skin through the thin fabric of David's stupid Coldplay tee.

She leaned against the back wall and drew up her legs, gging her knees. For some reason, she felt jet lagged. But could have been the exhaustion. She wanted to talk to one. No, she needed a long conversation with David.

She yearned for the comfort of his voice and the sureness of his presence. Ever since she had met him, that man had always been her harbor in every storm.

What was this cruel game he had decided to play with her?

And more importantly, why was he playing it?

It was just so impossible to believe that the David she knew could ever do a thing like this to her.

And that's when a new thought struck her.

What if the man at 2097 Longhorn wasn't really David at all? Jessica had some bizarre doppelgänger standing in her place. Maybe the same was true for him.

Or maybe he had a twin. She hadn't thought of that.

But one thing she was now quite certain of: that had not been her David who opened the door.

She shot up from the cot, then crossed her cell and banged on the cold metal. Over and over again until the guard finally came down the corridor.

She slid open the little metal face plate and looked inside. "This better be good."

"I need to speak with Officer Carlson."

"She's unavailable."

"You can't know that! You haven't even—"

"I don't need to. Officer Carlson—"

"Will want to hear what I have to say." Jessica glared at the guard, her jaw set and her teeth clenched, fists in determined balls at her side.

The guard sighed. "I'll be right back. But I can't promise anything."

"Thank you."

The little face plate slid shut. And Jessica paced. What if the guard was lying? What if she wasn't going to fetch Carlson at all? But she needn't have worried.

Less than twenty minutes later, the face plate slid open again.

This time, Officer Carlson looked inside. "What can I do for you, Amber?"

"What if he's not David?" Jessica said.

Carlson blinked. "What?"

"The man at the house. What if he's not David? What if it's his twin, or some kind of imposter? Maybe our doppelgängers did something to David and he needs our help—"

"Enough." Carlson looked genuinely disappointed. "Go to sleep, Amber. You'll feel better in the morning. When you can see things more—"

"I'M NOT AMBER!"

Carlson shut the face plate. Jessica kicked the door. "I SAID I'M NOT AMBER!"

There was no response.

Jessica walked over and collapsed on her cot. Why wouldn't anyone believe her?

She lay down. Not that there was any chance she could sleep.

But the mental and physical exhaustion of the day hung around her like a heavy chain, dragging her down. And as soon as she closed her eyes, she was asleep.

Chapter Ten

JESS LEANED back in her desk chair with a long sigh.

She had been working on her graphic design for the last couple of hours, and the T-shirt was now undoubtedly further along than it had been when she started, but it sure didn't feel that way.

Squinting at the screen, her work looked as generic as she suspected it was. "Dammit."

Maybe one day she'd be working for herself and could finally stop second-guessing what the big boss might think of her submission. After all, Jess knew what made a design visually click better than the people who paid her. But until that day, she knew she'd spend half her billable hours trying to read minds. The only thing she never questioned from MotionMosaic was the paycheck.

She yawned, and it surprised her. But at least Jess felt grateful that she was finally tired. Her eyelids had gained enough weight that she was confident that, despite a wired mind, her body would drag her deep into sleep once she hit the mattress.

She powered down her desktop, then left the office, stopping by the nursery to check on Bella.

She was fast asleep, laying like a doll in her crib. Her small chest rising and falling in a steady rhythm, her tiny hands curled into miniature fists, her head cradled against the bedding.

Jess leaned into the crib and smelled her. A sweet, almost sugary scent, blended with baby powder and a tease of that laundry detergent specially made for delicate skin.

She smiled and kissed Bella's cheeks, then slipped quietly back into the hallway, closing the door behind her before heading back to the bedroom.

David was loudly snoring. The kind of sound he only made in his deepest sleep.

She tiptoed across the carpet and slipped under the covers.

Then she closed her eyes and, taking deliberate breaths, pictured skies filled with stars. She redirected her imagination whenever it threatened to wander off and replay the evening's events. Then she nodded off, curled into a comma on the bed, her body tightly tucked under the covers.

A sudden sound woke her.

Jess kept her eyes closed, but her ears were alert and listening.

She heard the sound again and opened her eyes. It was still dark in the room. She turned to David's side of the bed but found it empty.

Another creak.

"David?"

No response, and Jess could feel his lack of presence in the bedroom. Maybe he couldn't sleep either and had gotten up to get a drink or a bite to eat.

She got out of bed and walked over to the window.

The backyard was quiet.

But something didn't feel right.

Jess went to the en suite bathroom and grabbed her robe off the hook on the back of the door.

Then she headed back into the bedroom and out into the hall.

"David?" Her voice was slightly louder now that she had passed the nursery. There was no response. She took the stairs down to the first level.

As soon as her foot hit the floor, she tried again. "David?"

Still no response.

And now her heart was pounding against her ribcage.

"DAVID!"

Shit, where was he? And why was the air so cool down here?

Jess went down to the front hallway and stopped cold. The front door was ajar.

She swallowed hard. There was a shelf in the hallway next to the closet that held David's various awards. She grabbed *Salesman of the Year 2021,* then pushed the door open and stepped out onto the front porch.

The crescent moon hung high in the sky like the Cheshire cat's mischievous smile. Countless stars glittered around it. The air was still, the neighborhood an inky black except for a few select streetlights glowing in the distance.

Why were the ones on their block out? Had someone done that deliberately?

Her heart continued to pound, insistent that something was wrong.

She squinted into the dark. Was that a flash of a passing shadow?

"David?"

Still no response. Jess stepped out onto the porch and jumped down the stairs, heading down the front walk toward the fence surrounding the property.

God. If Patsy were to look outside her window right now, she would have to conclude that Jess was crazy, or sleepwalking under a haze of Ambien. Albeit with a salesman of the year award in her hands.

A part of her felt like a predator.

But what prey? There was no one around.

"David?" she tried one more time.

Still no answer, but that's when she saw it.

That goddamned U-Haul. Parked just up the street under one of the broken streetlights. If it hadn't been off, she would have seen it from her office window.

She turned back to the house. A shadow moved in the window of the nursery.

An involuntary whimper of fear bubbled up from her throat. "Bella!"

She dropped David's award and bolted for the front door, barreling inside and bounding up the stairs, two at a time. She almost tripped on the top step, but caught herself before she could fall, dashing down the hall and into her daughter's room.

But David wasn't standing next to the crib. It was a woman, cradling Bella in her arms.

Jess tried to scream but couldn't.

Bella gurgled.

"Hush, Gwen," Amber said.

Gwen. The name sat like rancid, rotting meat in her mind.

"Put her down," Jess said.

But Amber ignored her. Keeping her back to Jess, stroking Bella's head as she crooned. "*Hush now, darling, close your eyes, in the moonlight, dreams will rise. A distant lullaby fills the air, whispered secrets from a stranger fair."*

"Stop singing to her! She's not your daughter!"

"Darkness holds a melody, a tale yet untold, a chilling—"

"I said stop singing!" Jess stepped closer. "Put her down right now or I'll call the police."

Amber stopped singing but didn't turn around.

Bella gave a small cry.

"It's alright, Bella," Jess said. "Mama's here."

"Her name is Gwen," Amber said. And then she started singing again. *"Hush now, darling, close your eyes, in the moonlight, dreams will rise. A distant lullaby fills the air, whispered secrets—"*

"STOP SINGING!"

Amber laughed, adjusting Bella in her arms.

So Jess screamed until her lungs were raw. "PUT DOWN MY BABY!"

And still Amber ignored her.

Jess lunged across the room, her face twisted into knots of rage, her hands like claws. She grabbed Amber's arm and whipped her around. "GIVE ME BACK MY BABY!"

But it wasn't Amber who stared back at her. It was her, Jessica Clarke, married to David and mother to Bella.

And she looked terrified to see Jess. "Who are you?"

Jess blinked. *Who the hell was she?*

Jess darted across the room to the mirror on the wall to see Amber Brown's face staring back at her.

Jess screamed again.

Then so did the other version of her.

And then Jess fell. And jolted awake.

She was lying on the floor of her office. She sat, confused. Then realized she must have fallen asleep and toppled out of her chair.

So the nightmare wasn't real.

But it sure felt real by the way her heart was hammering in her chest.

The bedroom door flew open. David was standing in the entry.

Jess got to her feet, embarrassed. "I'm sorry."

"What is it?" He looked around the room, holding one of his shoes up as though it were a club. "Is it that Amber woman? Did she come back?"

The sound of Amber's name got Jess's heart pounding even harder.

"No." Jess shook her head. "Or I guess she was, but only in my dream." She gave a nervous laugh to lighten the mood. "Or nightmare, since dates with a psycho aren't exactly something I want to dream about. Like, not ever again."

David walked over and gently took Jess by the arm, pulling her into a kiss. Then he rested his forehead against hers. "I'm so sorry about all of this."

"You have nothing to be sorry about."

"And you need to get to bed. You'll feel better when you've had some sleep."

She pulled back, looking up at him. "Do you?"

He raised a brow.

"Feel better? Now that you've had some sleep."

"Hell no."

She laughed. And this time it felt more natural.

He tugged her out into the hall. "Come on."

She followed him, then paused in front of Bella's open bedroom door. "I just want to check on—"

"Of course." David smiled, then squeezed her hand before letting her go.

She waited until he'd gone into their bedroom, then she poked her head in the room. Bella was fast asleep. But she entered anyway.

Now Jess didn't care if she woke her. But Bella was apparently as exhausted as her parents. She didn't even stir as Mommy leaned into the crib and smelled her, kissing her on the cheeks. It was only then that Jess joined David in the bedroom.

He was already fast asleep.

She knew she wasn't going to join him in slumber. Not now that fear had lit her mind on fire. But at the same time, she knew her body needed rest. So she climbed into bed beside him.

She tried not to look at the clock as the night slowly drained away, leaving dawn behind. But no way in hell was she going to sleep. She had no intention of allowing that nightmare to claw its way back into her brain.

Chapter Eleven

THANK God it was only a nightmare.

Jessica felt like she could finally exhale as she soared past the *Welcome to Texas* sign, splashed with a bullseye made of bird shit, right where the X in Texas came together. Of course, no bird had actually aimed for the sign, but Jessica still saw the feat as impressive, intentional or not.

She kept her left hand on the steering wheel as she reached over to grab her phone from the passenger seat, swiping over to *Whiskerface*. She hit the green phone icon.

And let it ring.

And ring.

And ring.

But still David didn't answer.

She glanced down at the screen. His contact no longer said *Whiskerface*. It read *WRONG NUMBER*, right as she flew past the *Welcome to Texas* sign.

Another one?

That was odd. Especially as it had bird shit on it as well.

All the birds in the state must have loved hitting targets as much as those gun-toting Texans.

She glanced back at the phone. It said *Whiskerface* again. Maybe she had misread it. After all, she was tired. She hit the green icon.

"Yeah?" It was a strange voice.

"David?"

"Jesus, lady," the man said. "How many times do I gotta tell you? This is not David Clarke's phone. It never has been. And unless you're offering me a wheelbarrow full of hot wings, don't call back!"

Such an odd thing for the man to say, especially that part about the hot wings. And he didn't sound like her David at all.

Jessica passed the *Welcome to Texas* sign again. It had that same smear of bird shit.

"What the fuck?"

She glanced back over her shoulder, gripping the steering wheel tight. The Manhattan skyline shimmered in the distance. A chill ran down her spine.

What the hell was going on?

New York didn't border Texas.

Was someone playing a trick on her?

She turned back to the road just in time to see the *Welcome to Texas* sign again, bird shit still marking the heart of that X.

She felt panic creeping toward her.

She gripped the steering wheel even tighter, her heart pounding, her forehead wrinkling with worry. She was nearing another sign. She almost didn't want to look. It couldn't possibly be—

But it was. Another *Welcome to Texas* sign.

Her breath grew shallow, and a heavy unease settled over her.

And then a horn brayed.

Jessica turned and looked out the driver's window. A semi-trailer barreled toward her. It was belching black clouds of exhaust, its horn screaming, grill flashing in the afternoon sun. Gaining speed with every second.

She threw up her hands to protect her face.

Too late. The semi smashed into the side of the U-Haul and—

She sat with a start, a scream still trapped in her throat.

Where the hell was she? The walls were made of cement cinderblocks. The door was—

Right. Jail.

The nightmare before her nightmare had been the one that was true.

Jessica rubbed her temples. She had a splitting headache. No doubt she was dehydrated as well. In addition to being hungry. The last thing she'd eaten had been that stale granola bar.

And she felt gross. How long had she been wearing these clothes? It must be close to twenty-four hours now. Her jeans and tee were both rumpled, her skin was slick with sweat, and her hair was matted and damp.

Even without any mirrors, Jessica was sure she had dark circles under her eyes that made her look like a raccoon that had pulled an all-nighter. She sniffed an armpit. Almost passed out.

The face plate on the door opened. A new jail guard looked in on her. "Amber Brown?"

"Jessica Clarke."

"Right. I heard that's what you're calling yourself."

Jessica glared at him.

"You want breakfast here or at home?" he asked.

"Home."

He jerked his head. "Then let's go." He closed the faceplate.

She heard the jangle of keys, metal scraping against metal. A second later, the door opened.

She jumped off the bench. "What about my things?"

"They'll be waiting for you at reception."

He walked her down the hall, unlocked the second metal door and opened it wide. She stepped through. But unlike last night, he didn't accompany her. Simply closed it and relocked it.

Jessica was back in the area where Barton had finger-printed and photographed her, but he no longer sat behind the desk. He'd been replaced by a new cop.

The officer glanced at her. "Amber Brown?"

She opened her mouth to argue, then snapped it closed again. "Yeah."

He pulled out her overnight bag, shoes, and purse, then handed Jessica the clear bag with her phone, ring, and necklace. "Anything else?"

She shook her head.

He placed a piece of paper on the counter that listed all of her items and gestured to it. "Sign here."

She did.

Then he gave her a stern look. "If you return to the Clarke home, you'll be charged with mischief or trespassing. Do you understand?"

Jessica nodded, still numb.

"Then you're free to go."

Jessica stared at him. "What?"

"You've been arrested, but not charged. Seems Carlson took pity on you." He pulled a card from beneath the counter and set it before you. "You can collect your U-Haul at the impound lot. It's at 905 Chestnut." The card had the same address and a phone number.

"My phone is dead," Jessica said.

"They usually are." The cop nodded and then turned back to his computer.

Jessica got the message and made quick work of shoving her feet into her shoes. Then she grabbed her property. Last thing she wanted was for him to change his mind.

She walked outside, then made her way around to the front of the station, blinking in the early morning light.

Jessica looked around for someone to help her. Her chest felt tight. Everyone was going to be a stranger. Why would they want to help her?

She watched a couple of early morning joggers pass by. But she didn't want to interfere with their run. Then she spotted an older woman with gray hair pulled back into a tight bun. She wore a plain skirt and sensible shoes. Looked like she didn't want to be fucked with.

But Jessica tried anyway. "Excuse me."

The woman stopped, eyeing her with suspicion.

"I just got into town, and I'm not sure where anything is." At least it was the truth. "Is there a community center around?"

The woman's face softened into a genuine smile, her eyes crinkling at the edges. "Well, of course, dear." She pointed down the street. "You want to head two blocks down there. See the blue building?"

Jessica nodded.

"Take a right when you reach there. The center will be about a half a block farther on."

"Thank you."

The woman reached into her purse and plucked out a five-dollar bill. She held it out to Jessica. "You look like you could use a little good will."

Jessica nodded, not daring to speak. Tears clogged her

throat, fingers folding around the bill as though it were a lifeline. She must look even worse than she had imagined.

The woman walked on, disappearing moments later. If it hadn't been for the five dollars clutched in her hand, Jessica might have thought she imagined the whole thing.

She tucked the money into her purse, then started walking toward the blue building.

Now that it was daylight, she had a better sense of Dallas. Wide boulevards and highways cut crisscross paths through the city, mingling with green spaces and buildings.

When she'd first studied the city on a map, David had identified a few standout structures. Landmarks like Reunion Tower, with its spherical top, and the sharply angular Bank of America Plaza. The skyline was a tapestry of southern charm and urban hustle, woven with threads of glass, steel, and Texas grit.

Right now, it didn't feel like home. Neither did New York. For the first time in her life, Jessica felt like she didn't belong anywhere.

She turned the corner, approaching the community center. The windows were tinted a deep blue green, the steel supports painted a dull gray. It looked as though it had been built in the Seventies.

She entered. It was cool inside. The reception desk was long and low. Paintings on the walls did the hard work of cheering the place up, though they mostly failed. Jessica stopped before a canvas of multicolored poppies, sure that she had seen a similar, if not identical, print during her last trip to IKEA.

An old CPR dummy was propped up behind the desk in a chair. Adjacent to it was a posted sign that read, *CPR CLASSES EVERY SATURDAY!*

Jessica walked over and smiled at the receptionist. The

woman wore a white collared shirt and looked like she woke up reporting for duty.

"How much is it to use the pool?" Jessica asked.

The woman pointed to the very obvious sign that listed prices. "Four dollars."

Jessica pulled the five-dollar bill from her purse and handed it over. A moment later, she had her change.

There was a lost and found box outside of the change rooms. She snagged a clean towel, then stepped into the women's room. Found an empty shower. Then hung her overnight bag and purse from a hook on the door.

She turned on the tap, stripping while the water warmed up. Then she stepped beneath the spray. It was too hot. But she didn't care. Letting the water warm her body.

She squeezed some soap from the container affixed to the wall and washed her hair. When she finished, she felt almost human again. But no way was she putting on yesterday's clothes and the ones in her overnight bag were dirty as well.

She wrapped the towel around her and inspected the lockers that filled the room. Several were closed, but not locked. She stole a pair of sweatpants, a T-shirt, and a hoodie.

God, it made her feel like crap.

But she felt even worse when she rummaged through the woman's purse, looking for cash. She found close to fifty bucks. She took it all.

Then she grabbed her bags and pulled her hood all the way up. She practically ran out of the community center, feeling more like a criminal than she ever thought possible.

Two blocks later, she spotted a McDonald's and walked inside. It was practically empty.

Jessica made her way to the counter. Before the worker

could even ask, she gave her order. "Quarter Pounder with fries and a Coke, please. And yes, I'll have the meal or whatever. And an extra fry."

The crew member looked bored. "For here or to go?"

Jessica saw outlets where she could charge her phone. "Here."

Within minutes, she had her meal. It was garbage, of course, and exactly what she wanted. The burger was juicy, savory with a hint of smoky char that she knew was actually a chemical making the meat taste fresh from the grill (was it David that told her that?). The fries were both salty and crispy, deep fried in she didn't even know what, probably something that was less biodegradable than plastic. And they tasted absolutely perfect.

Jessica got two refills of her Coke before finally deciding that she had been sitting in the McDonald's parking lot for too long and that it was time to get the fuck out of Dodge. Her phone wasn't charged, but it was charged enough.

She looked down the block when leaving the restaurant and saw that there was a police car nearing the community center.

She kept on going, trying and failing to book an Uber as she walked.

The app wasn't letting her schedule a pickup. Not without verifying her credit card first.

She stopped and rummaged through her purse. Her overnight bag. Crap. She forgot to get it back from Carlson and she didn't know the number off by heart.

"GODDAMMIT!"

A man walking toward her stopped, then crossed the road and continued on the other side.

Jessica glared at him as though he'd offended her, then

ducked into an alley. She googled her bank, then dialed customer service.

"Welcome to World Fidelity, this is Celeste, how can I help you?" Celeste sounded more excited by her question than the cashier at McDonald's had been, but Jessica felt sure that she'd just had more practice.

"I'm having trouble with my credit card," Jessica said.

"I'll need you to answer a series of security questions," Celeste said.

"Go on."

"Date of birth."

"August 19, 1994."

"Mother's maiden name."

Jessica grimaced. "Sparks."

"Address."

"2097 Longhorn, Dallas, Texas."

Celeste hesitated.

"Wait," Jessica said. "That's my new address. 1706 - 547 Arbor Street, New York." There was a moment of silence.

"You canceled your credit card," said Celeste.

That was a slap to Jessica's face, because no, she had absolutely not canceled her credit card, and never would have done such a ridiculous thing before taking a cross-country trip.

"No," she said. "I never canceled my credit card."

"Someone did." Celeste sounded sympathetic.

"I've been on the road for three days. Why would I cancel my credit card? I needed to use it."

"Maybe you thought it was stolen and—"

"No." Jessica cut her off, angry at the wrong person. "I want it reinstated."

"I'm afraid that's impossible. You can apply for a new

one if you like. All you need to do is come into one of our branches and show your ID."

"My ID is in the wallet that I left at home in New York. What can I do right now? How can I fix this?"

"Without ID?" Celeste said, as though needing to confirm that Jessica wasn't an idiot.

"Right. Without ID."

"You can't do anything. We need to see your identification to prove your identity."

"What about the security questions?"

"That won't get you a new credit card." Celeste was starting to sound impatient.

"I don't want a new card, I want my old card. The one I already have because I never canceled it. Can you help me with that?"

"I'm sorry, ma'am, but—"

Jessica hung up. Whatever came after *but* was going to make zero difference to her life.

She googled the nearest branch of her bank and found one that was a twenty-three-minute walk away. She returned to the road, then pressed the crosswalk button.

A half hour later, Jessica surveyed the branch's three tellers. She picked the dorky-looking guy who seemed closest to her in age, despite his line being the longest. Then she patiently waited for her turn, hoping to take a stab at getting *someone* to help her.

But from the moment he pushed his glasses up onto the bridge of his nose, she knew the battle was already lost.

"I understand that you lost your debit card in New York and that you're now here in Texas," he said, repeating her question as a statement, "but I'll still need two pieces of identification before you can issue another one."

"But my ID was lost," Jessica said. "I know my account number and my pin. Shouldn't that be enough?"

The teller shook his head. "Unfortunately, it's not."

"Is there any way you can make an exception?" Jessica leaned forward, hating herself for what she was doing before it was even a quarter done. She plastered an artificial smile on her face. "*For me?*"

"I'll be right back," said the teller.

And he was, just a few moments later, with the manager in tow.

"I'm afraid I'm going to have to ask you to leave." The manager glanced over at the security guard. "Unless you need an escort."

"No, I do not." Jessica shook her head and headed for the door.

Never had she felt more furious. Or stupid. Or ashamed.

She punched 2097 Longhorn Drive into her phone. It was a forty-five-minute walk away. She got started.

Chapter Twelve

THE MORNING SUN painted the breakfast table in soft strokes of light.

"You sure you'll be okay if I head into work?" David asked.

"For the third time, yes." Jess gave her husband a smile she barely felt.

They had gotten up at the same time, but he'd actually managed to snag a couple hours of sleep. The only shuteye Jess managed came with that goddamn nightmare.

"Okay…" He glanced at her, apprehensive.

"Stop sounding so unsure," said Jess, cradling her mug of coffee. "This isn't up for debate. You have that big sales meeting for the Sumner account today, and I don't want you missing that because of me."

"I love that you know I have a meeting for Sumner today."

"I try to pay attention when you talk."

He laughed. She smiled again, and that one came easier.

It didn't take long for him to look serious again. "I really don't like leaving you alone after last night, Jess."

"David." She locked eyes with him. "That woman is gone. She's been arrested, and she won't be coming back." She said it like a mantra, a prayer meant to restore their disrupted life. "Besides, I won't be alone. Clare and I are meeting up after my meeting. Now, go."

He leaned across the table and pressed a lingering kiss to her forehead. "I'm going."

And then he was gone.

She drew a deep breath, admiring the early morning sun streaming through her window, listening to the birds chirp outside. For the first time since that cop led Amber Brown away in handcuffs, Jess almost felt serene.

She poured herself another cup of coffee, hoping the feeling would last. Then she checked on Bella. David had already changed her diaper and given her a bottle. And she was back to sleep. At least someone in their family was getting rest.

But she'd be awake soon. Bella's after-breakfast nap never lasted long. So Jess wanted to get as much of the T-shirt design finished as possible. It wasn't yet due, but the deadline had triggered some mild contention at Motion-Mosaic, and they would be firming up the date during this afternoon's Zoom meeting.

Jess used to find her flow by sitting down in front of her design, but it had been forever since she felt consumed by her craft. She wanted to feel like a maestro conducting a symphony while working, but instead it was more like Jess clutching her baton as the orchestra played a dirge.

Her movements were laborious, her design maudlin. And though it was much easier for Jess to blame her creative struggle on the bosses who critiqued her work, she also knew the truth was that this gig kept a leash on her courage.

She was circling the edges of a design she might actually like when Bella started crying. Jess persisted for a few minutes, thinking Bella might go back to sleep. But no. She continued to cry. Jess abandoned her work.

After feeding Bella and engaging in some desperately needed playtime — for both of them — Jess didn't get back to her desktop until a few minutes before the meeting started.

Opening her design would be a mistake. The sight of even one little thing she could tweak would either have her making the adjustment and running late, or obsessing over the alteration she would already be making in her head, over and over and over.

Bella was wiggling happily on a blanket, staring up at the ceiling, or nothing in particular. She was settled. Jess didn't want to distract her.

So she counted down the minutes until the meeting started, staring out the window at the empty spot the U-Haul had occupied the previous night. But finally, it was time to sign on. The meeting proceeded smoothly enough until it came to Jess's deadline. She suspected it would be moved up. Just not as much as it was.

"We'll need the finished design by Friday," Gary said.

"Wait." Jess shook her head. "I was supposed to have until next Wednesday."

"That's not going to work anymore. Muriel needs to sign off on the artwork by next Tuesday, or it will seriously impede production. And I don't have to tell you—"

"No, you don't," Jess said. "I'm well aware of exactly what the bottleneck does to the entire line without you telling me." Again.

"Is Friday going to be a problem?" Gary asked.

"I could have it to you on Friday, but I suggest relaxing a day on this one. I promise to have the images to Muriel by the weekend, then based on her feedback, I can make any required changes on Monday."

Gary nodded. "Sounds good."

And then, since the boss thought it was cool, everyone else felt safe to start nodding along.

"Sounds good," echoed a couple of sycophants.

Everyone said their goodbyes, and Jess hurried to close the Zoom window, returning to her design, hoping to reignite the flow she'd found before Bella woke up.

Flow was easy enough to find. But after five minutes, Jess stopped cold and stared at her work.

Her design was supposed to be edgy. She had never intended to scare the shit out of herself with it. But that's what she had done by drawing two nearly identical faces staring each other down.

Jess blinked.

What the hell was wrong with her? And why had she drawn that?

Though, of course, she knew.

Maybe Bella sensed her mood shift, because she suddenly started crying, and Jess wanted to join her.

She turned off the computer, giving it a dirty look, as though it were responsible for the design and not Jess, before gathering Bella into her arms and leaving her office behind.

She went downstairs to the kitchen, singing "Itsy Bitsy Spider" on the way. She followed it up with a soaring rendition of "Three Blind Mice" as she made Bella's bottle. She tried to block out the nightmare from last night, with Amber (or was it Jess?) singing the homemade lullaby to Bella.

Bella grabbed the bottle, giggling. Jess smiled. It was

hard not to when looking down at her perfect face. "How would you like to see Aunty Clare?"

Bella farted.

"That is not the answer I'm looking for," Jess said.

Bella cooed.

"That's better."

After Bella finished her milk, Jess got her cleaned up. Then she grabbed the diaper bag and locked up the house with more intention than she remembered ever committing to that task before.

With Bella in her car seat and some classical music playing on the radio, she backed the Volvo out of the garage and pulled around to the front of the house.

Her heart was beating hard for no reason.

Jess knew full well that it was completely illogical, but for some reason she still half-expected to see the damned U-Haul, Amber standing in front of it, arms crossed as she stared at their house.

But, of course, Jess saw no U-Hauls or Ambers either in front of the house or on her short drive to the park.

She pulled into a space adjacent to Clare's Infinity, then climbed out. She spotted her friend and Clare's toddler, Evan, both sitting on a nearby bench. She waved.

Jess had met Clare in the adoptive mom's support group. And Clare was better than everyone else in her life when it came to all that self-development stuff. Especially when it came to listening, although Jess would never confess that to David.

"What's up?" Clare asked as Jess sat next to her. "Why do you look like that?"

"What do I look like?"

"Oh, I think you know what you look like," Clare said.

Jess laughed. "You'll have to spell it out for me."

"Death. You look like death, Jess. More than the

mommy fatigue. So let me guess, your latest T-shirt design is killing you, because you don't know what 'edgy' means anymore."

"I know what edgy means."

Clare nodded. "That could be a word to describe your current mood."

"See," Jess said, laughing, "this is why I needed to see you."

"To not talk about the thing on your mind?"

"Are you kidding? I'm dying to talk about it." Then Jess launched into her tale, telling her all about the weirdness that had transpired the previous evening.

"What the fuck?" Clare mouthed several times, as though not wanting to say it out loud on account of two-year-old Evan.

But Clare also had some serious questions similar to the ones that Jess had asked the previous night. "Could this Amber Brown be Bella's biological mother?"

"I wondered the same thing," Jess said, still not quite convincing herself. "But David says that would be impossible."

"*Unlikely* is the word he's looking for. Nothing is impossible."

"His sister not being a bitch is impossible." Jess laughed.

"Okay, I've gotta say something."

"You always do."

"First, the word 'impossible' bothers me. It's so … dismissive."

"And second? Just get right to it, Clare. I don't need any warmup."

"You're obviously agitated with David, otherwise you wouldn't have taken that jab at his sister."

"I'm agitated in general right now, because of last

night." Bella clapped to agree with her mommy. "But I also took the jab at Leanne because she's a total—"

"Don't say it!"

"I wasn't going to."

"I think you were." Clare laughed.

"I was going to say 'brat.'"

"Uh-huh. Are you sure that David isn't messing around on you?" And then, because of course she couldn't help it, she added, "Again."

"It's possible," Jess said. "Except that David seemed just as confused by the woman as I was."

"You're right. That would be *sooooper* hard to fake."

"She didn't just know his name, Clare. She knew my name, too. And that we had a baby. And she had *my* credit card. Not his. So it's not like she singled one of us out."

"She could have singled you out to fuck with him. Or she's fucking with him to hurt you."

"Direct hit if that's what she was trying to do. I barely slept. And I think—"

Bella burped up some milk.

Jessica dove into her diaper bag. "Fuck."

"What?"

"My wallet."

"Did you lose it?"

"No. Goddammit." She rubbed her brow, trying to remember. "Oh. I took it out to get my driver's license last night when the cop was there. I'm pretty sure I left it on David's cabinet in the hallway."

"You need sleep, my friend. When Bella goes down, you go down with her."

"Okay. I'll be a good girl."

"That means not staring at the screen and tweaking your work for two hours," Clare said.

"I know what being a good girl means. Also, can you

just say the thing you're holding off on? Because it's written all over your face."

Clare sighed. "Are you positive that David doesn't know Amber?"

"I already told you that I wasn't."

"I'm asking how certain you are. Be honest."

"I'm always honest."

"You're usually honest."

"Ninety-five percent."

"So that leaves five," Clare said.

"And you are excellent at math. Can we change the subject now?"

"Sure. Do you want to talk about something gruesome?"

"Always."

"My neighbor's brother was coming home from an estate sale out in Texarkana. A semi plowed right into him on the highway."

"Oh, shit…"

"Killed him instantly."

Jess felt chilled to the bone.

Chapter Thirteen

JESSICA CROUCHED behind a cluster of bushes in the alley, watching as the replacement that David insisted on calling by her name backed out of her garage in a hunter green Volvo and drove toward her.

She ducked into the bushes, holding her breath, expecting to be caught. The vehicle pulled around the corner. She knew Gwen was in that car. She stifled an urge to scream her name.

Then she counted ten Mississippis before scurrying out of her hiding place in the bushes between David's yard and his (their) neighbor's. She knew no one was home, but it didn't stop her from knocking.

No one answered.

Jessica knocked again, louder this second time, but still no response.

She looked around the backyard. Lush green grass, with a few trees for some light shade. A small herb garden and a modest sized outdoor seating area for entertaining guests. A barbecue, and a small rock garden. *BINGO*.

She looked all around. The backyard was fairly

secluded, but the last thing Jessica wanted was another night in jail. She had a feeling the cops wouldn't be so lenient this time.

She picked up a rock from the garden, took off her hoodie, and bundled it up. Then she marched toward the back door, not breaking her stride. If she hesitated, she knew she was going to talk herself out of—

Too late.

Jessica slammed the hoodie wrapped rock into the window of the back door.

But the glass didn't shatter, or even crack. The rock bounced right back at her and upsetting her balance. She caught herself from falling, then removed the rock from her hoodie and chucked it at the window.

That did the trick. The window shattered, sending shards of glass spraying across the ground and presumably the kitchen floor.

Jessica dashed back to her hiding space, cowering among the trees, holding her breath as she worked her way through more Mississippis. Finally, she poked her head out and took a timid look around.

The breaking glass hadn't set off any alarm, and she didn't see that any neighbors had been alerted by the sound.

She counted again, but now she was deliberately wasting time. "Come on, Jessica. Move your ass."

She crept out from the trees and ran across the yard to the back door.

She used the hoodie to reach through the broken window carefully to avoid cutting herself, and turned the deadbolt, letting herself inside.

Jessica entered, taking extra care to wipe her fingerprints off the outside knob and the lock. Her blood pumped with adrenaline. The whole situation was messed up. She felt like a burglar. But how was that possible, considering this was her house?

She made herself step into the center of the kitchen. Then the fury hit her hard. She had to monitor her breath, otherwise she was going to hyperventilate.

How dare David show her pictures of this place, tease her with hopes and dreams of a new life, and then what? Snatch it all away?

She had no idea how to finish that sentence. She felt lost. Which was odd, considering this was her home. Wasn't it? She sure as hell had signed enough paperwork to suggest that it was.

She looked around the kitchen. The room was homey and comforting. Jessica could practically smell the goddamned cookies she was sure Replacement Jessica made from scratch. And there was a laptop plugged into the wall that she no doubt looked up recipes on while the cookies were baking.

She took another few moments to breathe through the rage. Getting angry wasn't going to get her closer to the truth. At least not yet.

With a final exhale, she strode to the sink. Crouched down and opened the lower cabinet door to find a pair of rubber gloves inside.

She pulled them on, then started exploring the house, keeping her eye on the time. She figured she had at least a half an hour to an hour.

She started in the kitchen, fastidiously sifting through each cabinet, leaving nothing untouched, from plates to baby bottles, while making sure to leave everything exactly as she left it. All of these things were supposed to be hers. Or maybe not. She and David were going to shop for their home together.

She made her way into the hallway, venturing down

toward the front door. Now she was standing on the opposite side of where she had been the previous evening. What would she have done if the Replacement had strolled up, saying everything that had come out of her own mouth? Probably wouldn't have believed her either. She spotted a wallet on a cabinet full of awards for David.

She picked it up, opening it, staring at the driver's license. Jessica Clarke.

Her fingers tightened on the square of plastic and then she jammed the entire wallet into the pocket of her hoodie.

She entered the living room. It was full of bright colors and plush furniture, with a cozy atmosphere. Artwork filled the walls, bringing memories of her apartment in New York to mind.

There had to be some simple explanation for all of this.

She and David would be laughing about this soon. Although Jessica wanted to laugh right now. This was all so stupid. The man she knew as her husband would never do anything to hurt her like this.

She adjusted a chair, taking a moment to picture herself picking out new furniture. Maybe a couch with more stuffing. Then imagined her and David making love and getting lost in the cushions.

She spotted a large photo of David and the Replacement laughing at something. It brought her crashing back to reality, as though someone had thrown a rock at her chest.

She made her way upstairs and into the main bedroom.

Tears pricked her eyes as she searched through drawers and closets, as though the secret to whatever was happening might be located inside.

Finally she gave up looking around and sat on the bed.

She hugged a pillow to her chest, fighting off more tears. This was the bed where she should be sleeping with David.

Since that couldn't be her husband, who was the man who had taken his place? *Their places*.

She needed to find out.

Jessica wiped her face, then returned to the closet.

She spied an empty backpack tucked into the corner and took it out, tossed it on the bed, and gathered some clothes. Pants and shirts, socks and underwear. She filled the bag, feeling more like herself, still sure that there had to be some stupid explanation to all of this. The kind that would make her feel dumb the moment she heard it.

Of course! she would say. *How could I not have seen that?*

For the first time in her life, she was looking forward to feeling that way. Especially if it helped her make sense of her current predicament.

With the backpack full, Jessica went back to the closet for a last time, staring at David's side of the closet. And suddenly, as though possessed, she started yanking his clothes from the hangers. She didn't care about being caught. Why should she? She was his wife!

The other side of the closet was supposed to be hers. She pulled shoe boxes off the top shelf and searched through them until she found the box with the old pair of slippers.

Something clicked, and she knew even before shoving her hand inside the slipper that she would find a stash rolled up inside. And she did. She pulled out the roll of bills, fingering the currency.

If she didn't know the David Clarke who lived at 2097 Longhorn Drive, then how the hell did she know his secret hiding spot?

If the man who lived here wasn't her David, then he

sure as shit was doing a better job at impersonation than the woman playing Jessica.

She looked down at the money and gave it a quick count. There was almost two grand in her hands. She stuffed it into the backpack. She pulled Jessica's wallet from the hoodie and dumped that in as well. Then she zipped it closed.

Time was running short now. Who knew when the Volvo might be easing back into the garage? She supposed she wouldn't mind 'David' catching her in the house, but she had no idea what Replacement Jessica was capable of.

But she couldn't leave yet. Not without looking in that final room. She opened the nursery room door. And it was like a cold blade between her ribs.

She walked inside.

The room smelled of Gwen.

It was serene and calm. Jessica even approved of the warm yellow paint on the walls. It was something she would have chosen. At least this woman appeared to be taking good care of Gwen.

She walked over to the empty crib and looked inside. Tears pricked her eyes.

She picked up a light green baby blanket bunched in the corner and brought it to her nose. She inhaled. The fabric was soft and gentle, smelling of baby powder and laundered cotton.

She felt like she was going to be sick. Is this why everything was happening? Someone didn't think she deserved Gwen?

She set the blanket down, then grabbed a nightgown draped over the side of the crib. It had little embroidered forget-me-nots and a scalloped hem — exactly the kind of nightgown she would have bought Gwen.

Jessica stuffed that into the backpack.

There wasn't anything else to do in the house now. And she had been here far too long.

She retraced her steps to the kitchen, pausing by the small secretary desk at the end of the hall. There was a stack of mail.

She flipped through the envelopes, all of them addressed to Jessica Clarke, but not a single one reflecting her life.

She dumped the mail back on the desk, then grabbed the combo house/car keys from a hook on the wall. She snagged a coat — Jessica Clarke's, by the look of it — and pulled it on.

Now who was imitating who?

She headed for the back door, then paused, staring at the laptop.

Why the hell not?

She walked over, yanked the cord from the wall, and wrapped it around the computer. Might as well go all the way and commit to her *Ocean's 11* behavior. She crammed the Replacement's computer into her already overstuffed backpack.

Jessica stood idle for several more moments, studying the kitchen. She didn't know if there were any answers in the imposter's wallet or on the laptop, but it was as good a place to start as any. She would assemble the pieces of this puzzle at some point. Even if it wasn't right now.

She opened the door and exited into the backyard, peeling the rubber gloves off her hands. She stuffed them into the coat pocket and—

"Jessica."

She stopped cold. A woman was standing on the other side of the hedges.

"I'm sorry," the woman said, shaking her head in

embarrassed apology. "I thought you were Jessica. You look so much like her."

"Sisters."

The woman looked confused. "I wasn't aware Jessica had a sister."

Jessica nodded. "I don't see her much. Because I live in New York. How long have they been here on Longhorn Drive?"

"Who? David and Jessica?"

"Yeah."

"I guess it's been about three years now. But wouldn't you know that if you're her sister?"

She didn't know what answer she was expecting, but it sure wasn't that. If this woman had said a week or even a month, Jessica could have come up with an answer for what was going on. But three years left her in a vacuum of confusion.

The woman narrowed her eyes at Jessica. "What did you say your name was?"

"Alice."

"Hm." She glanced toward the back door. The shattered window glinted in the afternoon light.

"It was nice to meet you. I'll be sure to tell Jessica you said hello."

"You wait right there," the woman said.

But it was too late. Jessica was already running.

She made it three blocks before the sound of police sirens started to scream behind her.

Chapter Fourteen

JESS HUNG up the phone and turned to Clare. "You will never guess what just happened."

"Bella's pediatrician is calling about some recent test results? That bitch Muriel at MotionMosaic wants to see your finished design yesterday? The plumbing is blowing up at your house?"

"Jesus, no." Jess made a face. "Are these things that you want happening to me?"

"Not at all. Just hoping that it is has nothing to do with the woman who looks like you that David could not possibly be fucking around with." Clare glanced at Evan, but he seemed way more interested in figuring out how far he could get his finger jammed up his nose.

Jessica sighed. "You were probably closest with the last guess."

"About the plumbing?"

"Our house was just broken into."

"Christ on a cross with your last two days. You want company?"

Jess shook her head. "I'll be alright. The cops are there now. I should go."

Clare stood, then pulled Jessica into a hug once she was on her feet. "Give me a call later and let me know that everything is okay."

"Of course," Jess said, hugging her back.

Then she quickly walked to the car, loading Bella into the car seat. Then she drove home. Slow because she always tried to heed the signs that read *DRIVE LIKE YOU LIVE HERE*. But still faster than her regular speed. It felt like it took hours to get there.

She pulled up in front of her house to find a police cruiser parked the curb. She half expected to see Officer Carlson. But there were two male officers talking to Patsy instead.

Jess pulled up to the curb and parked. She rolled down the windows so Bella wouldn't get too hot, then got out of the vehicle and approached the officers.

"See what I mean?" Patsy said, gesturing to Jess. "I told them I was sorry that I didn't call when I saw her snooping in the back yard, but I thought it was you. And so I said, 'Wait until you see her!'" Patsy turned back to the officers. "You see what I mean, right?"

Both officers looked at Jess.

Then the one on the right, Officer Boddicker according to his name tag, said, "We weren't here to see the other woman, ma'am."

"She said she was Jess's sister, Alice. From New York. But I know Jess doesn't have a sister. And she's never been to New York. She's from Austin."

Jess felt cold.

Amber.

Amber Brown had been in her house.

Clearly, the woman wasn't finished with her family.

What good did a night in jail do if the first thing Amber did after getting out was break into the one place she had been ordered to stay the hell away from?

The second officer, Frederickson, said, "Do you know who she's talking about, Mrs. Clarke?"

"Can I talk to you inside?" Jess found it hard not to look pointedly at Patsy.

The officers appeared to understand perfectly.

"That would be great," Boddicker said.

"Excellent idea," Frederickson added, nodding and glancing at the house.

"It is rather warm out here," Patsy said.

"That won't be necessary, ma'am," Boddicker said. "We've got everything we need from you."

Patsy looked disappointed. "Well, you know where to find me if you have more questions."

"Indeed, we do," Boddicker said.

"Thanks, Patsy." Jess didn't mean it. Or maybe she did. Who the hell knew? She certainly didn't.

"Yes, thank you." Frederickson nodded again, this time at Patsy. But Jess would bet every box of cereal in her pantry that the officer didn't mean his *thank you* either.

Jess glanced back at the Volvo. "Just give me a sec to collect my baby."

She returned to the car, turned on the ignition, and rolled up the windows. Then she pulled out the keys, scooped Bella from her car seat, and walked back to the police officers.

"This way," Jess said.

Patsy stayed in the front yard, standing off to the side as if looking for something to do.

"Patsy," Jess said.

Then she led the officers up to the front door. They all

entered together. She led them into the living room, and they all sat.

"I know who the woman was."

"Yeah?" Boddicker raised his eyebrows.

"Her name is Amber Brown. She was arrested here last night after trying to get into the house."

"You mean 'break in,'" Frederickson said.

"No." She shook her head. "I mean get in. She knocked on the door, pretended to know my husband—"

"Pretended to know your husband?" Boddicker repeated, clearly dubious.

"Not like that. The woman said she was me, she used my name. She also said that my baby, Bella, was really hers. But she called her by a different name. Gwen, I think it was."

The officers looked at one another.

"Don't suppose you have an address or a telephone number for this Amber Brown?" Boddicker asked.

Jess shook her head, shifting Bella to her other arm. "But you can talk to the officer who arrested Amber last night. Carlson."

Fredericton got up and walked into the hallway. She heard him speaking to someone on his radio.

Boddicker said, "Why don't you look around with me, see if anything is missing?"

Jess nodded. Nothing seemed to have been touched in the living room.

But soon as she entered the kitchen, she spotted the broken glass on the floor and felt a jolt of anger. How dare that Amber bitch break their window!

She saw that her laptop was missing immediately.

"My computer." She gestured to the empty wall socket. "My laptop was plugged in right over there when I left the house. I'm sure of it."

Her office didn't look to have been touched.

And the nursery appeared unmolested.

But Jess could definitely feel what she believed to be Amber's energy radiating through the room. Or maybe that was leftover anxiety from her nightmare.

Even if it was only her imagination, that wasn't something she had proven herself especially capable of shutting off.

"This room seems fine," Jess said after tucking Bella into her crib.

Then she led the officers across the hall to her and David's bedroom. Something was definitely wrong in here.

Their closet had been obviously rummaged through. Clothes lay on the floor, drawers were half open. Jess noticed what was missing right away, because there wasn't much of a wardrobe; she liked to lounge and rarely went out, not since she started working from home.

"Jeans. T-shirts, socks, underwear." She grimaced.

So Amber wasn't content with stealing her name. She also wanted to dress like her?

Every missing item hollowed out another piece of her, and fear filled the emptiness.

Why was Amber Brown so desperate to be her?

"Just a bunch of clothes. Nothing I can't replace," said Jess.

Then she spotted the shoeboxes and knew that the cash would be gone. That didn't bother her nearly as much as the thought that Amber had known exactly where to look.

Did she find it by accident? Or did she know David hid emergency cash there? Because that would be a truth that Jess did not want to believe.

"There's $2000 missing. My husband kept it in a shoebox in an old slipper."

Boddicker whistled.

Frederickson asked, "Security system?"

"No." Jess shook her head. "Did you take fingerprints? Is that what's next?" She tried to remember the CSI-type shows she and David occasionally watched.

"No, ma'am." Boddicker said. "Nothing like that."

"Why not?"

"The intruder was seen with gloves," Frederickson said. "The odds of finding anything are … not good."

"We'll follow up with Officer Carlson," Boddicker added.

"In the meantime, if you have the serial number for your laptop, you can get that to us. But maybe consider getting a security company out here to install an alarm."

Jess felt like crying. "I just want her to leave me alone."

"We'll take a look around the neighborhood. See if there's anyone that matches her description."

She nodded. Feeling miserable.

"Is there anything else you can think of? Something we haven't asked, but you think we should know?"

Jess rubbed her temples. No. She didn't want to talk to them. She only wanted to talk to David. She shook her head. "Thank you for your time."

She walked with them downstairs.

"If she comes back," Boddicker said, "don't interact with her. Just call us. We'll deal with her."

Jess nodded. Not that she agreed. She almost wished Amber Brown would knock on her door. She would love to give that woman a piece of her mind. Maybe claw her eyes out of their sockets.

She closed the door behind the officers, then stared out the frosted window until she saw the blurry image of the police cruiser driving away.

She remained where she was. As though she were glued in place.

A shadow eventually crossed the door, and Jess nearly jumped out of her skin. *Amber!*

She rang the doorbell.

And of course, Bella started crying.

Dammit.

Jess lunged at the door and threw it open.

But it was Patsy, not Amber.

Ugh.

"Ooh. I hope I didn't wake the baby up!"

Bella cried louder.

"You did." Jess gave her neighbor a thin-lipped smile.

"I was thinking that you must be rattled after what happened. I've got the coffee pot on. I'd offer wine if it was later. You shouldn't be alone."

Loneliness had nothing to do with it, Jess figured. Patsy just wanted the gossip before anyone else.

"The first part of that is true," said Jess. "I am pretty rattled. But I need to get Bella back to sleep, and I could really use some quiet time for myself. That seems to be an endangered species these days."

Bella started screeching.

"See?" Jess gave the most performative face she could muster. "A new mommy's work is never done. But thank you so much for thinking of me!"

Jess started to close the door.

"Just let me know if—"

"I promise I will, Patsy. But Bella needs me."

She closed the door and locked it. Didn't even bother to watch Patsy leave. She just headed for the stairs and made her way up.

Bella had made the escape from Patsy much easier than it would have been otherwise.

She picked the baby up, cradling her. "Good baby, Bella."

But the baby refused her comfort. Her bawling grew louder, the sound bouncing against the nursery walls, amplifying Jess's headache.

She rocked her. Sang to her. Checked her diaper. Got a bottle from downstairs, warmed it up and tried to feed her.

But nothing worked.

She was probably picking up on her mother's upset mood. So Jess tried to calm herself, but only succeeded in making herself more anxious.

She really needed David.

She grabbed her phone and rang him. No answer. His cell phone rang through to voicemail.

So she tried the landline. Got his receptionist. David was apparently out of the office.

"Just tell him to please call me, or come home as soon as possible, if he can." Then, just in case Jess hadn't sounded urgent enough, she added, "It's important."

"I understand," the receptionist said.

Jess ended the call. Bella was still crying.

She warmed up a second bottle of milk and tried feeding Bella again. This time she took the bottle.

Bella calmed down, and Jess felt her entire body exhale. *Thank God.*

She glanced at her phone on the counter. Which made her think of her wallet.

She walked back into the hallway and headed for the cabinet. She remembered setting it on the top shelf last night.

It was gone. Maybe David had moved it?

But Jess didn't think so.

She'd ask him when he called.

But she had a sinking feeling she knew exactly where her wallet was. In Amber Brown's hands.

She clenched her teeth, resisting the urge to spew every

swear word she ever learned. She didn't want to upset Bella, not now that she was finally settling down.

Jess leaned against the counter, considering what the cops had said about getting a security camera.

She walked back to the living room and pulled the blinds, looking out the window to the street. Maybe that was a good idea. They'd be able to keep watch for Amber Brown even if she didn't approach the house.

She spotted Patsy out front talking to a group of neighbors, absolutely-no-doubt-about-it gossiping about what had happened over at the Clarke residence.

And with that new baby upstairs! she could imagine Patsy saying.

Maybe she should just hire Patsy as security.

Jess laughed long and hard, fueled by anxiety more than humor.

She sat on the couch, tucking Bella into the crook of her arm. Then she opened a browser on her phone. Googled local security companies in Dallas. She took a screenshot of the numbers. Then she pulled up notes and made a list of pros and cons for her and David to discuss later.

The more she thought about it, the more she liked the idea of getting a security system. Even if they never needed one before, having one installed and monitored now would go a long way to making her feel safe again.

And as a side benefit, it might even keep Patsy off of their property for once.

Chapter Fifteen

JESSICA STOOD outside the Sunset Plains motel, eyeing its faded exterior.

The two-story building had been worn down to an ancient echo of what the place probably used to look like and was now at least ten percent peeling paint.

"Two nights," she said to the man working the front counter. The front of his shirt was stained with God knew what, and she didn't want to know what he was watching on mute, broadcast from the small TV perched atop his desk.

The way he looked at her made Jessica think that not only did most customers in this place probably pay by the hour, but two days must have sounded like a marathon stay.

"Enjoy your time at the Sunset Plains." He handed her a key, not a keycard, then wiped his nose on the back of his hand.

She held the strip of plastic indicating room number seventeen by the very edges. Soon as she was out of sight, she got one of Gwen's wet wipes from her overnight bag and gave it a clean.

Then she walked to the last room on the lower level, right next to the stairwell. There was an empty parking stall labeled *seventeen* right outside the door. Not that she would be needing it.

She unlocked the door and entered.

The interior of the room was even worse than she had imagined. Older and grosser. There was barely any light. One glowing bulb hung in obvious embarrassment from the ceiling. Who knows where its shade had gone. The walls were a faded gray, decorated with scuff marks and stains. The tattered blue carpet was so threadbare that the concrete floor was visible in several places. There was an old wooden table, two chairs, and a bed with worn blankets atop it. Jessica wouldn't have paid five dollars for this furniture at a yard sale.

The room also smelled musty and dank. But there was a working table and chair, and right now that was her baseline requirement.

She plugged in the laptop and made herself as comfortable as was possible, then got to work.

Password. Of course the Replacement would have it password protected. She tried David's birthday. Nope. Gwen's birthday. No. Her own birthday. Thank God that one didn't work. It would have freaked her out more than the current situation already had.

She drummed her fingers against the desk, thinking. Then retrieved Jessica Clarke's (it annoyed her to no end, calling that woman by *her* name) driver's license from the stolen wallet.

She typed in the Replacement's date of birth.

The computer opened.

Jessica grinned. She wasn't so dumb after all.

She immediately turned off location services and got right to an online search engine. First, she looked up David Clarke. There were a bajillion results, with the most notable among them being a former law enforcement official who served as Sheriff of Milwaukee County, Wisconsin, from 2002 to 2017, and not her David at all.

She tried New York and that led to nothing, so she opted for Dallas next. And there he was, right where Jessica would have expected him to be, employed by the Prairie Corporation, Director of Sales, Region A — meaning all states east of Texas.

So at least that much was true.

But so what? How did that help her? She'd never considered David a liar before. In fact, she'd told him when they first started dating how she much detested liars, thanks to some wretched experiences with several prior boyfriends. David had sworn to always tell her the truth; he'd even included that promise in his wedding vows.

Right now it felt like she was working on a thousand-piece puzzle with half the pieces still upside down. And Jessica had no idea what sort of picture she was even trying to put together.

She punched the digits for the Prairie Corporation into her phone.

A helium-voiced receptionist answered the call. "Prairie Corporation. How may I direct your call?"

"David Clarke?" Jessica said.

"One moment."

It rang twice.

"Hello?" It was David. She was sure of it. But for some reason, she was expecting someone else. Maybe the doppelgänger currently living in his house.

"Hello?"

She cleared her throat. "David, it's me."

"Who?"

"Jessica." Then, "You know who this is."

"How did you find out where I worked?"

"What are you talking about? I've always known where you work! It's safe to talk now."

"If you call me at this number again, or any number, I'll call the police."

Jessica clenched her teeth. "Why are you doing this to me?"

"I don't know how to make this any clearer to you, Ms. Brown. I don't know you. We have never met. Leave me and my family alone." He spoke every word slowly and loudly, as though he thought she was stupid.

"But David, you're not even—"

He'd already hung up. The sound of his silence screamed in her ear.

She hit redial.

"He's out," said the receptionist, with only a quarter of her earlier helium.

"I just talked to him."

"And now he's out."

"He's not out," Jessica said.

But then the receptionist hung up on her.

She called back.

This time, she didn't answer. Damn.

Jessica scrolled through the Prairie Corp website until she found the company directory. Grant Miller was listed as being Head of Region A. He had a slightly different phone number than the one she'd used to call David, only one digit off. David's boss maybe?

She rang him.

"Prairie Corporation. Grant Miller's office."

Hallelujah, it was a different receptionist.

"Grant Miller, please."

"May I ask who's calling?"

"Absolutely. This is Mandy Maroka from Prizedale." Jessica did not know a Mandy and Maroka was the name of her favorite English teacher in high school. As for Prizedale? It was the first imaginary company name she could pull out of her ass.

"One moment, please."

After a two-minute hold, the phone finally rang. Mr. Miller answered immediately.

"Grant Miller."

She cut straight to the chase. "I'm calling about David Clarke."

"Oh?" he said.

She could practically feel him leaning forward.

"David applied for a job with our company and gave your name for a reference check." There was a moment of silence.

"David? David Clarke?" Grant sounded both ambushed and gobsmacked.

"Yes."

"But he just got a raise." And then, as if muttering to himself, "I had no idea he was discontented."

"He didn't mention he was looking elsewhere?" Jessica asked.

"No, he did not." Grant sounded pissed.

"Can you tell me what David is like?"

"Historically, David has always been an excellent employee." Now that he understood the nature of the call, Grant's professional voice had slid back into place. "One of our best, without a doubt. But I must admit to him seeming a bit distracted lately."

"Distracted how?"

"He and his wife adopted a baby."

"That is a big life change," Jessica said, trying to make

it sound like she wasn't gritting her teeth. "How long has David been with the Prairie Corporation?"

"Seven years."

"Did you look that up, or do you know it off the top of your head?" She had plenty of questions, but keeping her rage to a simmer as she asked them was like trying to keep a firecracker from popping on the Fourth of July.

"Off the top of my head." Grant gave her a light laugh. "David has made my life easier ever since the day he got here, so it's been seven great years. I'm disappointed to hear it might not have been the same for him."

"And never a problem until recently?"

"I don't see David's recent family distraction as a problem." Now Grant sounded slightly bothered.

"No, of course not. Thank you for your time, Mr. Miller."

"By all means." He didn't sound happy.

"Oh, one more question. How long has David lived in Texas?"

Grant sounded confused. "His whole life."

Jessica felt as though she had been shoved into a quicksand of disbelief. She could barely hold the phone.

"His whole life?" she said. "In Texas? What about New York? Has he ever lived there?"

"Not that I'm aware of," Grant said. "What company did you say you were calling from again?"

Jessica ended the call.

Could it be another David?

It had to be another David.

A person couldn't live in two places at the same time. There had to be two of them. Because at least one David Clarke had been living with her in their New York apartment for the last three years. Twins? But twins didn't usually share the same name.

And the photo of the David Clarke, Prairie Corporation Sales Rep for Region A, unmistakably matched the man she had been living, loving, and dreaming with for what Jessica considered the best three years of her life.

Jessica clicked through more websites, trying to scrape together whatever fragments of David Clarke's life she could assemble, but there were scant traces. A handful of photographs surfaced from Prairie Corp work events, charity soirées, and local community award nights.

Beyond that, the man was a digital ghost, apparently hating social media as much as he said he did.

She typed her own name into the search bar next. It was a strange sensation that put her temporarily out of body. There were a bajillion Jessica Clarkes. She added *Dallas* to her search phrase, hoping for a more relevant revelation.

It didn't help.

She opened her phone's camera and snapped a picture of the Replacement's driver's license, her hands shaking at the sheer absurdity of it all.

Then she uploaded the photo and initiated an image search.

Finally, some worthy results.

Jessica's doppelgänger led a comparatively public life, working as a graphic designer for a local sportswear company.

But there was also another page-one result that captured Jessica's attention. A five-year-old article from the Dallas *Daily News*. The headline would have been catchy even if she hadn't been looking for any lead to follow: *Naked Woman Causes Mayhem in Downtown Dallas.*

She clicked on the article, which detailed a bizarre incident involving a woman named Jessica Clarke, found wandering aimlessly through traffic, stark naked and evidently under the influence of some mind-altering substance.

She'd been taken into custody and subsequently admitted to the hospital. The age of the woman correlated with the Jessica she sought, but there was no way of knowing for sure if they were the same person.

Jessica leaned back in the worn motel chair, her skull pressed hard against the wall as she considered her digital rabbit hole.

If this woman was a sham, she was one hell of a performer, because she had maintained her charade for years on end. But this wasn't a Rip Van Winkle situation. Jessica wasn't missing any time; she was just juggling an awful lot of unexplainable shit in the timeline she had.

She peered at the date of the Dallas news article. It was from five years ago. Two years before she even met David. How did that make any sense? How could she know what Jessica's name was going to be before David even met her?

She banged her head against the wall, trying to keep herself from feeling crazy.

And the question of motive was haunting as well. What could possibly drive a person to assume someone else's identity?

Specifically Jessica's. She was a nobody. A lower-class girl from New York who never got any breaks, at least not until she had met David and felt like she'd won the lottery.

But most disturbing of all, why was David playing along with the woman's grotesque masquerade?

Could it have been his idea?

But again, *why*?

Jessica powered down the laptop and slapped its lid shut. Then she called for a cab, hiding the laptop beneath the pillow on the bed before leaving the room. Just in case Mr. Front Desk decided to snoop.

Fifteen minutes later, Jessica found herself in the back-seat of a surprisingly modern taxi and was en route to the Prairie Corporation.

The building was both imposing and impressive. Vast glass frontage with concrete and steel walls, and an entrance framed with sleek black columns. There were security cameras everywhere. A miniature oil derrick sculpture stood proudly in front of the entrance and cast a long shadow toward the visitor parking lot.

Jessica paid the driver and got out. She studied the building, wondering which office belonged to David, then walked away from the entrance, circling around to the rear of the building. She pushed her way through a dense hedge behind the Prairie Corporation headquarters and found herself in the sprawling employee parking lot.

David's car would be—

She paused. Then dug into her coat pocket and pulled out the keys she had stolen. With an anxious push, she hit the lock button. Twice.

A horn blipped. Lights flickered. David's BMW.

She made her way through the maze of cars, trucks, and SUVs. Hitting the button twice more to guide her steps.

And then there it was. She stared into the vehicle. His phone had been abandoned in the cup holder. She hit the trunk button. Not knowing what she intended to find. If anything. The real David Clarke, maybe?

But it held only a toolbox. She slammed it shut.

Then she opened the driver's side door and slid into the driver's seat. The familiar scent of David's cologne punched her in the nostrils.

She shut herself inside.

She picked up his phone and brought the screen to life. It flickered with notifications: twelve frantic calls from the imposter. And numerous texts. But his phone was locked. She couldn't read them.

She set it back down.

Then settled herself in the seat, slid the key in the ignition, and turned it on. Then she put both hands on the wheel. Ten and two. She looked around the parking lot. No one was around.

She drew a deep breath, then drove out of the parking lot. And kept driving.

Eventually, she spotted a sign indicating the airport. She followed it along, heeding directions that ultimately led her to long-term parking.

She found an empty space out of range of any security camera and pulled in next to a ten-year-old Camry.

She got out of the Beemer, then went around to the trunk. She sorted through the toolbox until she found a screwdriver. Then she hunkered down and unscrewed the license plates on the Camry, swapping them with those on David's BMW.

Once finished, she returned the screwdriver back to the toolbox and drove away.

Chapter Sixteen

Jess stood in the nursery, girding herself against the edges of panic.

She had been through Bella's closet several times already. Where was the nightgown — the one with the little forget-me-nots and a scalloped hem? It was Bella's (okay, really, Jess's) favorite nightgown.

It was missing. And no amount of tearing apart the closet was going to change that.

She looked in the crib one last time, knowing that it wouldn't be there. Because she'd already checked three times. But she kept hoping her memory was playing tricks on her. Maybe she only thought she remembered folding it over the rail of Bella's crib.

Maybe it would be like that time when she couldn't find the cumin and looked in every cabinet twice before David came into the kitchen and pointed to it after only a few seconds of looking. It had been *right there* on the second shelf, next to all the other spices. Once Jess had missed it the first time, her eyes had kept passing over it.

But with Bella's closet now in disarray, Jess was positive that she was not overlooking the nightgown.

And she was also confident in having left it on the rail of the crib. She always did that. In a very short time span, it had become automatic.

So, fuck. It could only mean one thing.

That goddamned woman, Madam Batshit Amber Brown, had stolen it.

Her throat suddenly tightened. She found it hard to breathe. The woman had been in the nursery after all. Just like her nightmare had shown her.

She had to leave the room.

Jess tucked Bella into bed again, made her way downstairs, sat on the couch and pull out her phone.

She hit Clare's number.

"What's up, Orphan Black?" Clare said.

"Please don't call me that."

"Oh wow. You really do sound upset. Was your clone hiding in the closet?"

"I don't feel safe," Jess said.

"Oh fuck, I'm sorry," Clare said, her voice turning serious.

"Can you spend the night?"

"Absolutely. Have you talked to David? What did he say?"

"I've been trying to get a hold of him, but he isn't answering his phone."

"What about calling work?"

"I left a message," Jess said. "But he hasn't called back."

A long silence from Clare. "Why don't you bring Bella here? Just in case she comes back."

"You don't mind?"

"Hell, no. I'll pick you up."

"I can drive."

"No. You sound like you're in shock. I don't think you should be driving. I'll come and get you."

"Thank you. I'll be ready soon."

"Can I pour some wine?" asked Clare. "Please tell me that you're in the mood to drink."

"I'll know how I feel when I get there."

"I'll open a bottle so it can breathe, just in case."

"Of course you will," Jess said, laughing. She ended the call, then went back upstairs and packed a bag for Bella. Then went into her own bedroom to pack one for herself.

Her backpack was missing.

"Son of a—"

She grabbed a cloth shopping bag and loaded her clothes into that instead. Then she went and got Bella.

It was actually a good thing she was going to Clare's. She didn't want Bella back in this room. Not until the security system was installed.

"You ready for an adventure? We're going to spend the night with Auntie Clare. But don't worry, Mommy won't get too drunk until after you're sleeping. She promises."

Bella laughed. Jess hugged her tight.

She heard a car pull up outside. Her heart starting pounding.

Dammit, she was on edge. It had to be a car, not a truck. It sounded nothing like the U-Haul.

Regardless, she hugged Bella even tighter to her chest as she went to the window and looked outside. She was right. There was no U-Haul in sight.

But there was a shiny yellow cab, and David was climbing out of the back seat. Then he paused and glanced up at the nursery window.

He waved at her. She hesitated. Then waved back.

As David headed for the porch, she and Bella made for the stairs.

Halfway to the living room, Jess realized how pissed off she was at him. Why the hell hadn't he called her back? He'd left her to deal with a burglary and its aftermath all by herself.

Jess promised herself a deep and calming breath before talking to him.

But as soon as he entered the house, she was unable to throttle her emotions. "Where the hell have you been? I've been calling you all day! You didn't bother to return even one of my—"

"I had a shit day, Jess."

"You had a shit day? YOU?"

"Jesus." Bella started to fuss. "I'm sorry."

"You couldn't even text me? And why the hell were you in a cab? Where's your car?"

"My phone was stolen. And so was my car."

There was a moment of silence. *Fuck.*

"I'm so sorry. Did you call the police?"

"Of course, I called the police. Unfortunately there's not much they can do it about it until it turns up."

"So it's insured. If that's why you're—"

"I'm not upset about the goddamn car."

"Then what?"

"Amber Brown called Grant and told him that I was planning to leave Prairie. I had to spend all day doing damage control."

"She called your work?"

"Yeah."

Jessica felt a chill. "She was here as well."

"Who?"

"Amber."

David's face drained of color. "At the house?" He stepped toward her. "Are you okay?"

"NO, I AM NOT OKAY." Bella looked up startled and let out a wail. Jess looked down at her. "I'm sorry, baby. Mama's having a rough day."

"Did she hurt you?"

"I wasn't at home."

"That's a relief." His face gained a little more color.

Jess stared at him in disbelief. "How is that relief? She broke into OUR HOME, after she was specifically instructed not to return. She stole my laptop, my wallet, obviously our spare car keys."

"Anything else?"

"Some of my clothes, the money in your shoebox."

"Of course, she did."

"Why of course?"

"Because when it rains, it obviously pours." David ran a hand through his hair. "FUCK!"

"Worst of all, she was in Bella's room."

His jaw tightened and he marched toward the stairs. Seconds later, she heard his footsteps overhead.

Jess got Bella settled onto her play mat in the living room, surrounding her with three of her favorite stuffed animals.

Less than two minutes later, David was back. "I'll get it cleaned up."

"Bella's room too. I want the bedding all changed. Who knows what she touched?"

David nodded, then spotted the diaper bag. The cloth bag with Jess' clothes. "Are you going somewhere?"

"Me and Bella are staying at Clare's tonight."

"Why?" David asked.

"That lunatic broke into our house today, David. I'm

not spending another night here without some kind of security system."

"So, you're moving in with Clare?"

"I have SecureX coming tomorrow to install a system and a glazier to fix the window."

"You don't need to do that."

"I told you—"

"I understand the need for security." His voice turned calm and soothing. "I'm not saying we don't need to worry about it, I'm saying that you don't have to hire a company."

"And why not?"

"Prairie Corporation has contacts in private security."

"Like bodyguards?"

"Exactly." David gave her a reassuring nod. "I'll get one of them on it."

"What does that mean?"

"I'll ask one of them to have a little conversation with Amber. Tell her to back the fuck off."

"And how will they find her?"

"I don't fucking know. Dallas can't be that big a place."

"And if she doesn't?"

"That's what these people do for a living, Jess. One conversation with them, and this Amber Brown bitch won't come within five miles of our house ever again."

"Fine," Jess said. "Do what you want. But I'm still getting the security system installed."

David didn't answer. Instead, he studied her for several long seconds of quiet appraisal.

"What?" Jess finally said.

"Nothing."

"No, no," Jess said. "There's something else on your mind."

He sighed. "The events of the other night were stressful."

"Yeah. And?"

He gestured toward her. "Maybe you…"

"Maybe I what, David? Finish the sentence."

"You know…"

Fucking coward. "I what? Started using again?"

"You lied about a burglary once before."

"You are such a total asshole for bringing that up right now." She glanced over at Bella in apology, even though she couldn't possibly understand what Jess was saying. She leaned toward him and lowered her voice. "Fuck you, David."

"Whoa." He was perfectly calm, raising both hands, palms out as though to let her know he meant no offense. "I'm not trying to fight with you, Jess. But I would be remiss if didn't draw the parallel—"

"Oh, you would be remiss, would you? We—"

"We were going through a stressful time, and you faked a burglary and stole our savings to buy oxy. How am I not supposed to see that as possibly relevant to this situation right now?"

"Because, David, we both know why that happened, and I've not even anywhere close to a relapse. Do I seem like the same person I was after three miscarriages nearly destroyed me and then we received a hundred thousand rejections from all of those adoption agencies?"

"Six rejections, sweetie."

"Don't sweetie me," she said through clenched teeth. "Not after you just accused me of a relapse—"

"I didn't—"

"If you had been paying the least bit of attention, you would know I haven't used since that incident on the street."

"I'm—"

"And I'm having a hard time understanding why you've spent all of this time telling me how great I'm doing and how much you believe in me, when you obviously don't. All of our work has just gone straight out the window because—"

"It's not all out the window."

"—there's another explanation right in front of us. Why is it easier for you to believe that I'm relapsing than that Madam Batshit broke in?"

"You're right. I'm sorry, I just wasn't—"

"What if she had broken in when me and Bella were here alone? I only left for a few minutes to meet Clare, so it's a miracle that didn't happen. Which means the timing was coincidental. Or she'd been watching. WATCHING. We're talking about your wife and child here, David — don't you care about that?"

"Of course I do. Again, I'm sorry."

Jess took a breath to steady herself. But it didn't help. Her voice still cracked when she spoke. "She took Bella's nightgown. The one with the forget-me-nots."

"Your favorite."

Jess nodded, blinking back tears. "What kind of sick fuck does that?"

"I don't know." He stepped forward, reaching out a hand. But then appeared to think better of it. "I don't know. I'm so sorry. I promise I wasn't doubting you. This is all just a lot to process. I've never been through something like this before. And I'm doing my best."

"But you doubted me, David. Saying that you weren't doesn't help the situation."

"Why don't we go out to dinner? Wherever you want."

Jess looked over at Bella. She was sucking on her dolphin. "We have plans."

"You mean going to Clare's?" He seemed surprised that she still wanted to do that.

Like he hadn't been listening at all.

"Yes, I mean going to Clare's."

Her phone dinged with perfect timing.

Jess looked at the screen notification. "Clare's here. I'll see you tomorrow."

Jess gathered Bella, then grabbed both bags.

"Come on, Jess. Let's talk about this."

"I'm not gonna change my mind, David."

"So you're leaving me."

"Jesus, I'm not leaving you. I'll be back tomorrow. SecureX is scheduled to arrive between eight and eleven. I don't know how long it takes to install the system, but I'll be home for that."

"You're gonna let Amber Brown come between us?"

"I'm the one trying to shut her out."

David opened his mouth, but Jess didn't want to hear what he had to say.

She opened the front door and stepped out, closing it behind her

Chapter Seventeen

JESSICA DROVE until she finally felt safe and the airport was far behind her.

Her rumbling stomach might have put her slightly ahead of schedule. She looked for a restaurant, deciding against yet another McDonald's experience. Then she spotted what looked to be an old-fashioned diner named Griddle & Grits.

Faded yellow paint coated the exterior walls, a marked contrast to the green-tiled roof. A large wooden sign read: *WELCOME TO GRIDDLE & GRITS* in white paint that was now a bit ashen. The windows were lined with chrome facing, and the front door was a faded red.

She pulled into the parking lot and found a spot. There was a poster in the window of something called a Lone Star Legend triple cheeseburger with bacon. The photograph might be faded, but the hamburger still looked damn enticing. Her mouth watered as she imagined what it might taste like.

The inside of the restaurant was bathed in warm yellow light from the triple-bulbed ceiling fans scattered throughout. There was a bank of pay phones to her left. The wood walls were covered in license plates, sepia photos of Dallas, and a half-dozen neon signs. The most prominent shone with *HAVE A HAPPY DAY.*

Jessica stood staring at it for a moment.

"Sit anywhere you'd like, hon," said the bright-eyed cashier and hostess. She smiled from behind an old chrome and red vinyl counter.

"Thank you." Jessica looked around at all the booths, upholstered in red and white vinyl. They were all occupied, except for a giant one in the far corner that could sit a family of ten. Jessica could never justify occupying that by herself.

She sat at the counter instead, two seats down from a middle-aged man who, at a glance, made her think that he thought of himself as more handsome than he actually was.

She studied the large chalkboard menu, detailing an abundance of greasy fare. Then she grabbed a menu from its holder, deciding she would rather look at the pictures than read the descriptions.

She was still studying the appetizers when the waitress arrived.

According to the tag on the pocket of her dress, her name was *BERNICE.* She wore a pink and white uniform that looked like it was missing its gingham. Her friendly face and bright eyes were both probably big benefits when it came to her tips.

"You been here before?" Bernice asked.

"First time."

Bernice nodded knowingly. "First timers look at the menu, long timers look at the board."

"Makes sense." Jessica nodded, setting the menu down. "What's good?"

"It's all good, if you like greasy." Bernice laughed. "Just don't order like you're on a diet. If you expect a stomachache, then you won't be disappointed if you get one, and maybe even grateful if you don't."

"Aren't you supposed to be telling me how good all the food is?"

"I'm telling you that it tastes great." Bernice laughed again. "You'll either never be back, or you'll be back all the time. Try the trashcan fries if you want to know what side of the fence you're on."

"How about just a burger and fries?" She glanced toward the window. "The Lone Star?"

"First timer?"

Jessica nodded.

"Then I suggest the Dallas Days Double Decker."

"What's on that?"

"You want the short answer, or the full Griddle & Grits spiel?"

Jessica laughed. She was enjoying Bernice's company. "I guess I'll take the spiel."

Bernice smiled, either deciding she liked Jessica or working for her tip. "The Dallas Days Double Decker is a feast of juicy, locally sourced Angus beef patties, crowned with sharp, melted cheddar and sweet, crispy onion rings. Fresh lettuce, ripe tomato, tart pickles, and our secret Griddle & Grits sauce conduct a symphony of flavors tucked between our toasted, buttery brioche buns!"

"Wow," Jessica said. "That does sound impressive. Both the burger and your delivery. Consider me sold."

"Would you like fries with that?"

"Something would be wrong with me if I said no, right?"

Bernice nodded. "I might have to diagnose you. Or throw you out."

"Then yes, please, I would like to order the fries."

"Regular, seasoned, or trashcan?"

"Now I have to ask what's in the trashcan."

"The trashcan fries are an unforgettable medley of indulgence. Picture our hand-cut, golden fries, seasoned and perfectly crispy—"

"I can go with the short answer this time." Jessica said.

"Of course," nodded Bernice. "It's fries with cheese and bacon."

"And how about the seasoned part?"

"Different kind of salt." She shrugged.

"What would you get?"

"Regular fries always do it for me. But I'm a simple girl."

"Me too," Jessica said.

"Regular fries it is."

"Will you think I'm gross if I also order a shake?" Jessica asked, only slightly embarrassed by her gluttony.

"Ma'am, I've seen folks order the Lone Star with a side of trashcan fries, and a shake, plus a slice of pecan pie for dessert for a snack, then come in an hour later and order the same for lunch."

Jessica laughed.

"Which shake is the best?"

"Chocolate."

"Chocolate it is," Jessica said with a nod.

She was usually a vanilla girl, but she liked Bernice an awful lot for only having known her for a minute. And right now, she wanted to have what Bernice was having.

"I'll get that for you right away, ma'am."

Jessica almost told Bernice her name, but somehow it was starting to feel foreign, like a lie in her mouth. Even though it wasn't.

"Jessica." She said it out loud. Just to make sure it was still her name.

The man two seats away looked over at her. He had a full head of brown hair, graying lightly along the sides. Three or four days' worth of stubble on his strong jawline. Neatly dressed in a button-down shirt and tidy slacks. He smiled, making it perfectly clear that he thought they should be sitting closer.

She turned away, digging out her phone and pulling up Google. Pretending to read something.

But it didn't work.

"So it's your first time here." His voice rang with false bravado.

"Yep."

"You new to town?"

"Just visiting."

"You picked a good place to get hungry."

Jessica didn't answer.

"I come here all the time."

"That's nice."

"Next time you should get the Heath bar shake." He shook his head in faux disbelief. "The chocolate shake is good, but the Heath bar is out of this world."

"Maybe next time." She tried to make her tone resemble that of a hammer pounding a nail into a board.

But if the man heard a tone, he ignored it.

"Maybe next time we could share a shake."

Jessica held up her left hand and pointed to the ring. "Sorry. I'm married."

"Only trying to be friendly." Suddenly, his voice sounded anything but. "You obviously don't know nothing about Texans."

"And if you don't mind," she said, holding his eyes, "I'd like to enjoy my meal in peace."

"Your meal ain't even here," he said before turning to study the chalkboard menu.

"Asshole," Jessica muttered.

She stared down at her ring for a long minute before finally tugging it off of her finger.

Was she married? She had no fucking idea anymore.

Jessica knew she went to the courthouse, spoke vows, signed a piece of paper. But if nothing else about her life with David was true, was her marriage?

A cold chill ran down her back.

Was Gwen even hers?

Given everything that had happened in the last day, maybe they weren't actually married.

Married. Marriage.

She had a goddamn marriage certificate. And yay for that, but double fuck, the certificate was packed in one of her boxes in the back of the U-Haul.

Which was in the impound lot.

She had completely ignored the U-Haul in favor of trying to figure out what was going on with David. She needed to get to the truck. Before Replacement Jessica did.

She suddenly felt claustrophobic, sitting at the counter and waiting for her food. She had to get out of here. She glanced at the clock, saw that it was 4 p.m.

"Everything okay?" asked the man she didn't want to talk to.

"Everything is great." She slipped the ring back onto her finger just as Bernice walked toward her with a chocolate milkshake.

"Your food will be right up, hon." She set the milkshake down on the counter.

"Thank you, Bernice, but is it okay if I get this all to go? I'm so sorry. Family emergency."

"Nothing to be sorry about." She shook her head but

held her smile. "Just make sure you don't let those fries get cold. You're better off tossing them in the trash than reheating them."

"You can leave the milkshake." Jessica smiled and took her first sip. It tasted delicious. Cold and chocolaty. She guzzled as much of it as she could while Bernice boxed up her burgers and fries.

Soon as she had her paper bag meal, she threw down a twenty as a tip and ran out of the restaurant.

She raced back to the BMW. It was 4:08, according to the dashboard clock. Jessica found the card Officer Grumpy had given her at the police station.

She punched the address into Maps on her phone, then gunned the engine.

Boy, did she want to speed. But she was driving a stolen car to a police impound lot, so it probably wasn't the best idea. So she forced herself to follow every rule of the road, staying within the speed limit to avoid getting pulled over.

When Jessica got their marriage certificate, Replacement Jessica's gig would be up. And she couldn't wait to have her explain what the fuck was going on.

Chapter Eighteen

THE IMPOUND LOT looked like a prison. At the front was an imposing cinderblock building surrounded by a tall chain-link fence with thick coils of barbed wire at the top. A hulking security gate with a large sign that read *NO TRES-PASSING* blocked access to the driveway.

The lot was overflowing with cars, trucks, and vans parked hither and yon as far as Jessica could see. There didn't appear to be any discernible order. She drove past, then parked around the corner, being sure to lock the BMW. She glanced around the deserted street, hoping the vehicle would still be here when she got back.

She could always drive the U-Haul, she supposed. But she preferred the Beemer.

Jessica retraced her steps back to the cinderblock outpost and entered.

The office was large and rectangular, with a wide back window through which Jessica could see the lot. The room was ugly in both sight and odor, from the dark brown linoleum underfoot to the faint reek of motor oil and dust in the air.

A woman sat behind the desk. Her name tag read *MONICA*, and she looked like she hadn't taken shit from anyone in decades. She had a wide, solid frame with broad shoulders, like a tank ready to roll.

Jessica already felt intimidated. Maybe this was a stupid idea.

But Monica gestured for her to approach, so she did. "Vehicle plate?"

Jessica grimaced. "I don't know."

"What d'you mean, you don't know?"

"It's a rental. A U-Haul."

"When was it brought in?"

"Last night."

Monica studied her for a moment. "So you're Amber Brown."

Jessica flushed. *What had Carlson said about her?* "Sure, whatever."

"You need to pay the towing and storage fees before we release it."

"I don't want the vehicle. Not yet."

Monica narrowed her eyes. "Then why are you denting my linoleum?"

"I just need to get something from inside it."

"This isn't public parking. You do realize that the vehicle will continue to accrue fees until—"

"Yes." Jessica nodded. "I understand. I'll pick it up eventually. I just need to get something out of the back."

Monica sighed — obviously she would not be able to save this woman from herself. "ID?"

"About that." Jessica smiled, but Monica didn't smile back. "I don't have any—" She stopped. She had the Replacement's wallet. "Time to waste."

She smiled again to cover her awkwardness.

"Well, I wouldn't want to waste your time." Monica glared, tapping the Formica counter.

Jessica placed the driver's license down. Trying not to look worried. Monica glanced at the photo, glanced at Jessica. Then turned to her computer. "The vehicle in question belongs to an Amber Brown."

"The cops got my name wrong."

"Sure they did." Monica said. "I've heard that before. I'm afraid that I'm going to have to—"

"Call U-Haul."

"And why would I do that?"

"You can confirm that Jessica Clarke rented the vehicle." She touched her chest. "That's me. I'm Jessica Clarke."

"Yeah, I got that part." Monica sighed.

"Please. It's important."

"It always is." Monica's eyes sharpened. "You better not be wasting my time."

"I promise that I'm not." Jessica raised her hand like she was about to swear on a Bible. "U-Haul will tell you that Jessica Clarke is the person who rented that vehicle."

Monica nodded, then picked up the phone and dialed. Then she turned her back on Jessica and spoke with the person on the other end of the line. She kept her voice low. All that Jessica could hear was a multitude of uh-huhs. Finally, she hung up the phone and turned back to her.

"Well?" Jessica said.

"Seems there's a first time for everything." Monica tapped her license. "Cops did get your name wrong. But you gave the company an incorrect date of birth."

"I'm really sorry about that."

"It's not my paperwork." Monica shrugged. "But you might have an issue when returning the vehicle to U-Haul."

Jessica held out her hand. "Keys, please."

Another nod. Monica heaved herself up from her seat and went over to a bank of keys. Then she returned. "You try to drive that thing out of here and you'll kill all the tires and I'll have Benji drag you down to Dallas PD. Got it?"

"Benji?"

Monica pointed to a German Shepherd sleeping in the corner.

"Got it."

"Bring the keys back when you're finished."

"I will." Monica dropped them into her hand. Jessica jerked away before the woman could change her mind. "Thank you!"

She turned and ran for a side door.

"You'll need the stall number."

Jessica was in too much of a hurry. "How many U-Hauls could there be?" She gave a forced laugh.

The door slammed closed behind her.

Vehicles of every size, shape, and color — SUVs, pick-ups, and motorcycles — filled the whole of the lot. There was also a whole phalanx of U-Hauls, from short and boxy to the bigger box type that had held her and David's old life.

She turned around and went back inside. Monica was leaning on her elbow as though waiting for her.

"Sorry about that." Jessica tried to make herself appear as sheepish as she felt. "I guess I'll need a stall number after all."

"More than you thought?"

Jessica nodded.

"Number three-five-seven."

"Thank you," Jessica said. She went back outside, following the appropriate numbers until she saw her U-

Haul, with Montana on the side, parked toward the back of the lot.

It felt like it had been months since she'd seen the thing. She walked around to the back and unlocked the sliding door. She raised it, staring in a mélange of cardboard boxes. Remnants of her life with David. Packed and stacked, like she had last seen them.

She had no idea which box contained their marriage certificate, so she grabbed the first one, almost falling over. She had expected it to be heavy. But it was surprisingly weightless.

She peeled the tape back and looked inside.

The box was empty. That was weird.

She picked up a second box. It was equally light. She yanked the tape away. Empty.

What the fuck?

She grabbed the next box and then the next, her panic mounting as each proved empty. Where were their treasures? The framed photo of her and David in Central Park the day he proposed? The stuffed bear her grandmother had given her on her fifth birthday? The email David had sent her when they got approval from the adoption agency? The quilt she had inherited from her great grandmother?

None of it was here.

Every box was empty.

Her entire life, both before and with David, was gone. Swallowed by a black hole.

Jessica closed the U-Haul door and locked it. Though she didn't know why. There was nothing to keep safe.

She stalked back toward the impound office, threw the keys on the counter.

Monica looked up from her computer screen. "Did you get what you needed?"

"Someone stole everything from my truck."

"Impossible." There wasn't a lick of sympathy in Monica's expression.

"Why?"

"This lot is guarded like a fortress. We've got gates, cameras, and a security guard."

"Benji?"

"Oh, I got more than Benji. You wouldn't guess how many people try to avoid their fees."

"Maybe they broke in at night."

Monica shook her head. "At night, the dogs run loose. Besides, the whole place is alarmed. We've got more security here than the federal penitentiary system. Nothing gets in or out unnoticed. So whatever game you're playing, Miss Amber Clarke or Jessica Brown or whoever you are, your belongings were not stolen while your vehicle was at my lot."

"What the fuck, then?" Jessica asked.

"Ma'am, I'd appreciate it if you didn't swear at me."

"I'm sorry." She blinked back tears. "I'm having a shit day. And I'm not swearing at you. I just don't understand what's happening right now. Or last night. Or maybe the last three years of my life. I feel like I'm losing my mind."

Monica leaned forward. "You got a deranged ex?"

Jessica looked at her. And nodded.

Monica's expression softened into something that might have been sympathy. "Had one of those myself once. Fed him to Benji."

Jessica widened her eyes.

"Just kidding."

Jessica wasn't sure about that.

"Listen, don't let him make you crazy. Chances are he took your shit and is holding it hostage so you'll go back to him. Don't give him the satisfaction. Got it?"

Jessica nodded.

"Now, if you don't mind my saying so, it seems like you're in need of a good night's sleep."

"Yeah. You're right." Jessica turned to leave, then stopped. "You sure there's no way anyone could have come in here and taken my stuff out of the U-Haul?"

"I'm certain. And just to make you feel better, I'll review the security tapes. If anything comes up, then I'll give you a shout."

Jessica dropped her shoulders. "Thank you."

Monica swung her computer screen around. "This your phone number?"

Jessica checked the digits and nodded.

"Get some sleep."

Jessica smiled, then left the building.

She walked back to the BMW, which was mercifully still there. She unlocked it and slipped into the driver's seat, then sat for a long time staring out the window.

Then something inside her snapped. She started hitting the steering wheel, punching the seat and the door, screaming until her lungs ached and her throat was raw.

Chapter Nineteen

EVAN'S BEDROOM was a lot different from Bella's nursery. Jess preferred the yellow walls and blush-colored fabrics she had chosen for her daughter. Evan's bedroom was painted in bright primary colors. Cartoon character posters covered the walls. Toys were everywhere. A toddler bed was tucked in the corner, ready for when he outgrew his crib. Not that there would be room for him without moving the mountains of stuffed animals currently occupying it.

Not a single one of which looked like it had ever been touched.

Unlike the stuffed teddy bear in Evan's crib. That was frayed and worn.

Jess glanced down at the sleeping toddler and smiled. Thank God for Clare. She walked over to the second crib. Usually Clare had it in their bedroom. But now Bella was tucked up inside, gurgle-snoring.

Jess had had a shower and was now wrapped in a borrowed bathrobe. Maybe soon she would be able to remember what normal was supposed to feel like.

She stepped out of Evan's room and went downstairs to where Clare was waiting in the living room. She had poured two glasses of red wine, the half-full bottle standing between them.

Jess dropped onto the couch next to Clare. "Those two glasses look so perfectly balanced. Like down to the drop. I'm impressed."

"I appreciate you noticing. I wanted to make it visually obvious that I waited for you."

Jess laughed and picked up her glass. "That's why we're friends."

"How was your shower?"

"Invigorating." Jess took a sip. Delicious.

"I'm glad to hear that. Maybe—"

"Sorry to interrupt." Clare's husband, Mason, poked his head into the living room. He was a good-looking guy, though a bit nerdy, with a receding hairline and round glasses. But reasonably athletic and confident in his faded red tee and pajama bottoms. "Just wanted to say goodnight."

Clare bounced up from the couch went over to kiss him. "Goodnight. I love you."

"Love you too." Mason kissed her back. "Have fun. But don't rush to bed." Then he waved at Jess. "Goodnight. We're glad you're here."

Then he disappeared and Clare returned to the couch.

"I love your husband," said Jess, glancing at her friend.

"Me too, and that's another reason I love you so much."

"Because I think Mason is great, and that you're even greater together?"

"Most bitches be jealous," Clare said with a laugh. She took a swallow of wine. "Even if they're in happy relationships themselves, they still want to compete with yours. Or mine, in this case. I've never felt that from you at all. Makes it easy to talk without worrying about what I'm going to say." Clare took another sip.

"Well, your relationship has nothing to do with my relationship."

"Sure, but you even let me shit talk your husband without feeling like I'm rubbing it in your face that Mason is a great guy."

"You don't shit talk him." Jess took a sip of wine. "Do you shit talk him? Today doesn't count."

"No. I don't shit talk him, but I do tell you the truth. Until that psycho is found, I'm glad you're here."

"Me too."

"So, tell me what happened. Give me the tea and I promise not to tell another living soul."

Jessica knew she wouldn't. They had traded multiple fears over the years. Especially about not being able to have children of their own. And neither she nor Clare had ever shared a word of those late-night cry sessions. Not even to each other's husbands. Not even in the safety of their adoptive moms' group.

Jess needed several long swallows of wine before she was ready. But once she'd warmed her throat, she finally came up for air and told Clare everything about her day, ending with the especially uncomfortable part where David practically accused her of staging the break-in.

"Asshole."

"Yeah. I agree with that."

"You want to shit talk him more?"

Clare sighed. "No. Feels a bit like kicking him when he's down. Unless you want to?"

Jess shook her head. "No, I was hoping we could be more focused on solutions."

"Oh, hon, of course." Clare put a hand over Jess's.

"We can always shit talk later. But I do need to hear the rest of this story. Whatever you haven't told me yet, because I can see it in your eyes."

"When he asked me if I staged about the break-in, I actually…" Her voice cracked. Jess didn't want to finish, but she also knew that without getting it out of her mouth, they couldn't move onto the next thing. "When he asked me that, I actually had to stop for a moment and think, *Did I?*" She shook her head in embarrassment.

"Don't let that man put you in the hospital again."

She blinked the tears from her eyes. "David didn't put me in the hospital, Clare. I did that to myself. My relapse was one hundred percent my responsibility." She sniffed. "It bothered me, though, that he thought that I might have relapsed enough to say it out loud."

"It should bother you. It's a shit thing to say."

"And that he arrived at that conclusion so fast. Is that how David really sees me?" Clare still didn't answer, because they both knew that Jess wasn't ready to hear it. "Like, if I've moved on from not trusting him anymore after he…"

"Cheated on you."

"If I've moved on, then how come he hasn't moved on? I learned to trust David again, so why isn't he trusting me?"

"*Do you* trust him? Are we still at ninety-five percent? Or has the number fallen?"

Jess sighed. "Is this like how much charge I have left on my phone?"

Clare shrugged and topped up her wine.

"I'd say I'm at eighty percent."

"Jesus. He dropped fifteen percent in one day."

Jess laughed. No one could make her feel better about

a situation than Clare. "This whole thing makes me think that our marriage isn't nearly as sound as I thought it was."

"Okay. That's where I'm going to get really honest with you and hope I don't end up regretting this."

"Go on."

Clare took a long swallow of wine. "We both know I have some serious problems with David for cheating on you. If something is wrong in the relationship, you communicate that with your partner — you don't stick your dick into—"

"Women are guilty too."

"Sure. But we're talking about David right now. And when you relapsed? That's when you get super supportive of your wife. You don't trip and land dick first in some other woman. He should have been more supportive."

"He—"

"I've heard every one of your excuses, hon. You telling me he couldn't have taken a minute off of work to be with you? Has he ever asked for any time off? Even once? Even for Bella's first week at home?"

Jess tightened her fingers on the wine glass.

"I know he's been a prince ever since you guys went to therapy and agreed to work on the marriage. But even though I'm not someone who ever needs to be right, I really hope David is never going to pull that shit again."

"You don't think he knows Amber?"

Clare shook her head. "I got good instincts. So believe me when I say that even though I think David can be a shit, I really think your marriage is sound. At least from what I've seen around you guys."

Jess leaned forward and kissed Clare's cheek. "Thank you for saying that."

"But all that being said, I still have some serious questions about Amber Brown. And wonder if David knows more than he's saying."

"Imposter alert. Orphan Black."

"Yeah." Clare took another drink. "So, who do you think Amber is?"

"I have no idea."

"You must have some idea."

"I feel like it has something to do with Bella somehow, because she seemed fixated on the baby. Even though she called her Gwen."

"More to do with Bella than David?"

"I don't know," Jess said, not letting herself probe that question too deeply. Another reason it was good for her to be with Clare right now.

"You said her last name is Brown?"

"Yeah, that's what the cop said."

Clare nodded. "I'll be right back."

She returned less than a minute later with her laptop. She opened the lid and pulled up Google, then typed in: *Amber Brown, Dallas.*

Nothing came up. At least nothing that related to the woman that was attempting to steal her life.

Clare pursed her lips. "How do you think Amber found you?"

Jess shrugged. "No idea."

"She's obviously trying to be you, right? Copying your name, your look, even claiming to be Bella's mom."

"Gwen's mom."

"But why?"

"I don't know, Clare!"

"You're gonna make me ask, aren't you?"

Jess glared at her. "Don't do it. Your instincts said our marriage was sound."

"They've occasionally steered me wrong. I thought Mason was a nerd when I first met him."

"He is a nerd."

"Yes, but he's my nerd. When he first asked me out, I couldn't imagine myself dating him."

"Fine." Jess finished her wine. "Ask the question."

"You said Amber looks like you?"

"We could almost be twins."

"Do you think that David slept with her?"

"Maybe." That slipped from her lips far faster than she would have liked.

"Do you think he promised to marry her?"

"It's possible." Jess was feeling worse instead of better. "But she claimed they were already married."

Clare sighed again and drained her glass. "Well, it's the only reason I can come up with that would explain why Amber is behaving the way she is."

They sat in silence for a long time.

Finally Jess spoke. "Yeah, me too."

Clare squeezed her hand.

"Thank you for letting me stay here tonight," Jess said.

"Of course. I love you."

It was all too much. Jess started to cry.

Clare shuffled forward and hugged her, holding tight, making sure that her best friend felt loved.

Chapter Twenty

THE GRUNGY BATHROOM in her cheap motel room was dingy and dark, with moldy grout and worn fixtures. The plastic shower curtain was yellowed, and the shower head never stopped dripping. A musty scent hung ripe in the air.

But it was strange that what undoubtedly had to be the grossest shower of Jessica's life was also one of the most refreshing. Still, even as gross as the shower floor had been, she had savored every drop of the warm water cascading over her. She felt a much better version of herself after she left the bathroom.

Then she sat on the bed and turned on David's phone.

Of course it was password protected. His birthday did not work. She tried Gwen. Nope. She tried the Replacement's birthday.

The phone opened.

She felt equal parts furious and victorious.

She turned off location services, then checked his contacts, scrolling through a long list while looking for any reference to her number.

But after going through every contact, she came up empty.

It shouldn't really surprise her. She didn't remember him calling her from this number. But she certainly would have felt better if she'd found a link between them. Or would she have?

She honestly didn't know anymore.

She scrolled through his emails next.

But every reference frustratingly (and again, infuriatingly) only led to Replacement Jessica. She found an order confirmation for a self-watering bonsai tree; a congratulatory note for a five-year 'Mustacheversary,' which she couldn't even imagine because David swore he'd never had one, a thread of trash talk from his Fantasy Football League, a delivery notice for a monthly wine box.

Plenty of things to confuse and anger her, but nothing that got her any closer to what was going on.

She searched for *Amber* next and found exactly one mention. But just like all the Jessicas, it had nothing to do with her.

Amber was a reference to color, for a shade of yellow that Replacement Jessica decided not to go with for her home office but definitely wanted an opinion about. She also made a teasing comment about blowing him that night, making Jessica want to explode. Instead, she deleted the email.

She opened his photos next and was flooded with pictures of David standing next to the imposter, sitting next to her, or her sitting on him in a few of them.

Fucking bitch.

All of those photos of David and the Replacement were all taken before Gwen had arrived. Although there were a few painfully recent ones, where Gwen was swaddled to the point that she wasn't even visible in the photo.

None of this made any sense whatsoever.

It felt like a Black Mirror episode, where David had been given some sort of replacement wife technology. Where he'd chosen to replicate her face and body, but maybe not her personality.

Every time she tried adding two and two, Jessica ended up with *Why the fuck doesn't this make any sense?*

Replacement Jessica was living Jessica's life.

Looking at the pictures was like tossing gasoline on a fire of rage.

Jessica went back to his contacts, scrolling through every one, looking at each of them closer. She spotted *HOME* and scrolled past, only circling back after finding nothing else that seemed out of the ordinary. Just like she'd found nothing odd the first two times.

She was starting to feel like a ghost.

Her thumb hovered over the contact for *HOME*, pausing to consider what she would say if he answered.

But it was impossible to plan for what she did not (and could not) understand.

So she finally pressed down and braced herself for whatever was coming next.

She dialed, and he answered.

"Hey, you found my phone." David sounded so easy and relaxed, his tone filled with a warm calm.

Not what Jessica expected, especially if he knew about the break-in.

She said nothing.

"Hello?" David said after a heavy silence. "Hello? Is someone there?"

"Are you alone?"

"Who is this?"

"Jessica." And fuck him thrice. "You know who it is."

David disconnected the call.

Jessica rang him again.

No answer.

Then no answer on repeat.

Jessica decided she would not be ignored for even one second longer. If David refused to answer her this time, then she would drive to their house and make him regret the moment he ever decided to fuck with her.

Assuming that's what happened.

He answered.

But he wasn't in the mood to play ball. "Listen, I don't know who you are—"

"Liar. You know exactly who I am, David!"

"—or how you got my phone—"

"I got it out of your car, asshole!"

"—but you're going to leave my family alone starting right now, or I'm calling the cops."

"I know things about you." Jessica made her voice calm and inviting. A mystery box that he would be scared to open, but even more scared to leave untouched.

"Is that a threat?"

"You hate egg yolks, you wear your socks inside out because you say they itch the other way, you hate golfing but pretend to like it because it's your boss's favorite sport. I didn't know his name was Grant before today, but now I do."

"None of that proves anything," he said.

"You go to bed at exactly 11:07 pm whenever possible, because you read some article claiming that as the optimal sleep time. You don't like the taste of strawberries, but you pretend to because they were your mother's favorite fruit. You also like a finger in your asshole when you—"

"Fuck you, lady!"

"As long as it's before 11:05!"

"Do not call here, ever again."

"Answer my questions and I won't need to."

"What you need to do is fuck the hell off. Because that person you described is not me."

"I already fucked the hell off, David! Isn't that what I did when I drove across the country to be here with you *and our baby*!" Jessica took a breath to control herself. "Did you know the boxes in the back of the U-Haul are all empty? Of course you do, because you're the one who packed them! Why would you do that, David? It doesn't make any sense. Did you really think that I was never going to knock on your door?"

"I'm warning you one last time. If—"

"I don't know what she did to you, David. Maybe invented some kind of mind-altering drug. But we've been married for three years and—"

The line went dead.

Jessica called back and got a busy signal.

Then the same thing the next three times in a row.

But the tempest she had been feeling earlier was gone. Jessica was too angry to drive over there now. It was a rock-hard fact that she would end up in jail if she did, maybe even end up in prison for murder. That's how angry she was at him. And her.

She was picturing things she shouldn't have been imagining. Like her hands around Replacement Jessica's throat.

How could she have let this happen to her?

And how could she have never seen it coming?

She wanted to cry until she had nothing left. Instead, she screamed loud enough to make her nearest neighbor in the motel consider calling the police (assuming there was anyone else staying in this dump) while chucking David's phone across the room.

It bounced off the wall and landed with a surprisingly soft thud on the carpet.

A moment later, Jessica stood with a sigh and retrieved it.

Then she went climbed onto the sad little bed and curled into a fetal position, staring at a photo of the Replacement with Gwen.

She slid her thumb over the Replacement's face.

And finally found her smile.

Chapter Twenty-One

JESS RUBBED HER EYES, scooping the crust out with her thumb as she sat in bed.

Should she even have any crust in her eyes after such a rotten night's sleep?

She turned over, hugging a pillow to her chest.

Then she sat bolt upright. She wasn't at home.

She needed to take care of Bella.

As if on cue, her phone buzzed. She glanced at the nightstand to see a text from Clare.

She picked up the phone and swiped her messages open: *I've taken care of Bella. So please go back to sleep if you need to when you read this.*

That was the first message, sent about five minutes ago. The most recent one read, *Seriously everything is handled. And I hope you're not so indifferent to your mental health that you leave your phone on the nightstand and turn off do not disturb.*

Jess smiled, strongly considering taking Clare's advice and trying to get another fifteen minutes to three hours of shuteye.

But then the phone buzzed again. She was about to tell

Clare to fuck off in the kindest way possible when she saw it was from David.

Any ETA on coming home? Security company is here and I need to get to work.

Jess considered texting *Fuck you*, and unlike Clare's, she'd meant every word of it. She went with ignoring his message instead.

But she wasn't going back to sleep. She would end up doom scrolling or googling Amber Brown if she stayed in bed.

So she got up and went to the bathroom.

Only to come out to her phone ringing. It was David.

Jess picked up the phone, rejected his call, then sent him a text: *I'm on my way.*

She took a five-minute shower, got dressed fast, packed her and Bella's backpack, then scurried downstairs.

She found Clare in the kitchen with both kids. Evan was snacking on Cheerios, with Bella asleep in her arms. "I need to get home."

"You didn't get my text?"

"Yes, but I also got one from David. The security company is there, and he needs to leave for work."

Clare made a face that was full of opinions, but none were stated out loud.

"He seriously can't handle it?"

Jess shrugged. "I told him I'd do it yesterday."

Clare nodded. It looked like she wanted to say more, but she didn't.

"Mason!" she called out. He popped into the kitchen. "I'll be right back. I'm just driving Bella and Jess home real quick."

"No, no," Jess said. "We can get an Uber."

"Wouldn't hear of it," Clare said. "Besides, you'll need a car seat for Bella."

That was true.

Mason pretended to be sad. "I was just about to challenge you two to a pancake flipping contest, so I guess that's off the table."

Clare laughed and kissed him. Then she turned to Jess. "Coffee first. And I'm not taking no for an answer."

She made it as fast as any barista — and it was delicious. Strong with a hint of vanilla and a splash of coconut milk. Then she went into the living room and gathered Bella.

By the time Jess finished her coffee and went outside, Clare had their bags in the trunk and Bella already strapped into Evan's car seat. Bella giggled as Jess closed the car door.

"She's always so happy," Clare said.

Jess smiled. "I love that about her."

"Any last-minute questions before I drop you?" Clare asked, pulling onto the road. "Anything you want to talk about?"

"The better question might be, what are you hoping I wanted to talk about? Or even better, what is it that you've been wanting to say?"

"You seem a little paranoid."

"That's great." Jess nodded. "Then I am acting exactly how I feel. Someone broke into my fucking house and wants to wear my skin. Should I not feel paranoid?"

"I'm worried about you."

"I'm worried about me too."

"I'm serious."

"So am I." Jess nodded again. "As serious as a heart attack. I'm worried about Amber Brown and whether she's a psychopath."

"She might not be." Clare hit the indicator and turned right.

Jess stared at her. "Are you kidding me?"

"Psychopaths have persistent antisocial behavior."

"You don't think the shit she's put us through is antisocial?"

"I mean like impaired empathy and no remorse. Bold, disinhibited, and egotistical traits," Clare said. "We don't know what this woman's damage is. But we can agree that it's dangerous."

"So what should I do?"

"A restraining order. You don't know anything about this woman other than her name?"

"I've told you every single thing I know about her," Jess said as Clare pulled up in front of her house.

And she still had that look on her face.

"Can you please just finally say it?"

"What do you want me to say?" Clare asked.

Jess stared back at her. "You know."

"Fine." Clare put the car in park. "But don't hate me. I couldn't bear it."

"Jesus Christ, what?"

"If you're ever thinking of relapsing, please just promise that you'll call me first."

Jess stared at her. Tears sprang to her eyes. "Oh. Oh, of course, Clare. But I promise you that's not where I am."

"I believe you. But this shit is upsetting. And I wouldn't blame you if it crossed your mind. Just call me. I'll drop everything and come right over. I know how hard you fought for Bella's adoption, and I won't let Amber Brown or David Clarke stand in the way of your happiness."

Jess unbuckled her seatbelt and gave Clare a hug. "Thank you for being such an awesome friend."

"Of course. You know I—"

Clare stopped. David stood on the front porch, watching them. He saw the women notice him then, tapped his wrist as though to indicate they were wasting his time.

"Sometimes I really do wish that Mason wasn't such a great guy," Jess said. "David always looks like more of an asshole after I see you."

"I know, hon." Clare smiled. "But it's not a competition."

"Never." Jess shook her head and got out of the car.

Thank you! he mouthed, though *About time!* was also implied.

David walked around to the side of the house as Clare and Jess took their second hug. Then Clare unloaded the trunk while Jess retrieved Bella from her car seat.

"Love you," Clare said.

"Love you too."

Jess started toward the house and Clare toward her car. In the Volvo, David peeled around the corner. Clare jumped back to avoid being hit, raising her hands high in the air as though to tell him off.

David slowed, grimaced and waved as though that made up for the blunder. Then he drove off.

Jess dropped the bags and walked back to Clare.

"Oh my God, I'm so sorry! Double what I said about David being an asshole. Jesus, are you alright?"

"He sure was in a hurry," Clare said.

"Sorry."

"You said that. And you don't have to be. Another person's actions are not yours to defend."

Tears sprang to her eyes, and Jess wanted to hug her again.

Clare said, "You want me to stay while the security guys finish installing the system?"

"That would be nice, but I have work to do. I need to get that T-shirt done."

"Even more of a reason then. I'll stay out of the way. Mason is already watching Evan. He won't care if I stay a little longer." Then she sweetened the deal. "I'll even handle any questions from the security guys. Seriously, close your door and get as much work done as you can."

Jess tried to not cry. "You really are my best friend."

"I know. Now let me help you and myself. This way I don't have to listen to you bitching about Muriel later."

Jess laughed. She handed Bella to Clare, picked up the bags and they entered the house.

The security guys seemed to know what they were doing. So she went upstairs and sat in front of her computer, ready to work, eager to get her design done. She didn't know which she'd feel better about: getting another invoice sent off, or getting Muriel all the way off of her back.

A half hour felt like a long time to get started. And Jess could have been happy with that if she'd got rolling.

Ninety minutes, she still hadn't resolved her design, so much as drawn and erased the same thing multiple times and now only had the early buzz of a migraine to show for it.

Being creative was rarely this hard. She felt guilty for wasting Clare's time. And the security guys would no doubt be finished any minute. And then they'd all be gone.

Maybe that pressure was making her freeze up. Maybe once they were gone, she'd be able to focus. Though she wouldn't admit to Clare that she had gotten nothing done.

But then Jess made the mistake of checking her email and saw a new check-in from Muriel, wanting to know the status of her graphics.

Almost done! she emailed back. One sentence, two words, and zero detail.

Still, Jess would almost be done if only she could focus.

She needed to be honest with herself. Focusing would be impossible until she answered some nagging questions about the Replacement.

She googled *David Clarke and Amber Brown*. But nothing came up. That stayed true no matter how many variables she tried. Those two names were not linked anywhere, according to fifteen minutes on Google and another ten on Bing. That made her feel slightly better.

But it also brought her total time of doing nothing on the overdue design to nearly two hours.

Jess kept googling.

And lost more valuable minutes.

So she stopped, long enough to consider a better strategy than her haphazard variations on the name Amber. She'd run through them all. Ambur. Ambyr. Ahmber.

She'd wished she had thought to get the number Amber had called last night. She caught a glimpse of it on the phone when she'd insisted it belonged to David. But she couldn't even remember a single digit.

She played over last night's events. Then had a thought. Officer Carlson had impounded the U-Haul. *That's* what she should be googling.

Two minutes later, Jess knew exactly where the impound lot was. She put the address in her phone and tucked it into her pocket.

It would be hard to concentrate on her work now that she finally had a lead. But she needed to get the T-shirt design done.

At least Jess was smiling when she got back to it.

An idea came to her, but it felt instantly wrong once she started drawing. Again, she felt like she was forcing her creativity, instead of allowing it organically to reveal a concept.

She erased it and started something else.

But Jess was only two minutes into the work when Clare knocked on her office door.

"The security guys are done," she said. "They need to show you how everything works. I tried to get them to show me, and I promised to show you. But there's something you have to sign saying that you understood the demo and—"

"Of course." Jess put her screen to sleep. "I was almost finished anyway."

The technician's name was Stan. He was tall and fit, wearing a black uniform with a badge on the front. With short brown hair and a serious expression, he carried his clipboard like it added an inch to his height.

Stan led her through the intricacies of the system. Familiarized Jess with the surveillance cameras, showing her how to monitor the live feeds and enable the motion detectors. He demonstrated how everything worked, from syncing the cameras to understanding the alerts that would notify her should an unwelcome entity breach their boundaries.

Jess signed the documents to prove her understanding, set the passcode, then thanked Stan again, even waving at the man as he walked toward the work van. Soon as he was gone, she turned to Clare.

"You want to do some detecting?"

Clare blinked. "Not at all what I was expecting you to say."

"And?"

Clare grinned. "Hell, yeah."

Chapter Twenty-Two

"I NEED TO GRAB MY COAT," Jess said.

"Oh my God, hurry up. I feel like we're in a detective show. A good one. On a streamer."

"You're thinking too much about this." Jess laughed.

She reached for her coat. It wasn't there. Of course it wasn't. Because Amber had stolen it. So she grabbed one of David's instead.

Then she set the new SecureX alarm for the first time, exactly how Stan had shown her.

"And Mason seriously won't care if we drop Bella off again, even though you were supposed to be coming back home?"

"He only has one showing today, and it's not until this afternoon. But if it makes you feel better, we can just keep Bella with us. Seriously, your baby came with batteries included."

"Okay." Jess smiled, overjoyed with that decision. "Thank you."

They went back out to Clare's vehicle and got in.

As Jess put on her seat belt, she felt something crinkle in David's coat pocket.

She reached in and pulled out a piece of paper: the plane ticket from his most recent trip. She shoved it back in the pocket, then turned back to smile at Bella, who was strapped once again into Evan's car seat.

"We're going on an adventure, Bella."

Bella clapped.

Clare started the car.

"I know you like to listen to that Baby Einstein crap or whatever, but I think it's more important I don't put my head through a window in despair."

"So what does that mean?"

"Right now?" Clare fiddled with the radio. "It means Beatles or Stones."

"My mom used to be obsessed with The Beatles. Stones, please."

"Excellent choice."

"Paint It Black" filled the cabin as Clare pulled away from Longhorn Drive and headed to the impound lot.

Midway into the fifth song on Clare's Rolling Stones playlist ("Sympathy For The Devil"), they arrived at their destination. Clare killed the engine, cutting the song off.

They retrieved Bella, then head into the cinder-block building. They approached a Formica counter and a heavyset receptionist in uniform looked up at the three of them.

"You again?" Her name tag read *MONICA*. Jess glanced at Clare. She shrugged. "Let me guess, Ms. Amber Jessica Brown Clarke. You don't want to pick it up, just look in the back." She seemed slightly irritated.

"Sure."

She sighed, got up, and walked over to a board full of

keys. She pulled a set of keys and tossed them on the counter. "You remember the stall number?"

Jess shook her head.

"Three-five-seven," Monica said.

"Thanks."

"Thank you," Clare said, providing an extra helping of gratitude to make sure that Monica believed them. Then they exited through a side door and out into the impound lot.

"Jesus," Clare said as they reached the bottom of the concrete steps and walked into a sea of vehicles. "You must really look alike if she thinks you're Amber."

"That's what I've been trying to tell you."

"I know, but still, wow, she didn't even question that you were her for a second."

"How much Amber Brown looks like me is one of the weirdest things about this whole fucked-up mess."

"Is it wrong that I want to meet her?"

Jess gave her a look.

"I mean, this really is an Orphan Black situation."

"It is not. Stop saying that. There is nothing supernatural about this."

"There's nothing supernatural about Orphan Black," Clare said. "Have you seen the show?"

"Yes, I've seen the show," Jess said, walking toward a U-Haul with Montana on the side. "I just wasn't expecting to live it." She stopped before the vehicle.

"Is this it?"

Jess nodded.

Clare plucked the key from her hand. "What are we waiting for?"

Jess followed her around to the back of the truck. Clare unlocked the lock, lifted the latch, and threw the door up on its rails.

The inside was packed with boxes. A lot of them. Enough to move an entire life across the country. But they weren't stacked neatly. They were scattered about.

"This feels weird," said Jess. "Don't you think it's weird that the boxes are all over the place?"

"Yeah, it feels weird." She nodded. "But they could have fallen over during the drive. Remember, this thing was on a tow truck."

"They look more trashed than fallen over."

"Do you want to go first? I can hold Bella," Clare said. "Actually, let me rephrase that: hand me Bella, you're going first."

Jess followed the order and then climbed up and into the back of the U-Haul. She lifted the flaps of the first box. Staring inside.

"What is it?" Clare asked.

"It's empty." Jess opened the next closest box. "So is the one."

"Maybe she already moved everything?"

Another five boxes later, Jess said, "I think they're all empty."

"Holy cowbells. That is definitely weird."

"Cowbells?"

"I'm holding Bella."

"We were just listening to The Rolling Stones."

"What does one have to do with the other? You know what, never mind." Clare shook her head, glancing into the truck. "Look at that one."

Jess spun it around. It looked like someone had put their fist through the cardboard. Another had a shoe print on it.

"I think someone had a tantrum," Clare said.

"You think?"

"None of this makes any sense," Clare said. "Too bad we can't ask Monica."

"Who's Monica?"

"The guard in there." Clare gestured toward the reception building.

"Why can't we?"

"Because she thinks you're Amber," Clare said. "And I don't think we want to mess around there. Better to stay invisible, since what we just did here might be considered a crime."

"I can hardly impersonate myself."

"Still, it's not your vehicle."

"No, but it's not like we killed someone."

"Is that going to be your legal defense?"

Jess growled at her.

"Come on," Clare said. "Before Amber comes back."

"If she does, I'm chaining her to a chair 'cause I have a million questions."

"Now *that* is a crime," Clare said.

They went back into the office, and Jess put the keys on the Formica counter.

"You get what you need?" Monica asked.

Jess nodded.

"You find your stuff?"

"Huh?"

"Your things. You get them back from your boyfriend?"

"Yeah," Jess nodded. "I did."

Monica snagged the car keys. "Just so you know, fees are stacking up."

"Yeah. I'll get it tomorrow."

Monica grunted, slid off her chair, and walked back over to the peg board that contained all the keys.

The Beatles played as they drove back to Jess' house. Jess glanced at Clare. She met her eyes and they both burst out laughing while Bella rocked out to "Yellow Submarine" in the back.

"Jesus," Clare said. "We are the worst detectives."

"The worst," Jess agreed.

"But if you get any more ideas and don't call me, I'll never speak to you again," Clare said as she turned left onto Longhorn. "I'm always up for a spot of detecting. Playdates and Perpetrators."

"What's that?"

"The name of our show."

"No one would watch that."

"Some people would watch it," Clare said. "It has alliteration."

"That doesn't make it a good name."

"Love you," said Clare.

Jess smiled. "Love you too."

Five minutes later, Jess was on her way back to the house. She paused at the door to wave goodbye to Clare, and seconds later, her SUV disappeared down the road.

The Beatles had worn Bella out, and she was already falling asleep as Jess walked her into the house. She locked the front door, then carried her upstairs. She hesitated before entering the nursery.

But she wasn't about to let Amber keep her from living in her own home. She entered the room. At least David had done what he said. He'd changed Bella's sheets.

She lay her in the crib and pulled up her blanket.

Jess kissed her on the forehead and left the room. Then she grabbed David's ticket from the pocket of his coat. Taking it into her office to add it to their basket of receipts.

A word caught her eye. *NYC.*

Jess froze. New York City?

She blinked. And rubbed her eyes. New York City.

She checked the date on the ticket. Last week.

David was supposed to have been picking Bella up in Los Angeles. Not New York City. So what the fuck was he doing there?

Jess heard Clare in the back of her mind, demanding that David answer a few questions.

She got her phone and called Prairie Corp.

She got his receptionist. "Mr. Clarke isn't available at the moment."

"Okay." But it really wasn't. "Please, just tell him that I called."

"I'll do that."

But then she glanced at the clock. "Wait!"

"Yes, Mrs. Clarke?"

"It's really important."

"I understand. But he's not in his office. Mr. Clarke had a business lunch appointment. His calendar says that he should be back in the office by two. I'll tell him that you called if he comes in before then."

"I'd rather you didn't," said Jess.

"Pardon?" The receptionist sounded bewildered.

Jess hung up the phone.

Chapter Twenty-Three

JESSICA SAT in David's BMW at the end of Longhorn, watching house 2097.

All of those pictures, hours spent scrolling on his phone (clearly a different one from the phone she found in this car), showing her photos of her new house. Photos that turned out to be lies.

Same outside, different insides.

Just like David.

What the hell had happened to him?

Jessica had no idea, but she was back on Longhorn, determined to get some answers.

Surely the SecureX van parked out front had something to do with her.

Replacement Jessica must not feel very safe. Good.

Fuck Replacement Jessica in all of the ways.

David, too. Until she had reason to believe in him again. Assuming the man who lived here was David. The jury was definitely still out on that one.

Let them feel rattled. Give them a taste of what Jessica was feeling. At least *they* had Gwen for comfort.

Replacement Jessica had broken and entered into her life.

Right now she was watching him pace the front porch. He was talking on the phone. Probably the landline. He looked annoyed.

He got off his call, but the pacing didn't stop.

The SecureX technician approached David, and he seemed to provide a clipped answer, displaying a physicality to his temper that Jessica had never seen before. The technician held up his hands and went back into the house.

Jessica studied David. She couldn't really remember ever seeing any kind of temper on David before. It almost seemed robotic how throttled his emotions could be sometimes. Especially when it came to Gwen. She had cried with disbelief, nerves, joy, anxiety when they got the call from the adoption agency. Whereas David had seemed to take it all in stride. He almost seemed clinical in his response.

The only time she had seen him overwhelmed with emotion was when he declared that nothing would stand in the way of adoption. He almost had a brute force of determination about him. It had actually scared her a little.

Less than ten minutes later, a car pulled up to the house. The Replacement was inside, talking to the driver, another woman who looked around five years older than her (and Jessica).

They seemed to notice David pacing and concluded their discussion. They hugged and got out of the car, then David disappeared around the side of the house.

Replacement Jessica got Gwen out of the back seat.

And then the green Volvo came screaming around the corner and barreled into Longhorn Drive. He almost hit the Replacement's friend, who threw her hands up in the air, her meaning clear: *ASSHOLE!*

Jessica's eyes returned to Gwen. God, she wanted to run and grab her. But she knew exactly what would happen. She'd wind up back with Officer Grumpy.

And yet again, no one would believe her.

Jessica waited until the Volvo had almost disappeared, then she pulled onto the road, gunning it.

Within a few minutes, she'd caught up to him.

Then started to worry that she might be getting a little too close.

But David was clearly only paying attention to whatever was a few feet in front of him. He barely stopped at any of the four stop signs he hit, rolling through before finally making a left.

They drove out of the manicured lawns, neatly painted houses, and (Jessica was certain) well-kept streets, until they reached the highway. Considering David took the third exit, they should only have been on the road for a few short minutes.

But the concrete arteries were congested.

By the time David pulled off onto a frontage road fifteen minutes later, Jessica was convinced that he wasn't aware of her.

She didn't pull in behind him, but continued on, circling the block. Making sure it wasn't an attempt to ditch her.

But nope, the Volvo was still there, parked in front of a coffee shop. It was the only building in a surprisingly large lot.

The coffee must be great, because judging by the number of vehicles, Texpresso was packed.

The Volvo was empty, which meant that David was already inside. It was risky, but she parked the BMW at the far end of the lot and got out of the car. And then she hesitated.

What if he was waiting for her inside? What if he was hoping to confront her?

So what if he was? Maybe it was time for a confrontation.

Jessica chewed on her thumb for a full minute before finally stirring up enough courage to walk confidently over to the Texpresso and peek in the window. Pretending that she wanted to see the menu.

She saw David in line and watched him until he placed his order.

Then she waited until he carried his drink to a table that gave him a clear view of the parking lot. His back was to her for seconds. She darted inside, walking straight to the counter as though she'd been in the place countless times before.

Texpresso was modern and spacious, with floor-to-ceiling windows that drenched the place in natural light. The walls were decorated with eclectic yet overtly masculine artwork. And colorful rugs added a much-needed element of coziness to the place.

She approached the counter.

"Can I help you?"

She glanced up at the menu on the wall, picking the first thing that sparked her interest. "Pecan Prairie Mocha."

"Name?"

She almost said Jessica. Then Amber. What had she called herself when talking to Grant? Mandy? "Mandy."

The clerk noted her name on the sleeve of the coffee cup.

Jessica paid for her drink, then gestured to the washroom at the far wall. "Do I need a key?"

The clerk shook her head, and Jessica headed over. She relieved herself and then washed up. When she exited, she saw the counter was a direct line to where David was sitting.

So she stood in the corner, watching him and waiting for her drink. She should go over and talk to him.

Maybe now that he was alone, he'd be able to tell her what was really going on.

But she couldn't bring herself to do it. She didn't want to be yelled at again. Not here. In public.

And if she tried to explain, who was going to believe her?

Not even the cops did.

A woman entered, not bothering to glance at the menu. She made her way directly to David and sat opposite him at the table. She was an attractive blonde in shi-shi yoga clothes, with long golden locks cascading down her back. Her creamy skin practically glowed under Texpresso's friendly lighting. She had a slender physique from her long neck down to the tiny ankles peeking out of her brightly colored sneakers.

David stood to greet the woman.

Had the gall to kiss her on the cheek like a pile of shit.

He handed her something, but she couldn't see what it was.

Jessica took out David's phone and snapped several pictures of him and the woman.

She watched them talking and laughing. They seemed familiar with one another, laughing like lovers. Jessica wondered if Replacement Jessica knew about this woman. She imagined not.

They continued to talk for a few more minutes.

David finished his coffee, then stood up and kissed her on the cheek again. Too fast for Jessica to snap a photo.

They parted ways at the door.

Jessica kept watching, waiting for her moment.

She followed them to the door, watching through the window as David crossed the parking lot. The woman was already gone.

David spotted the BMW and paused. She saw his head lower as he took in the license plate. Obviously not recognizing it.

He shook his head and made his way over to the Volvo. "Mandy!"

A woman touched her arm. "I think she's talking to you."

Jessica glanced back at the barista. Right. *Mandy*.

But Jessica needed to follow David. If she went back for her drink, she'd lose him.

He was already pulling into the road. Jessica darted out the door and ran for the BMW.

She gunned the engine and raced toward the exit.

An old Honda Element cut right in front of her.

Jessica throttled the urge to lay on her horn. Soon as the Honda Element turned out, she floored it. Cutting around the driver and speeding up the road.

She slowed as she spotted a police car. But it turned the other direction.

She applied the gas again.

It was a lot harder to keep up with David coming out of Texpresso than it had been on his way here. She almost lost him. Twice. Thank God for the color of his (or the Replacement's?) Volvo.

She lost him a minute later. But by then they were close enough to the Prairie Corporation for her to guess his final destination.

When she spotted his Volvo in the parking lot, she felt victorious.

But she didn't stay, driving out of the parking lot and driving around the block. She found a parking spot on a side street that had a perfect view of anyone entering or leaving.

Whenever she felt like she'd been sitting for too long, she drove around the block. But then she became convinced that every trip probably drew more attention than if she just stayed put.

Her patience paid off at lunch time. David dipped out of the parking lot and pulled into the street. She slunk down in the driver's seat as he passed.

Seconds later, she was once again following the Volvo. David drove down into the city to a sketchy area under the highway. Dark and uninviting, the shadows were long and deep. The area buzzed with electricity. Trash littered the ground, and the concrete was plastered with graffiti.

Crap. Why the hell was David here? Jessica hoped that she hadn't driven right into a trap.

But he didn't leave the car, staying put behind one of the concrete barriers.

After three minutes, another car finally drove up. A black Dodge Charger with several dents in the passenger side door and a loudly rumbling engine.

Was this yoga woman? Maybe this is where they carried on their affair (if that's what was happening).

As the Charger approached, David got out of the vehicle. But it wasn't yoga woman who got out of the vehicle. It was another man. They made an odd couple for sure. David was dressed professionally in his slacks and dress shirt. His companion wore combat boots and carried a leather jacket. His jeans were torn from use, not because it was the style. And both his forearms displayed a full sleeve of tattoos.

The newcomer had the hard look of the men she'd seen in the photos with David at the Prairie Corporation's charity dinners. And even if it was only because Jessica was watching them from the shadows, the man radiated a sense of danger.

The tattooed man looked at David expectantly.

David reached into his suit jacket and pulled out an envelope. He looked reluctant to hand it over.

But he did.

Jessica took out her phone and snapped a few pictures.

The man opened the envelope and thumbed through the contents. He appeared to be counting money. When he finished, he shook his head and appeared to try to hand the envelope back.

And then they started arguing.

Both men were clearly angry. Tattoo Arms gesticulated wildly with his hands, while David's side of the conversation included a series of pacifying motions.

Jessica would have given just about anything to hear what they were fighting about. But no way in hell was she getting out of the BMW.

Eventually they calmed.

It was clear that David had talked the other man down.

Tattoo Arms nodded, seeming to acquiesce to whatever David had suggested.

David patted the man on his back, waited for another nod, then turned around and walked back to the Volvo.

Jessica was torn, unsure of whether she should continue to follow David to wherever he might be going next, or follow Tattoo Arms. Maybe he knew something about David that would help her make sense of the shit-show her life had become.

She put the car into drive and got ready to pull out after the Volvo, but it was impossible to tear her eyes away from Tattoo Arms. There was something about the way he was waiting for David to pull back out onto the road. Like he was still pissed. Like he'd only let David think he'd won the argument.

Jessica made the decision to let David go. She'd be able to find him again, but if she didn't follow Tattoo Arms right now, she might never know he was.

When the Volvo was gone, Tattoo Arms pulled out his phone and dialed.

Jessica's phone started to ring.

She dug it out, slouching down and staring at the contact information.

Whiskerface.

Chapter Twenty-Four

PETER GOT BACK into his Dodge charger and propped the phone up against the steering wheel, listening to it ring.

It kept ringing.

He flipped through the money in the envelope. Counting it once, and then again while managing not to chew his bottom lip through the second time.

Five grand was exactly half of what was promised. And more than anything in life, Peter did not appreciate being fucked with.

If David didn't make this right, then Peter would have to make it right in the only way he knew how.

The call went to voicemail. "You've reached Jessica Clarke—"

Peter snorted. Then disconnected and dialed again.

Bitch had better answer this time.

She did, three rings into the call, just before it went to voicemail.

But she didn't say *hi*, or anything else. Just a lot of breathing.

Peter waited it out, but exhibiting too much patience

would be a mistake. He had the upper hand. He had every intention of keeping it.

"Amber?" A little more breathing, but Peter could sense her discomfort. "Amber. You know I can hear you breathing, right?"

Still no response.

"I'm calling to help you."

"You're calling to help me?" Her voice was thin and reedy, like she was anxious.

"Yeah."

She rushed on, as though summoning courage. "My name is Jessica, not Amber."

"Okay."

"Who are you?"

"A friend."

"I want a name."

"Gary."

She was quiet for a moment, then asked, "Is that really your name?"

Peter snorted. "My name isn't important. What's important is I have information on David Clarke that I think you'll be interested in."

"What kind of information?"

"The kind that is best shared in person."

"You want to meet in person?" she scoffed. "I don't think so."

"Then you're gonna be shit out of luck. 'Cause I ain't talking over the phone."

"Why not?"

"You might be miked."

"What does that mean?"

"Working for the cops."

"Well, I'm not."

"Then let's meet."

"How am I supposed to trust you?"

"That's up to you. I ain't your shrink. You either do or you don't. I'm risking enough just talking to you. So if you want to know why David—"

She hung up.

"Bitch," Peter said, surprised by her lady balls.

He'd need to call her back eventually, but he had a feeling she was going to call him first. He forced himself to sit tight.

He pulled the gun out from inside his coat pocket and checked the chamber. Then he studied the number of bullets with a smile.

The phone rang. He returned the gun to his jacket.

"Get disconnected?" Peter asked.

"I hung up on you."

"I'm sorry to hear that."

"What do you want?" she asked.

"I already told you, I have information—"

"That's not what you want. Tell me what's in it for you. How can I trust you?"

"Look, I can't even get my old lady to trust me. So you either want to meet me or you don't."

Peter turned his engine, then pulled out from the dingy nook under the highway.

"You need to give me something," she said. "I don't make it a habit of meeting strange men."

"Too bad. It might loosen you up a little."

She hung up again.

Peter snorted again, but he knew he lost that round.

He kept driving but rang her back.

"What?" she said instead of hello.

"I know that you're not Amber."

"That's great. So you know what I already told you. We agree that I'm not Amber. Is that all you've got?"

Might as well throw out the whole hook. "I know why David is doing this to you."

Silence.

He grinned. She was bumping up against the bait. He could feel it.

"Why?"

"See, I'm selling, but you're angling for freebies."

"I don't have any money."

"We both know that's not true," Peter said.

She was quiet.

"Maybe you're the untrustworthy one." Peter paused to give her time to think. "'Cause we both know that you stole money from David."

She hesitated.

"It's only a couple grand," she said.

He almost slapped his knee. Hot damn. She had just swallowed the bait. The hook was now lodged in her throat. He had her.

"It's more than I got right now. Two-thousand dollars, you say?"

She paused again. "Fine."

"Fine what?"

"I'll meet you."

"Not now," Peter said, swinging his steering wheel to the right as his Dodge reached the corner. "I got a meeting."

"Then when?"

"At ten. Trammel Crow Park. There's a bench on the far side of the parking lot near a cluster of trees. It'll be private. We can meet there."

"Trammel Crow Park?"

"You know where it is?"

"I can find out. But I want to know why you're doing this. Does David know you're meeting me?"

Peter snorted. "Hell, no. You and me, Amber—"

"Jessica."

"We're in the same boat. David betrayed me. I want to get even."

He could hear her breathing again, probably wondering if she could believe him.

"Wouldn't you like that?" Peter asked. "To get even with David?"

"What's your name?" she said. "I know it's not Gary."

"Peter."

"Okay, Peter. How should I—"

He killed the call and tossed the phone onto the passenger seat. Then he glanced in the rearview mirror. He spotted the BMW. Knew it was hers.

Two blocks later, she slowed. And he sped up. She made no attempt to keep pace. He darted through a red light, turned left, then right. But she was gone.

Amateur.

He drove directly to Trammel Crow Park.

It was a large, open space with lush green grass, winding pathways, and tall trees. He circled a large playground surrounded by benches and pulled into a large lot across the park, populated only by a smattering of cars.

He scoped out the area several times, waiting until there were no more joggers. Then he added a silencer to his gun and walked toward the bench he'd picked out for tonight's liaison.

Once there, he shot out the park lights, one at a time. No one seemed to notice the sound of glass exploding. Then he returned to the car.

He had just started the Dodge and pulled onto the road when his phone dinged.

The contact read, *BALL & CHAIN.*

And the message read: *where r u?*

He waited for a red light, because there were some rules that even a man like Peter chose to follow if it meant he'd still be alive and able to see his kid. Then he tapped out his reply: *on my way.*

Apparently, that response wasn't good enough for her royal highness.

Joe just stopped a goal. He's asking for you.

Now he was driving and texting, and his own bad behavior was pissing Peter off.

I said I'd be there. And I meant it.

You've said that before.

"Bitch." He was approaching an intersection. The light was yellow. But he didn't hit the brake. Instead, he slammed his foot down on the gas, just as the light turned red, and roared down the street, heading for his son's game.

Chapter Twenty-Five

JESSICA HAD PULLED the BMW over to the side of the road and turned it off.

She chewed on her thumb while considering for the umpteenth time how ridiculous her life had become.

Was it even her life?

An odd question to ask, but the repeating query was like gum stuck to her heel. It just wouldn't let go.

And why the hell had she agreed to meet Peter? Let alone in a deserted park after dark?

Someone knocked on the car window.

She started.

Standing on the sidewalk was an old man, bare chested, age spots dappling his folds of wrinkled skin. He wore a not so fashionable combination of electrocardiogram (ECG) electrodes and hospital pants. She rolled the window down.

"Yes?"

He didn't speak, just held out a shaking hand.

She dug into her coat pocket and pulled a $100 from the stash she had stolen from David (though, according to the law, it was half hers). Then she crawled over to the passenger seat and held it out.

He hesitated.

"Go on," she said.

He took it, staring back at her, baffled. "Thank you?"

Jessica nodded, then she got back in the driver's seat. Rolled up the window and drove away.

She didn't know where she was going. She simply turned on the radio and drove. Her mind was consumed with thoughts of Peter. At least she knew what he looked like. She had the advantage over him. Or did she? If he knew the Replacement, then he would know her.

She pulled over, dug out her phone, and opened Google, looking for the closest hunting store. She was just a few minutes away from something called Rugged Republic Outfitters. She imagined a place like that would have a bunch of different options for a woman to protect herself.

When Stevie Nicks was done singing about thunder only happening when it rained, Jessica switched the radio off again. Listening to someone else at the moment was too distracting.

She needed to keep focused on tonight. Either Peter was being honest and truly wanted to get back at David, or she was being set up.

Neither option made her feel good.

She pulled into the Rugged Republic Outfitters parking lot. It was filled with trucks and SUVs, most with racks for hunting gear. David's BMW looked like a toy car when she parked it next to a truck with tires the size of oil drums.

Having lived in New York all her life, Jessica had no frame of reference for what a Texas hunting store might look like inside. She felt smacked in the face by the reality of it.

First, it had never even occurred to her that the shop

might be more than one story. And second, "shop" might be too quaint a word for the three-story structure. Gray stone walls and massive windows, all of them dark. An ornate wooden sign above the door read *Rugged Republic Outfitters* in thick, white letters.

There was a cluster of large trees around the entrance and a handful of benches and picnic tables were scattered about a front-facing courtyard. They were filled with either families or large men eating alone. Apparently, this hunting store also had a restaurant, barbecue by the smell of it.

Jessica passed a flagpole that flew American and Texas flags that were twice the size of her old bedsheets. Then she entered the store.

Rugged Republic Outfitters was the size of a ware-house, but the interior was much more organized than she expected. Each section was clearly labeled: fishin', huntin', barbecuin'. Weirdly, the shop (she decided that the word worked better than she would have expected) seemed almost homey.

A trio of signs helped her narrow down the search: *When Nature Calls, Answer With Precision; We Handle the Outdoors, You Handle the Knife;* and *Sharper Solutions for Savvy Sportsmen.*

The section made available a whole variety of tools, from knives with long jagged blades (for field dressing, apparently) to shorter serrated blades designed for skinning (or skinnin'). The handles came in a rainbow of colors and were made with a variety of materials, from wood and plastic to iron and stainless steel.

There was also a selection of sharpening stones and honing oils to maintain the sharpness of what now seemed like luxury blades.

Jessica didn't need anything fancy. Just something she could use if an asshole wanted her dead.

She must have looked helpless. Or lost. Or both.

An older man in a plaid shirt and overalls walked over. He was the same general size and shape as Santa Claus, but his white beard had been sheared into a trim goatee.

"You look like you have questions, ma'am."

Jessica nodded. "Yeah."

"My name is Curt. How may I help you?"

"I'm looking for a hunting knife."

Curt nodded at the display. "There ain't a better place in Dallas for you right now, then."

"But I don't know what kind to buy."

"What kind of hunting will you be doing?"

She hesitated, then gave him a helpless look.

Curt narrowed his eyes. He knew. He'd probably had plenty of women in his section asking for the same kind of thing.

"This way." He led her over to a display of knives that looked more ordinary than the others. "Anything strike your interest?"

She pointed to a large blade. "I like that one."

"That's the Ka-Bar Becker BK9 Combat Bowie Fixed Blade Knife." He nodded. "It's a great knife, but it's not for you."

"Why not?"

"Too big."

"Isn't bigger better?"

"It is if you're cutting something that's already dead. But if you're looking for personal protection, then you should strongly consider something smaller. Otherwise you'll make it too easy for the predator to take it off you."

"Oh. I don't want that to happen."

"Most don't, ma'am."

Jess looked at him. "Which one would you suggest?"

"Well, ma'am, that all depends on what feels best in

your hands. How about I get you three different knives to test?"

She smiled. "That sounds great."

Curt collected a trio of blades. And he was right. The one she liked best was small enough to feel like it belonged in her hand, like it was a part of her.

"Meet the CRKT Minimalist Bowie Neck." He gestured to the blade. "Don't be fooled by its compact size. She packs a punch with a sharp, 2.125-inch stainless steel edge. And that snug fit in your hand is thanks to the unique three-finger choil handle design. Light as a feather at just 1.6 ounces. Your perfect companion for personal protection and everyday tasks."

"Thank you, Curt."

He smiled. "I can help you with your purchase over here."

"Cash, please."

"Of course." He led Jessica to an adjacent register, then handed her a coupon for ten percent off a future purchase.

Jessica left Rugged Republic Outfitters feeling better. She got back into the BMW and opened the knife box. Holding it in her hand, drawing it through the air, getting comfortable with it. A good choice for sure.

She folded the blade closed and tucked it in her coat pocket.

Then she pulled out her phone. No one had called. Or texted. Not that she expected to them. Who was she waiting to hear from? David? Replacement Jessica? Peter? If that indeed was his name.

She opened up her photo app and scrolled through the pictures she had taken of David and the woman in the cafe. Jessica wished she had been quick enough to get a shot of him kissing her on the cheek. But still, these images were incriminating enough. Their heads close together. Smiles on both mouths.

She had a plan for those photos, but she had to make a pit stop first.

She dropped her phone into the cupholder and started the car.

She left the parking lot, leaving behind the gun rack-mounted vehicles, feeling far more lethal than when she arrived.

She drove back to the community center, steering clear of the police station.

She didn't even have to use the GPS.

She was starting to get used to Dallas.

And weirdly, despite the still chilling circumstances, that familiarity and sense of direction made her feel like she was indeed home.

Jessica parked in front of the community center.

Then she got out of the car and walked toward the entrance, pulling her hood up, the CRKT Minimalist Bowie Neck Knife tucked into her pocket, just in case.

Chapter Twenty-Six

JESS HADN'T SPOKEN to David since he got home.

Of course he knew she was angry. And he had known her long enough to understand the glaring difference between the right moment and an adjacent time.

A few seconds sometimes meant everything.

But there were so many things on her mind, and she felt a pressing need to say them all. At once. Jess was afraid that when she opened her mouth, everything would spill out in a way that she might never be able to take the words back.

But at least he'd brought dinner home with him. Her favorite. Thai. So they sat down to a meal of plump shrimp spring rolls with a tangy tamarind sauce, fragrant chicken green curry rich with coconut milk and spices, a spicy beef pad Thai tossed with crushed peanuts, and a vibrant mango salad, all garnished with basil and cilantro.

The heavy aroma lightened her mood. A little.

She waited for him to ask her what was wrong. But he kept his full attention on his noodles. So she gave up waiting.

"How was L.A.?"

The chopsticks paused midway to his mouth. "What?"

"L.A. How was the trip?"

"I told you."

"No, you told me about picking Bella up. How was the trip itself? Good flight?"

David eyed her. "What's wrong?"

Now he asked. She yanked the plane ticket out of her pocket and tossed it on the table. He glanced at, paling.

Then he bit into his egg roll. Filling the silenced with chewing. As though he was trying to buy enough time to come up with some kind of answer. Or excuse.

"The adoption company fucked up."

"How did they fuck up?"

"Some new employee got our file mixed up with another couple. But believe me, Roberta at Forever Home has been dealt with."

"What does that mean? Got our files mixed up?"

David cleared his throat. "They told me the pick-up was in L.A. But it wasn't. It was in New York."

"And you didn't think to tell me?"

"I literally found out at the airport! I was standing in line when I got the call. Can you believe that shit?"

"I don't know."

He blinked. "What?"

"I don't know if I believe you."

He gestured to the phone. "I can call Forever Home. They can tell you."

She studied him. He didn't appear to be lying. But maybe she couldn't tell anymore.

He set down his chopsticks and wiped his mouth. "When was I supposed to tell you?"

"What kind of question is that?" She dropped her fork and threw her hands in the air. "How when you found out that you had to go to New York instead of L.A.? Don't you think *that* would have been the perfect fucking time?"

"Don't swear at me, Jess." He shook his head, clearly trying to keep his cool. "It never works out when you swear at me. I was just trying to do the right thing."

"And what was the right thing, David?"

"My number one priority was getting to Bella. Same for numbers two and three and all the rest of them after I got that call from Roberta. There was a flight leaving in twenty minutes and all I could think of was getting a ticket and getting on the damn plane. Apologies if my first thought wasn't, *Oh better tell my wife about this mix-up at the adoption agency. They gave me the wrong city. Ha ha.*"

Jess licked a bit of sauce from the corner of her mouth as he continued.

"I — *we* — were so desperate for Bella my lizard brain had me terrified that if I couldn't get to her that day, Forever Home might take her away from us. I know that's not true, but I just wanted to get to our daughter. Even one more night without her seemed like too long. We worked too hard to get Bella. Sorry, *you* worked so hard to get her. I wasn't thinking rationally. I'm sorry about that."

"Okay. I might understand your initial reaction. But why didn't you say anything when you got back?"

David didn't answer.

"Would it have been that hard to say, 'Oh my God, babe, you're not going to believe what happened to me. I was at the airport when I got this call.'"

"I didn't want you to be worried." He looked down at the floor, rubbing his jaw. Jess couldn't figure out if he was being performative or not. "And—"

"And what?"

"Roberta took responsibility for the blunder, but I still didn't want you to think that I had screwed up somehow."

There was a long moment of silence.

"Why would you think that? When do I ever behave like that?"

He shrugged. "I wasn't thinking straight."

"No shit."

"And then it didn't seem to matter. Because Bella was here. And who cares if I picked her up in L.A. or New York? She was here. She was ours. I didn't care about what happened in the past. I just wanted to think about the future. *Our* future. I'm sorry, Jess. I messed up."

"Yeah, you did."

He didn't say anything further. Just picked up his chopsticks and started pushing his noodles around.

Her phone pinged.

Jess glanced over to where it was plugged into the wall. Then got up and glanced at it. She stared down at the screen, furrowing her brow.

David set his chopsticks down. "What's wrong?"

"It says that I'm getting an AirDrop from your phone."

"It's not from mine," David said. "It was stolen."

They looked at one another.

"Amber," Jess said. "She's here."

"Shit." David lurched up from the table and ran toward the back door.

"Where are you going?" But he was already gone. Jesus. They should have just stayed inside and called the cops.

She looked at her phone. For some reason, she accepted the AirDrop, her curiosity burning too hot for her to reject it.

The photos were of David and a blonde woman. They were seated at a table in a cafe, Texpresso by the look of it. The two of them had their heads together in most of the shots. They sure looked cozy.

She lost any desire to call the cops.

She set the phone down and waited, folding her arms across her chest. David had left the back door open. Warm wind blew inside. The air conditioning kicked on. She still didn't move.

A car door slammed. Followed by a car screeching into the night. David was back seconds later.

"She's gone," David said, closing and locking the door behind him.

"Did you see her?" She sounded calm. Almost no tone in her voice. Surprising, considering the way she was boiling inside.

"No." He shook his head. "Who knows if it was her?"

"It was her."

He finally looked at her. As though realizing she might be upset. "Shit. Sorry. I should have just punched in the alarm code. Or called the cops."

"Yeah. But then you'd have to explain these to them." She held out her phone.

He looked at her curiously, then took her phone. He saw the photo of him and the woman. Then scrolled through the others.

"Fuck. She followed me."

"To think I actually believed Helen when she said you were at a business meeting today."

"Jess—"

"How long have you been seeing her?"

"It's not what you think."

"Uh huh." She got to her feet. "Like you going to New York instead of L.A. wasn't what I thought? Any other lies you want to come clean on?"

"Jesus, Jess. It's Erin Green."

Jess blinked. "Am I supposed to know who that is?"

"She's one of the new sales reps at Prairie. I told you

we were hiring last month. Bringing her on board will help to alleviate some of my duties. I thought you were happy about that."

Jess chewed on her lip. Okay, she remembered that. Mainly because it had come on the heels of an intense argument about how much he had been working for the past few years.

"She doesn't look like a sales rep."

"What is a sales rep supposed to look like?"

"Why are you acting like I'm crazy for asking?" Jess asked. "I'm pretty damn sure it's a reasonable question, given how comfortable the two of you look. If this is a business meeting, why is she dressed like that?"

"In yoga clothes?" His tone implied her paranoia.

"Yes, in yoga clothes, David. That's hardly business professional."

David gritted his teeth. "Because it wasn't a business meeting. At least not an official one."

"Then why were you meeting with her?"

"Because she starts work on Monday." He made it sound like she should understand.

"So?"

"So, did you forget that I would be in New York?"

She sat. She actually had. "And?"

"I won't be at the office on Monday. I needed to get her the keys to the building and the office."

"And it was too inconvenient for her to go down to Prairie Corp. You needed to meet her in sexy yoga clothes instead."

"They're just yoga clothes, Jess." David sighed, like he was tired of the conversation. He picked up a piece of shrimp and tossed it into his mouth. A moment later, he spit it out. "Jesus Christ. Now our food is cold. I'm sick of this conversation. Of you suspecting my behavior is questionable. You are very welcome to call Grant if you don't believe me. If I had my goddamn phone, I could show you Erin's resume. Or better yet, we can go into the office together and look at her resume there."

He sounded agitated, like she had really hurt his feelings. Was it possible that everything he was telling her was true? He had promised to never lie to her again. Not after his previous affair. And as far as she knew, he hadn't.

"No, that's fine."

He got to his feet. "Well, I'd prefer it. Because sometimes I think you act like this Amber Brown bullshit isn't affecting me as well."

Her cheeks grew hot. "I have never said that."

"You haven't needed to. You've been implying it left, right, and center. I would rather deal with Amber Brown than your recent paranoia. So grab your coat and let's go. You can explain to Erin and her husband how you think we're having an affair."

Jess felt the hairs go up on the back of her neck. *"Paranoia?* I have every right to feel the way I do, given what you've put me through the years. Celeste was also married. That didn't stop the two of you from fucking."

"See, there it is. You're never going to let me forget that one mistake."

"It wasn't one time, David. And it wasn't a mistake. Unless you somehow tripped and fell dick first into Celeste four times."

"I agreed to therapy. You told me you had worked through your feelings around the affair."

"I thought I had."

"Well, clearly that was a lie."

Jess shoved her dinner plate away from her. "It wasn't a lie, David. I did think I'd worked through my feelings."

"Well, I haven't cheated on you since then, Jess, so you're just gonna have to deal with it."

"Oh, goody. Give the man a prize. He's managed to stay faithful."

"You know what I mean."

"It's profound how fast the hurt drained away. I feel so much better now."

"Don't be sarcastic with me," he said.

"Then don't swear at me!"

"Jesus Christ. I'm not swearing at you."

"You have. Twice."

He walked through the doorway and retrieved the Volvo keys from the wall. "Come on. Let's go to Prairie Corp."

"No, I said, it's fine."

"But it's not fine. Not if you keep accusing me of shit I didn't do."

"I wasn't accusing you of anything." She felt like screaming. It took everything in her to remain calm. "I was simply asking a question."

"Bullshit, Jess. You didn't want to know about her yoga pants. You wanted to know if we were fucking. If I didn't know—" He broke off, leaning against the counter. "Holy shit."

"What?"

"You thought me and this Amber Brown were fucking as well."

"I did not." But her cheeks flushed.

He shook his head. "I don't believe it."

"I never thought that, David."

"It's written all over your face. Did you tell Clare that you thought that?"

Jess didn't reply.

"Great, so she thinks I'm sleeping around too."

"I never accused you of that in front of Clare."

"But I bet you never denied it. I don't know why you think Amber was here for me, when she's clearly trying to look like you. And I'll say it again: I think she's probably related to your adoptive mommy group."

"Based on what?"

"Based on the fact that she tried to say Gwen was her daughter."

Jess froze. "Bella."

"What?" David said.

"Our daughter's name is Bella. Only Amber called her Gwen."

David rubbed his jaw. "Jesus fuck. This goddamn situation is getting to me. I can't even keep my baby's name straight." He looked like he was going to cry. His eyes were red and watery. "We had an agreement, Jess. If you stayed in the marriage, then you would learn to trust me again. Especially if we went ahead with the adoption. This is both sounding and feeling like the opposite of that."

"I know," Jess said. "And I swear I'm doing my best. But this Amber Brown shit has stirred up a lot of old crap inside me. Crap I thought I'd dealt with at therapy. But apparently not. But just so you know, I'm also not the only one that's throwing accusations."

David looked confused. "What do you mean?"

"You accused me of relapsing earlier. Of staging the burglary. Did you really mean that?"

"That was a mistake."

"Right. Another mistake."

"Jess—"

"Our deal went both ways, David. You were supposed to learn to trust me again as well. In case you forgot, trust is a two-way street. Dr. Pearson told us that many a time."

"You're right." He nodded. "So how do we clear the slate and start trusting each other again?"

"I don't know. It's hard to think straight when I'm nervous about Amber."

"What exactly are you nervous about? We have the security system that you wanted installed. I arranged for my guy to have a chat with her. Isn't that enough?"

"Are you fucking kidding me?"

"*Swearing*," David said.

Jess picked up her phone. "She was just outside our house. Dropping photos. The security system and 'your guy' are obviously not working."

"She's trying to destroy us."

"Yeah. But why?"

David sighed. "I don't know. Stop looking to me for the answers. Besides, she didn't actually get close to us."

"I can't believe you're not more concerned about her."

"I'm plenty concerned," David said. "I'm just trying to be rational about it."

"Because one of us needs to be, right?"

"That's not what I'm saying."

"I think it is what you're saying. You think I'm being too emotional."

"Maybe you are. Or maybe you're just refusing to see the situation for what it really is."

"And what's that, David? Please enlighten me with your version of reality."

"There's only one reality, but one of us has a perspective that isn't clouded by fear."

"Clouded by fear?" Jess echoed, her voice a brittle shell. "You think I'm just a scared little girl?"

"I didn't say that. You're twisting my words."

"Then please enlighten me. Because I'm pretty fucking

clear that Amber Brown shouldn't be coming anywhere near my baby. While you seem to think I'm overreacting."

"That's not what I meant." His voice sounded swollen with anger.

"You practically called me emotional and irrational."

"I'm trying to keep us focused on the facts instead of imaginary threats."

"Imaginary threats?" Jess's chair screeched against the floor as she stood. "I can't believe you're trivializing this."

"I am not trivializing anything. I'm trying to save our marriage!"

"And I'm not?"

They stared at each other, David breathing hard through his nostrils. "I'm fed up with arguing. Let's get in the car."

"No." She shook her head. "I just put Bella down for bed."

He marched out of the room. She heard his feet on the stairs. Jesus Christ, he wasn't actually going to get Bella, was he?

She ran to the bottom of the stairs and called up: "You better not be waking her!"

But of course he was. A second later, she heard Bella cry. *Damn it.*

She started up the stairs, but he was already coming down.

He walked to the back door and flung it open. Heading outside to the Volvo. He opened the back door and got Bella strapped into her car seat.

Then he turned back and met her eyes. "You coming or not?"

Like she had any other choice.

She punched the security code into the pad, then

stepped out and closed the door. While she got into the passenger seat, he retraced his steps and locked the door.

Then he joined her in the car. For a few minutes, they drove in silence. Jess was trying to calm herself. Not wanting Bella to pick up on their hostility.

"I don't care about seeing her resume," said Jess at their second red light. "I already told you that."

He didn't answer her.

Nor did David get on the highway.

"This doesn't feel like we're going to Prairie."

"We're not."

But that's all he said.

"Where are we going?" she asked.

He still didn't answer.

"This isn't funny, David. You're scaring me. So tell me where we're going or I'm going to call the cops. It's not okay to—"

"You'll see in a minute."

It was actually more like five. But then David was swinging the Volvo into a parking space right at the front entrance of Southern Lead Supply. The slogan burned into the wood beneath the shop's name read: *Your Second Amendment Sanctuary*.

"Nope." Jess shook her head. "I'm not going in there."

"You are."

"I don't want a gun, David."

"I don't give a shit what you want. Not anymore. I'm sick of this crap. I'm sick of Amber Brown. I'm sick of my wife feeling goddamn scared in her own home. So if the security system wasn't enough, maybe a gun will make you feel better."

He got out and walked around to the passenger side, opened her door. "Now get out of the fucking car."

David didn't wait for her. Instead, he opened the rear

door and got Bella out of the backseat. She was cranky and fussing. He tucked her into his arm, cooing at her. Jess got out and followed him inside.

They passed rows of gleaming weapons and made their way up to a counter display filled with handguns and rifles of all shapes and sizes.

The place smelled of oil and gunpowder.

"Can I help you?" asked a lean man with small eyes.

David nodded at Jess. "I need a gun for my wife."

"Sure thing." The man nodded. "Do you know what kind you're interested in?"

"The kind that stops nightmares."

Chapter Twenty-Seven

STREETLIGHTS SPLASHED an orange glow on the asphalt, outlining the vehicles in front of Peter in dark shadows. Neon signs glimmered in the night, bars and restaurants broadcasting their temptations to the drivers passing by.

He glanced at the car clock. He was about ten minutes away from Trammel Crow Park. He'd be there fifteen minutes before Amber. He wanted to arrive first.

He braked as a cab stopped suddenly in front of him, vomiting a gaggle of college girls. He blasted his horn. One of them turned and gave him the finger. He responded in kind. Then they all ran inside to the club. How anyone could run in those heels, Peter had no idea.

It seemed odd to him that the world spun on despite his bad mood. Shouldn't it all stop? At least for a fucking minute or two?

The cab drove off. No doubt to pick up another fare. Peter blasted his horn again. Just because he felt pissy.

Why did even the good things in life always turn into bullshit?

Like Joe's team winning the game. Even though his kid

let six goals get right by him. Not that Peter gave a shit. It was Linda who wouldn't shut the fuck up about it. She cared ten times more than Joe did, and it was his goddam team. If the kid didn't care, why did she?

In fact, Joe barely seemed to give a dripping dick about the game, or even that his old man was there. He barely acknowledged Peter's presence. Not that Linda fared any better. He didn't see Joe look for her once in the stands. She might as well have been a pile of shit to the kid.

The only time that Joe was remotely civil to either one of them was when he asked if he could stay at Mattie's for the night.

The boys wanted to stop at Dallas Deep Dish first. Joe was going to order a meat lover's and try some of that volcano cake for dessert.

Peter was a little irritated, as they had made plans to go to BB-CUE, a restaurant where you could get pulled pork and then shoot pool. But he allowed himself to get excited about the idea of going to Dallas Deep Dish instead. They hadn't been there since the kid was, well, a kid. He allowed himself a moment to remember the taste of their gourmet pizza. Then a mental picture of Joe thanking him, a wide smile of appreciation on his face, formed in his head. Only to have it all come crashing down.

"Yeah, sure," he'd said. "Let's go."

But Joe declined. "I'd rather hang with the guys."

And not to act like a little bitch or anything, but Peter had a much bigger problem with how the kid had said it than his actual words. On paper it sounded fine, but Peter had learned to read subtext like a preschool primer while in prison.

"We had plans," Peter said. "As a family."

After a long and uncomfortable pause during which Joe

was supposed to fold to his father's will, Linda did the cuntiest possible thing. She undermined him.

"Just let him go." As if those four words didn't piss him off enough, her next eight got Peter picturing his hands fastening around her throat. "Jesus Christ, you can be such an asshole."

The kid was gone before Peter could respond. Not even waiting for his approval. As soon as Linda gave her assent, he tore out of there like a fart in the wind.

And then he let her have it.

He supposed it wasn't all her fault he was pissed. He was in a shit mood because he'd put his work on hold to make time for his son, and then the kid flipped him the bird and did whatever his fucking bitch whore of a mother let him do anyway.

"You know it's bullshit that you always let him do whatever the fuck he wants," Peter had said.

His ex had glared at him. "I don't let him do whatever the fuck he wants, asshole. But hanging out with his team after the game is a regular, normal thing. Joe doesn't like to miss out. But I'm guessing you don't really understand that because you're so used to missing out on everything. Like his childhood."

"You better watch yourself."

"Or what, Peter? You going to hit me? I'm pretty sure you probation officer wouldn't be happy with that."

"You know I wouldn't do that." Again.

"You weren't there the first six years of his life, Peter. So it shouldn't be any surprise that he doesn't want to spend time with you. I don't give a shit at all if that bothers you. You caused that. And you have to sit in it. And if you can't, then fuck the hell off."

Linda must have been listening to Tony Robbins or some shit. She had never mouthed off to him like that before. Peter didn't like it, and she'd just made a really big fucking mistake by talking to him like that.

He had been planning to give her the five grand for child support. Seeing is how he was in arrears. But now he would be keeping the entire haul for himself.

Fuck her, and fuck their offspring. They could both suck dicks like lollipops for all he cared.

Soon as David got him the rest of his cash, he'd be booking a ticket to Hawaii. And David was gonna pay. Tonight. If not, then Peter would be stopping by that swanky ass house of his and he'd be having a conversation with Mrs. Jessica Clarke.

Peter had always wanted to see the islands in person. Maybe it was also the kind of place where he could make a brand-new start. It had sunshine like Texas. But he also heard there were cool ocean breezes.

He bet the heat didn't make island women as cranky as those in Texas.

He glanced at his GPS. Five more minutes to Trammel Crow. Soon as he finished up there, he could close the lid on this particular box of bullshit.

Then he'd pick up his payment and get the hell on with his life in Hawaii or otherwise. Maybe he should stop by Linda's first. Have a little chat with her. Remind her she had no right talking to him like that.

To hell with Hawaii. Maybe he should go to Brazil. Or Costa Rica. Then he could really go to town on Linda. Only, he'd have to be careful. The kid would be the one to find her.

Three minutes later, a full minute ahead of schedule, Peter spied the entrance to Trammel Crow Park.

There were a couple of cars still parked, but they were both pulled into spots under street lamps.

The only car that Peter cared about was a silver BMW.

He was startled to see it parked near the entrance, in a similarly lit area. Fuck.

That did nothing for his mood. He'd wanted to be first to the park. But she'd come even earlier than him. Well, unless he rebooked (and he wasn't about to do that with his money on the line), he might as well make contact.

Peter pulled out his phone and sent a text: *parking*.

He waited, watching the shadows and leaves rustling in the wind. Several cars drove by in the distance.

He glanced at his phone. Still no response.

Where the fuck was she?

He texted again: *u here?*

This time he got a reply: *I'm at the bench.*

Peter nodded in satisfaction, glad that this would be over soon. He texted: *be there soon.* He pulled out his gun and checked it again, not that there was anything to check. It was just the comfort of routine.

He shoved the weapon into his waistband and pulled his shirt down over it.

Then he took out the knife from his pocket and flicked the blade open. He'd prefer to use the knife. He liked being up close and personal to his prey. It made him feel energized. Like his blood was charged with electrons.

He got out of the car and closed the door as silently as possible. Then he walked over to the BMW.

He looked inside but didn't see anything of note. Amber wasn't hiding inside. Maybe she really was at the bench.

But he didn't take the path he used before to shoot out the park lights. He walked up and over the rise so that he would now be approaching her from behind.

And sure enough, she was there.

A dark shadow sitting on the bench, engulfed by other dark shadows.

He checked to make sure no one was around. But all the pedestrians had turned in for the night. The only witnesses to his presence (or hers) were a symphony of crickets playing a melodic rhythm. Dumb insects didn't even realize they were helping him. For a big man, he could move awfully quietly when he wanted to. But the insects covered whatever remaining sound his footsteps made.

He approached the bench in silence.

She sat still, facing the parking lot.

Stupid bitch.

For a moment, the back of her reminded him of Linda.

He bolted toward her. Knife in hand, he grabbed her from behind, then dragged the blade across her throat.

Chapter Twenty-Eight

JESSICA CLAPPED her hand over her mouth, but cold chills rippled through her as she watched Peter draw his knife and cut her throat.

Or what that motherfucker thought was her throat.

Thank God she had trusted her instincts.

She'd been smart enough to grab the CPR dummy from the community center and stay one step ahead of this murdering man. Who David had sent after her. David. Her goddamn husband.

She watched Peter look down at his knife. Then he stepped around, yanking the dummy up.

He stared at it.

Then his phone lit up. He used the flashlight app to inspect the dummy. She saw him rip a piece of paper from the dummy's head.

After the community center, she'd gone to the Walmart Photo Center and printed a photo of him talking to David under the highway. And for some reason she had written, *He's setting you up*.

Peter jammed the paper in his pocket and scanned the park.

"Come on out, Amber."

She didn't move.

"Let's talk."

She resisted the urge to snort. Just in case he heard her above the crickets. She was sitting so still they had forgotten she was there and started up their song again.

"Jessica?"

She still didn't answer. Though how the crickets couldn't hear her heart pounding like a racquetball in her ribcage was astounding. God. What if she had actually trusted Peter? Or David? What if she'd still been blinded enough by her love for him to make the meet?

Then she would be lying in a pool of her own blood right now.

She got a text. Careful to keep her screen hidden, she glanced down at the message: *where r u?*

But of course she didn't respond. The screen went black.

And then he strode toward her. She almost ran. But then she realized he hadn't seen her at all. He was just slinking deeper into the shadows. He still had his phone out. Hit the screen. Then raised it to his ear.

She was going to be close enough to hear every word of the call he was about to make.

But a part of her wished that he would take at least a couple of steps away. He was far too close.

If he caught wind of her, she'd be dead.

She heard the murmur of another voice.

"No, it's not fucking done." He paced in the shadows. "She's not here. You wanna know what was?" He didn't leave time for an answer, just barreled on. "Some crash test dummy shit … fine then, CPR. What the fuck difference does it make? She also has photos, man ... of us ... you and me asshole, what the fuck do you think?"

Peter spun around and walked toward Jessica again. If his voice hadn't been raised, he surely would have heard her breathing or sensed a trembling human only hairs away from him.

"She's not my problem. She's yours. And if you don't get me my fucking money, I'm gonna carve up your entire fucking family, starting with your goddamn baby."

Jess froze, slipping her hand into her pocket, feeling for the knife. If this man thought he was gonna hurt Gwen...

"In fact, I'm gonna make my way over there right now." He disconnected and shoved the phone back in his pocket.

Crap. He was gonna hurt Gwen.

But how was she supposed to stop him? He was twice her size.

Fuck! This wasn't what she had wanted at all.

She opened David's phone and pulled up his contacts. Scrolling through until she found *Jessica*. She dialed. The call was rejected, so she texted: *You're in danger*.

The reply message came immediately: *Leave us the fuck alone.*

But fear had clawed into her conscience; there wasn't a chance in the world that she could leave this alone.

She texted again: *I'm trying to help you. You and Gwen are in danger.*

Message not delivered.

Double fuck. Real Jessica had been blocked by Replacement Jessica.

Peter was halfway to the Charger now. The Dodge would be faster than the BMW if for no other reason than Peter surely knew Dallas better than her. Not only that, Peter could drive. Like really drive. Jessica was a New York girl — yeah, she had a driver's license, but she wasn't exactly fast or confident on the road. The drive west had proved that. She had probably taken twice as long as anyone else who made that trek.

She needed a head start.

But the odds of her making it past Peter to the BMW without him seeing her were 50/50 at best, and probably a lot closer to a snowball's chance in hell if Jessica was being straight with herself.

She crept from her hiding spot. Still keeping to the shadows. But her hesitancy was slowing her down. Gwen. Her daughter was in danger.

That was all she needed to light a fire under her ass.

She bolted for her car.

Peter spotted her. And for a moment, he seemed perplexed.

But then he tore right, heading straight for her. A tree trunk exploded next to her.

What? And then again. And she realized he was shooting at her.

She ran.

And he chased.

She zigzagged through the park, Peter gaining behind her. Closing the space between them with what seemed relative ease. Not fair. Her lungs were already burning. She wanted to stop and walk.

She yanked out the car keys.

Don't drop them, don't drop them, don't drop them.

She hit the unlock button, arriving at the BMW. She flung the car door open, dove inside, and slammed the door shut.

She jammed the key in the ignition and turned the key. Nothing happened. Fuck. She'd forgotten to put it in park.

She slammed the gear shift. Twisted the key and tried again.

This time, the car started.

She threw it into reverse, racing across the gravel. Then shifted into drive. The headlights caught him. He aimed the gun.

OH SHIT!

She turned the car. The driver's window shattered. Safety glass sprayed.

Stunned, she instinctively slammed on the brakes, throwing up her hands to protect her face.

And then Peter was reaching in through the window. She saw the gun barrel. She screamed, pushing his arm away.

He pulled the trigger a second time, and that bullet THUNKED into the backseat. He bunched his left hand into a fist and punched her in the face. Her head hit the seat rest. She saw him swing the gun around again.

Jessica yanked out the cold, comforting steel of the CRKT Minimalist Bowie Neck. With a fluid thrust, she lunged forward, burying the blade in Peter's arm. Fuck. She had been aiming for his chest.

But it didn't matter.

Like a punctured balloon, Peter recoiled, dropping the gun. It clattered onto the asphalt. He stumbled backward, away from the BMW.

For some bizarre reason, she nearly asked him if he was okay.

But she came to her senses and threw the car into gear, her foot mashing the gas pedal all the way to the floor.

The BMW roared to life like a hunting lion that finally made the decision to go after its prey. The tires spun on the gravel, then caught, and the car catapulted forward.

Jessica aimed for the entrance, only glancing back in

the rearview mirror when she hit the road. She half expected to see his headlights fill the car. But they didn't.

She kept driving. Fast. She didn't care about speeding. Not even a gun to her head would convince her to slow down at this point. Her hands were clenched around the wheel as if superglued.

Streets, landmarks, and signs whizzed by in a dizzying blur.

She careened down the road, narrowly missing another vehicle, driving through a red light (thank God for minimal traffic). She swerved down a dark alley, hit a garbage can, and sent it rolling. The sound startled her, making her think Peter had caught up and started shooting again.

But there was no sign of the Charger. She drove down a few more alleys, just to make sure. Just in case he was in pursuit. But if he was, he never caught up to her.

So she pulled over, threw the driver's side door open, then leaned out and vomited. Bits of glass fell onto the road. And she realized she was covered in the stuff. Where the fuck had that come from?

The window.

Right.

He had shot it.

Jessica remembered now. He had aimed a gun at her and pulled the trigger. But it wasn't Peter's hand. It was David's. Peter was just the one holding the weapon.

David had pulled the trigger. David. Her husband. The man who swore to love, honor, and cherish her. The man she had adopted a baby with.

And then a thought dropped into her head like a coal through plastic. What if Mrs. Jessica Clarke living at 2097 Longhorn Drive wasn't the Replacement Jessica? What if Jessica Amber of New York City was the Replacement?

She blinked back tears. She would not shed one more

goddamn tear for David. Not after he tried to kill her. Instead, she got out of the vehicle, shaking the glass from her hair and shoulders. She removed the hoodie, giving it a shake, then used it to wipe the glass from the driver's seat.

She shivered in the hot air. Pulled the hoodie back on. Then got back in the car and opened up her phone. GPS.

She had no fucking idea where she was.

And had only one destination in mind. She typed in: *2097 Longhorn Drive.*

Ten minutes away. She felt invincible now. She bet she could even beat Peter there.

She put the car back in drive and sped away.

Chapter Twenty-Nine

Jess woke to screaming.

What the—

She sat upright. The room was dark. She listened. But didn't hear anything.

Was she having another nightmare?

She glanced over at David, to see if he'd heard anything. Even in the dark, she could tell his side of the bed was empty. But then she confirmed it with her hand.

Maybe he had gone in to see Bella. Or had chosen to sleep on the couch. They weren't exactly talking to one another when they got home.

"Jessica!"

She bolted out of bed, standing beside it, hand on the mattress as though for support.

Was that her name being called?

Or was it her imagination?

Maybe she only thought she heard her name.

What did people call that thing? Pareidolia? When you make familiar patterns out of something abstract. But that didn't apply to sound, did it?

"Jessica!"

Okay, that time she heard it. That was her name the woman was screaming.

Jesus Christ. Was that Amber Brown?

She grabbed her housecoat. She yanked it on and headed for the hall. She threw open the linen closet and grabbed the bath towels off of the second shelf so she could access the safe.

Then she punched in the electronic code.

It whirred, then the door popped open.

She pulled it out, then got a bullet from the box of ammunition. Maybe David had been right after all about getting a gun. She loaded a bullet into the chamber. Then reached for another.

And hesitated.

In truth, she didn't trust herself with more than the one. Multiple shots in the intruder would probably make it harder to claim self-defense.

You're in danger.

You and Gwen are in danger.

Fucking Amber. That would be the last time she threatened either one of them.

"JESSICA!"

At this point, Amber was going to wake the whole goddamn neighborhood up.

She whirled around and headed for the stairs.

But then she spied a shadow moving in Bella's room and paused before kicking the door open, while gripping the gun tight in her hand.

Even though Amber sounded like she was outside, she half expected to see her standing at the crib.

But it was David.

He had Bella curled in his arm. "Sorry, didn't mean to wake you. She was crying, so I came in to rock her."

"You didn't wake me."

"Then why are you up?" He caught sight of the gun. "What's that for?"

"Did you hear Amber?"

"Amber?"

"Yelling?"

He shook his head. "What are you talking about?"

"She's outside screaming my name."

David looked confused. "I didn't hear anything."

"JESSICA!"

"There."

He continued to stare at her. "What?"

"You didn't hear that?"

He shook his head.

Jess stepped back into the hallway. "This is bullshit."

She whirled around and hit the stairs.

David trotted after her. "Where are you going?" Bella started crying.

Jess stopped on the stairs, turning around to look at him. "I'm putting an end to this once and for all."

"Jesus, Jess—"

"One of us needs to deal with the problem."

"There's nothing out there!"

Bella cried louder.

"I thought your personal security guy was going to make Amber Brown back all the fucking way off?"

"I don't think she listened to him."

"No shit?"

Bella started screeching.

Jess wanted to take her from him. But more than that, she wanted to deal with Amber. Then maybe she'd leave them the hell alone.

She stalked down the rest of the stairs.

"Jesus Christ." But he must have gone and put Bella back in her crib, because her sobs faded away.

Jess had almost reached the front door when she heard his footsteps on the stairs. Seconds later, he'd caught up to her. He grabbed her arm.

She recoiled, pulling away from his grip. "Fuck off."

"I don't think this is a good idea, Jess."

"Apparently."

"You're escalated. Let's just call the cops."

"We tried that. And you know what happened? She came the fuck back."

She reached for the door.

"JESSICA!"

She whirled to face David. "Well?"

"Well what?"

"Are you telling me that you don't hear that?"

"Hear what?" He looked frustrated.

She sucked in a lungful of air and yelled: "JESSICA!"

He took a step back. "I heard that."

"But not what came before?"

He shook his head.

She curled her lip, then flung the front door open, not bothering to turn the SecureX system off. The little pad began beeping.

David leapt over to it and punched in the code.

A second later, it silenced.

But Jess only had eyes for Amber Brown. She stood on the front lawn. Staring. Then she took a step forward. Jess pointed the gun at her.

Amber's eyes widened, and she froze.

"I told you I heard her," Jess said.

She raised her hands. But now Amber looked less like a predator and more like prey.

A lot less.

Enough to make Jess wonder why she was holding a gun on the woman.

"He's gonna kill you," Amber said.

Hearing her voice was enough to set her on edge once again. Her hand shook on the gun. "Shut the fuck up!"

"Who are you talking to?" David asked.

Jess ignored him.

"You have to listen to me," Amber said, keeping her hands in the air. "He's going to kill you."

Who? Jess wanted to ask.

But it was just a trick to distract her.

Who knew what Amber had up her sleeve?

David grabbed her arm again. "Who the fuck are you talking to?"

Jessica stared at him. "What?"

He placed a hand on each shoulder. *"Who are you talking to?"*

"Amber."

"My name is Jessica."

"Babe. There's no one there."

Jess yanked away from David and pointed the gun at Amber. "SHE'S RIGHT THERE!"

Amber ducked, cowering.

David shook his head. There were tears in his eyes. "There's no one there, Jess."

Her breath hitched in her throat. What?

"You can see me, asshole!" Amber yelled. Then she lowered her arms. "He can see me just fine."

"Give me the gun and come inside." David had Jess by her arm again, but his grip was gentle.

"Don't give him the gun," Amber said. "He'll kill me."

"Please, babe, there's no one here."

"Stop calling me babe!" Jess kept her arm steady.

David dropped his arms and stepped back.

"You're really telling me you can't see her?" Jess asked.

David scanned the yard, his eyes passing over Amber with the same detachment as he looked at the fence, the trees, the road.

Then he turned back to her. Shook his head.

Jess pulled the trigger.

Her arm jerked back, the shot went wide. Amber bolted.

Jess tore after her.

But David grabbed her arm.

"Let me go!"

But he wouldn't. They grappled for a moment, then he yanked the gun from her hand. By the time he released her and Jess had run into the street, Amber had disappeared into the shadows.

Jess kicked the fence and returned to the yard.

"Are you goddamn done? You want Patsy to call the police?"

"There's only one bullet."

He glanced at her and checked the chamber. Then he grabbed her arm. "Get back in the goddamned house. *Now*."

She shoved him with all of her might. He tried to grab her again. She stumbled away from him. "GET THE FUCK AWAY FROM ME!"

Patsy's bedroom light flicked on.

It had the same effect of someone throwing a bucket of cold water over the both of them. They froze, trading a look.

And for the moment they shifted to the same side.

David reached out and took her hand and she let him hold it.

A second later Patsy's door opened, and she stepped out onto the front porch. "Did I just hear a gunshot?"

"We did too," Jess said.

"Sounded like a car backfiring," David said.

"I lived in Detroit for seventeen years," Pasty said. "I know what a gunshot sounds like."

David stuck to his story. "I'm pretty sure it was a car."

Patsy glanced at the road. "Then where's the car?"

"Gone," Jess said.

"It wasn't only a gunshot I heard," Patsy pressed.

"No?" Jess said.

"Seemed like there was a lot of screaming as well."

Jess imagined Patsy sitting up in bed, gleefully listening to their argument in eager anticipation of sharing it with the neighbors.

"Television," David kept lying. "We were watching a movie."

"Seems to me I heard someone calling out for your wife."

"Fine. We were having sex. Got a little loud."

Patsy recoiled.

"Jesus," said Jess.

"Come on." David held out his hand. "Let's go back inside."

Jess hesitated, then turned and followed him to the porch without taking his hand. Patsy stayed put, watching them.

David entered, making sure to keep the gun hidden from Patsy's view.

"Jessica," Patsy said.

Jess paused. And glanced over at her.

"You sure you're okay?" This time there was no sense of snoopiness in Patsy's tone. In fact, she sounded worried. "If you and Bella need somewhere to go, you're welcome to come here."

Jess felt like a shit. If it had been anyone other than

Patsy, she would have probably taken them up on the offer. Clare, for sure. But not Patsy.

"No, I'm good."

Then Jess entered the house, closing the door and locking it behind her.

She punched in the SecureX code. The light was on in the kitchen.

She walked down the hallway. It was quiet upstairs. Mercifully, Bella must have cried herself back to sleep.

David had the whisky out. "I'm going to make you some hot honey and whisky, okay?"

She nodded. "Okay."

"I'll bring it upstairs."

She glanced at the gun sitting on the kitchen table. A blight in her colorful kitchen. Suddenly, she hated it. "You'll put that away?"

He nodded.

She turned and made her way upstairs. Listening at Bella's door. All she heard was soft breathing.

Then she went into the bedroom and climbed into bed. She kept her robe on. She needed an extra layer between her and David.

How had he not seen Amber? She was standing there right in front of them.

Unless she hadn't been there.

Oh, Jesus. Had she had another nightmare? What did people call them? Night terrors?

What if she shot at someone innocent? By the time David came upstairs, her whole body was shaking, and she felt cold.

He walked over to the bed and crouched beside it.

"Here you go." He handed her the hot honey and whisky.

She looked at him. "She really wasn't there, was she?"

He hesitated. Then shook his head.

Tears pricked her eyes. "What did I do, David?"

"Hey, it's all right."

"No, I could have hurt someone."

He kissed her brow. "You've been under a lot of stress. We both have. Drink up."

She raised the glass and swallowed. It burned hot all the way down. But she didn't feel any warmer.

And the whisky tasted bitter.

She tried to hand it back to him.

"All of it," he said.

She sighed. But the last thing she wanted was another argument. Bella was sleeping. She wasn't about to risk waking her. God, if Forever Home ever found out about this shit, they would regret ever placing Bella with them.

She swallowed the last of the whisky, handing him the cup. Then she squinted. The room got blurry. That was odd.

She tried to stand, but he gave her a gentle push back on to the bed.

And she realized. He wasn't surprised she was dizzy.

"You drugged me?" She wasn't even sure if she said the words out loud, because her tongue didn't seem to be working.

Neither was her head. It felt back onto the pillows.

And there was only darkness after that.

Chapter Thirty

Jessica ran to David's BMW and scrambled inside.

She started the engine and tore away from Longhorn, leaving only a fading roar from her engine and the smell of burning rubber in her wake.

This was the second time she had been shot at tonight. Peter, she understood. But *Jessica*?

For some reason, she hadn't imagined that Jessica had been as disturbed by this situation as she had. That was a mistake.

One that she wouldn't make again.

Jessica realized she was speeding and managed to slow. The warm Texas air blew in, warming her. Despite the fact that the window was gone, she turned on the air conditioning.

She didn't know where she was going.

She just drove.

And kept driving.

All the way to the outskirts of Dallas. The landscape was desolate, stretching out in every direction, disappearing into the dark.

Jessica was still shaking even after twenty minutes of driving. She still didn't know how Jess had missed. Maybe she wanted to?

She kept driving. Maybe she should keep going. All the way east. All the way back to New York City.

No, she wasn't leaving.

David had destroyed her life there.

And incinerated the one here.

She wasn't going anywhere.

And not just for herself.

But for Jessica and Gwen as well.

Didn't matter that she shot at Jessica.

David had stood on their porch insisting that his wife couldn't see her. His gaslighting had gone to a whole new level.

She pulled over and killed the engine.

Staring out at the darkness.

If David was capable of doing that to his wife, then he was certainly capable of doing everything that had happened recently to Jessica. There was no doubt about it. That was her David. He hadn't been replaced at all.

He had wooed her deliberately. Married her. And stolen their child.

What kind of sick game was he playing?

She didn't know. But she was sure as shit going to find out. Not only for herself. But for Gwen. She wasn't going to allow her daughter to grow up with a monster for a father.

For some reason, she felt better knowing that he was a lying asshole. And had been all along. It meant she wasn't crazy. Exhausted, but not insane.

She yawned. Hit the car lock. Probably for the tenth time.

Which was dumb because the driver's window was blown out. But still, it made her feel better.

She hit the seat button, pressing it until it was almost horizontal. Then she curled into the fetal position.

But she was still tense.

She told herself all the truths that mattered. Like that no one knew where she was. That she was going to be okay. That she had already survived more danger and misadventure than most people would ever see in a lifetime.

And that whatever David was doing, she didn't deserve it. Her eyes welled up.

"You don't deserve this." She said it out loud because she was having trouble believing it. Because maybe there was a part of her that always felt that David was too good for her. Or that she was beneath him.

"Fuck that noise," she said.

She was gonna fight for what was hers.

David could fuck himself with a two-by-four. Gwen was *her baby*, and Jessica would not rest until she was back in her arms.

She bunched her coat into a small bundle and cradled it in her arms, imagining it to be Gwen. She closed her eyes, humming slightly, and fell into a restless slumber.

Later, she woke, disoriented. She felt like she had slept. But she really had no idea. Although she must have, because it was lighter now. Approaching dawn. And she wasn't as far out of the city as she thought.

It looked like she was in some kind of industrial area.

She glanced out her window.

A man stood watching her from across the street.

She started.

But it wasn't David or Peter. He was a stranger. And he

kept on staring. She glared at him, raising the back of her seat. Then she wiped the drool from her chin. When she looked back at him, he was still staring.

Her muscles groaned. She needed to stretch.

She flung the car door open and got out. He still didn't move. She did her best to ignore him.

He kept on watching.

"What's your problem?"

He gave her the finger.

She glared at him and got back in the car. The seat still wasn't where it needed to be. She adjusted it. And her fingers brushed something loose and metal.

She grabbed it.

What—

She drew it out from beneath the seat. Peter's gun. It hadn't fallen onto the gravel at all. It had fallen into the car.

Jessica didn't know her firearms, but this one seemed like a classic. It had a polished black handle and a silver-gray barrel. It was heavy in her hand, but the balance felt nice.

Holding it, Jessica felt a goddamn goddess.

The man who had been watching her backed away.

"That's right, fucker," she said.

He dipped into an alley and disappeared.

Jessica set the gun on her passenger seat, then pulled the coat over it to hide it.

She turned the car on and looked at the time. It was already four in the morning, so she had been way off about how long she had been asleep.

She pulled into the road.

The man in the alley watched her go.

Jessica gave him the finger.

She drove in silence. The night was dark, and the

streets were quiet. She only passed a few cars. But now that she knew where she was, she was able to navigate back to her shit heap motel without using the GPS.

She parked in the spot right outside of her room. She barely had the energy to get out of the car.

She leaned her forehead on the steering wheel. Maybe she could just sleep there.

But no, she needed a shower. That nap in the car almost felt like a subtraction of rest.

She bundled the gun into her coat, then cradled it against her chest like a baby. She rolled out of the car, locking it, then went to her room. She was inside within seconds. Closing and locking the door. Sliding across the little chain.

Then she pressed her back against the cheap wood.

She didn't move for half a minute.

But she was starting to feel that jetlagged feeling again. She was exhausted.

She flicked on the light. The grimy lightbulb flickered once, twice, but stayed burning, casting long shadows around the room. She yanked the stale motel curtains closed, then kicked off her shoes, toeing them under the end of the nondescript motel bed.

She kept a tight grip on the gun and coat, trudging into the bathroom. Only then could she finally release the weapon. Setting it on the floor. She peed and washed her hands. Then yanked back the shower curtain from around the tub.

And stared.

Peter lay in the grungy tub. The hilt of the CRKT Minimalist Bowie Neck jutted from his chest. Now that she could see him, the metallic stench of his blood mingled with the bathroom's musty scent.

Jessica stood, rooted to the floor, her gaze anchored on

Peter's pallid face. Then she closed the curtain. She waited a moment, then opened it again.

He was still there.

She whirled around to the toilet. And vomited. Not that she had anything in her stomach. She couldn't remember the last time she ate.

When she finished retching, she rinsed out her mouth. Then she stepped back to the tub. With a slow and trembling hand, she searched for a pulse in his neck. She couldn't find one. His skin was cold. His eyes were open, unblinking.

His mouth was slack. He didn't even look surprised that he was dead. For some reason, she thought that odd.

"Dead." She said it out loud once again, to make it real. But he was dead alright. Undeniably, irrevocably dead.

A distant wail broke the heavy silence.

She froze.

Police siren.

And it grew louder with each passing second.

"Fuck," she muttered.

She felt like her heartbeat was as loud as thunder. Her fingers closed around the hilt of the knife, and she yanked, ripping it out of Peter's chest, ignoring the sickening sound that accompanied it, like a wet rope being torn in two.

Then she scooped up the coat and gun and ran into the bedroom, shoving both weapons and the coat into Jessica's knapsack. Then, in a frantic panic, she gathered the rest of her scattered possessions, her movements fast yet mechanical.

The room felt too small, the walls closing in on her with every echoing wail.

And the sirens drew closer.

Then she fled from the room, slamming the door behind her.

She tossed everything into the BMW, her fingers shaking as she found the keys and turned the ignition. Once again, she was launching David's stolen car into the night.

But she was too late.

A pair of police cruisers filled her rearview mirror, their headlights blinding her.

Outrunning them would be impossible.

She was cornered. This was it.

One of them flashed their headlights. She waved. Then eased over to the side of the road.

What an idiot she was. She should have left the knife. Thrown the gun as soon as she'd found it.

She'd never been smart. Her mother had told her that constantly. She'd even confessed it to David when they were dating. *I've never felt smart.*

And she'd just proven it. To herself. And to them.

But the cop cars didn't slow down. They raced right past her, disappearing into the night.

They weren't after her.

THEY WEREN'T AFTER HER.

The sirens receded into the distance.

Jessica sat in silence as the adrenaline drained from her system.

Then, without warning, she dropped her head to the steering wheel and cried. It was a torrent of relief, fear, grief, despair, and loss.

She cried until snot ran from her nose.

Until her throat was raw.

Until she had a pounding headache.

And then she fell asleep.

But it wasn't for long. Fifteen minutes by the clock in the car. But it was enough. Because Jessica woke knowing exactly where she needed to go next.

And what she needed to do.

Chapter Thirty-One

JESS WOKE to muted light bouncing off the walls in a garishly ruthless ballet.

She groaned, raising a hand to massage her temple. She had a nasty migraine.

Foggy remnants of whisky clung to her tongue.

The whisky. The memory jolted her wide awake, the venomous taste of betrayal cutting through the alcohol. She curled her mouth into a snarl and sat.

Pain shot through her skull. She winced.

David had drugged her.

A tidal wave of anger washed over her. Her joints and muscles creaked in protest when she swung her legs over the side of the bed.

She curled her toes into the plush carpet, trying to regain a sense of balance. But still the world swirled around her like a cruel carousel spinning out of control.

She pressed her palms into the mattress, riding the wave of nausea until it retreated.

David.

He'd crossed a line that he should never ever have been crossed, no matter the circumstances.

Even if she had imagined Amber Brown on their doorstep last night (and fuck her four ways from Sunday if she was wrong about that), it still didn't forgive her husband for MOTHERFUCKING DRUGGING HER.

She felt like she'd forgot how to breathe. So she calmed herself, then got up. She still had her robe on, so went out into the hall.

She peeked in on Bella. But the baby wasn't in her crib.

She went down the stairs, telling herself to be cool.

But as soon as she reached the kitchen, she spotted David feeding Bella. A few days ago, that sight would have filled with joy. Now it filled her with venom. And she needed to spit.

David glanced up at her. "Good morning."

"What the hell were you thinking?"

"I was thinking about a lot of things…" He sounded oddly calm. "Can you be more specific?"

"Why would you give me a sleeping pill? You know how dangerous that is for me."

"Jess." The look on his face, like he was about to explain softly how mistaken she was, made her want to grab one of the frying pans hanging over the stove and wallop him over the head with it.

So she turned around and walked out.

Bella cooed.

And she felt like shit. She hadn't even said good morning to her daughter.

She walked back upstairs and into the bathroom. She locked the door, then turned the shower on hot.

When the room was thick with enough steam to rival a spa, she shed her nightgown and stepped under the water.

She stood in the mist, staring at the condensation licking the tiles, her skin tingling under the heat.

She closed her eyes, drawing in deep breaths, releasing any tension. She didn't know how long she stayed like that. Could have been minutes. Could have been twelve hours.

The water started to cool. She had drained the hot water tank.

She stepped out, grabbing her bath towel and wrapping it around her. Then she wiped the steam from the mirror.

She stared at her reflection. Amber looked back at her. She flinched, screaming. Jesus. She was losing it.

Of course her eyes were lying.

She gripped the edge of the sink and stared deep into the mirror.

She didn't want to believe that David was right, and that she was just seeing things. But Jesus Christ, she could have sworn she had just seen Amber in the mirror.

She was rattled. That's all this was.

Lack of sleep.

Fear.

It did things to you.

David knocked on the bathroom door.

Jess ignored him.

He knocked again.

"I'll be out in a minute."

"Are you okay?"

"I'm fine."

"Are you sure?"

She opened the bathroom and pushed past him into the bedroom.

"Jess. Hey. I'm right here."

"Yay, you can see me."

"What the fuck is that supposed to mean?"

"You know exactly what it means." Jess walked to the closet and pulled out a pair of jeans. Grabbed her bra and a T-shirt. Went to the dresser and grabbed underwear. Then she discarded her towel.

"Can you please get out of here and go watch Bella? And forget I said please."

"You're mad."

"Of course I'm fucking mad!" He didn't move. So she ignored him and continued dressing. Bra, panties, jeans and tee.

She walked to the door.

He stepped in front of her. "Jess—"

"Get out of my way."

She nearly put her hands on him, but he stepped back. "Where are you going?"

"Out."

"That's not an answer."

"How about *none of your fucking business*. That's where I'm going."

She stalked down the hallway and hit the stairs.

He caught up to her in the living room. "We need to talk."

She ignored him, sliding her feet into her shoes. Reaching for the diaper bag. Goddamn it. She held out a hand. "Credit card."

"What?"

"Give me your credit card."

He crossed his arms. "Not until you tell me where you're going."

"Groceries."

"We have plenty of food."

"And I want more. Give me your card."

He hesitated. Then pulled his wallet out and slid out his card. She snatched it from him before he could change his mind.

She turned, reaching for the doorknob. She opened it. But he planted his palm on it, closing it.

"We need to talk."

"About what?" She turned to face him.

He gestured to each of them. "This."

She shrugged. "So talk."

He sighed. "I want to help you."

"Of course you do."

"I'm serious, Jess. You need help. And this time I don't want to leave it until too late."

She stared at him. "What in the actual fuck is that supposed to mean, David?"

He almost looked embarrassed. "I think that maybe you should consider—"

"Consider what?"

"Consider going away for a bit and resting."

"Resting? Maybe you could just keep giving me sleeping pills without my consent. Then I could get all the rest you want me to have. How does that sound, David?"

"I understand that you're mad. And maybe it was a mistake to give you one. But I was worried."

"A mistake? Is that your go-to word now? For every time you fuck up?"

"You're being unreasonable."

"I'm being unreasonable?"

"Spiraling, then."

"Fuck off, David. I'm not going back to the psych ward. Because I'm not having a breakdown. I'm pissed. Those are two very different things. And I don't know what your game is."

"I'm not playing a game, Jess. I'm really worried."

"Or why you're claiming that you couldn't see Amber."

"BECAUSE I LITERALLY DIDN'T SEE HER."

"I know for a fact that we have a stalker."

"Okay, Jess." He held up his hands and backed away. "Do what you want. I'll be here with our daughter when you get back." Translation: *I'm so sorry that you can't see reality right now.*

She yanked the door open, then strode down the front stairs and out to the Volvo, half hoping he would be dumb enough to get in front of it. She could claim it was an accident, right?

My husband drugged me last night, Your Honor. I didn't know what I was doing.

She got into the car and slammed the door.

And then he appeared at the passenger window. Knocking on it.

She ignored him.

"Jess, wait!"

She rolled down the window a crack. "What, David? What?"

"What about Bella?"

"Consider yourself lucky that she's not old enough to know what's going on, so that you don't have to go back in there and explain how you drugged her mother last night."

"Jess—"

"Get the fuck away from me."

"But—"

That's all he got out.

Or if there was more, she missed it. Because Jess threw the car into drive.

Then she hit the road and kept going.

Chapter Thirty-Two

JESS WAS a full block away from the house before she could finally exhale. Not that she relaxed. She kept her eye out for any silver BMWs, U-Hauls, or strange vehicles that might be harboring Amber Brown behind the wheel.

What the hell was up with David?

Her husband was acting like she was delusional. But Jess knew full well the only drugs in her system were the ones that ass-fuck had given her last night in his special hot honey and whisky.

She wasn't the crazy one here.

It was David.

He was obviously hiding something.

There was no rational reason for him to have been actively ignoring Amber Brown. Jess had seen enough breadcrumbs (like that ticket to L.A.) to believe that she knew for sure he was lying, just not what he was lying about.

Or why.

But there was no doubt whatsoever that David was

gaslighting her. Because this was all starting to feel too damn familiar.

He'd pulled this shit before. Back when he was sticking it to that stupid bitch, Celeste, during her consulting stint at Prairie. She'd felt something was off in their marriage.

But he'd convinced her it was all in her imagination. And like an idiot, she'd believed him. Goddamn low self-esteem.

As soon as her hands stopped shaking, she pulled over and parked in front of a handsome Craftsman house. Then she pulled out her phone and pulled up Clare's contacts. Her finger hovered over the number.

But then she decided against it.

She had a much harder call to make. Fabiola's number was still a favorite, according to her phone, even though Jess hadn't had reason to call the number for a while now. She had considered deleting her therapist's number just a week ago, as a sign of bravery, telling herself that she would never need it again.

But she'd hesitated. And decided to keep it just in case.

And now here they were.

Was it a mistake for her to put it out there like that? Maybe this was some kind of test from the universe.

She reached Fabiola's receptionist on the first ring.

"Good morning, this is Rose for Fabiola Rodriguez. How can I help you?" Rose. So that meant Jackie had moved on. Or was away on vacation.

"Hi there, good morning, this is Jessica Clarke. I'm a client of Dr. Fabi."

There was some clicking on a keyboard, then, "Nice to speak with you, Mrs. Clarke."

Sure. Whatever. She just wanted to get this done. "It's Jess. And I would love to make an appointment."

"Of course." More tapping.

"The soonest available, please."

"We currently have a two-month wait list."

"Two months?"

"Yes."

"That's not going to work for me. Please, I need to see Dr. Fabi before then."

"I'm afraid there's nothing that I can do."

"Can you ask her? Please. She'll remember me."

"Of course she'll remember you, Mrs. Clarke. Dr. Fabi remembers everyone she helps, but that familiarity can't open additional spots on the calendar, I'm afraid to say."

Jessica almost snorted. Rose didn't sound afraid to say it at all. "Is there a wait list?" Jessica asked.

"Yes, of course."

"How many are on the list before me?"

"You'll be eighty-five."

Jesus. "There are eighty-five ahead of me?"

"No, you would be eighty-five. There are eighty-four before you."

Who knew Dr. Fabi even had that many patients?

"There's nothing you can do?" Jess asked.

"I can help you to make an appointment. The first available opening will be two months from now, on—"

Jess hung up. Knowing the exact date two months out from now would only make her angrier.

She tossed her phone on the passenger seat, put the car back in drive, and circled the block, staring at the road, studying it all as if for the first time.

But there were still no strange cars. No U-Hauls or silver BMWs. Just Mrs. Whitman's ancient daisy-yellow Volkswagen Beetle, its peeling paint standing out like a sunflower in a field of stones. Mr. Larson's newish F-150, the Hendersons' sleek black Range Rover, and several other cars that Jess had no idea who they belonged to, including three Toyota Siennas from three different decades.

But none of them contained Amber Brown.

She finally drove out of the neighborhood and headed over to a mall where a small Provisions grocery store sat. She'd always loved shopping there, but only did so during those intermittent eras when David seemed less uptight about money. The man's emotions about what she spent or didn't spend revolved around seasonal transitions she had yet to map or understand.

She wasn't going to go in, but then she spotted a silver BMW in the parking lot. So she hung a left and took a hard left into the lot.

The driver was a woman, though she didn't get a clear look as she sidled by (trying not to make herself too obvious). But she would have bet all the former cash in David's shoebox that was Amber Brown, trying to hide from the world in a red hoodie.

She was doing a real shit job of it.

Amber got out of the BMW and hurried into Provisions.

Jess did the same, following the woman into the store. But she'd lost sight of her. Provisions was bustling with customers. Light poured in from the large windows, drenching the buckets of cut flowers in sun. The smell of fresh produce filled the store, but she couldn't afford to get lost in that right now.

Instead, she wandered the aisles, looking for Amber. She stepped past large displays full of organic and locally sourced produce, stands of artisanal meats, baskets of freshly baked breads. The surrounding air was fragrant with the scent of spices.

She hurried past the deli counter to the fish market.

Scurried past the aisles of healthy snack options, catching several fleeting glimpses of Amber.

But she was always just at the end of an aisle, disappearing around the corner as soon as Jess spotted her. She felt like the universe itself was toying with her sanity.

A Provisions employee, either helpful or suspicious of her, watched her with an odd expression, then approached her. "Can I help you with something?"

"I'm good," said Jess.

The man put his hands on either side of his waist, perfectly framing the bright red Provisions uniform. Despite his forty-something years, he looked almost boyish with that mess of brown hair falling over his forehead.

"You sure about that?" He gave her a friendly smile. "Maybe there's something I can help you find?"

She stopped. Maybe he could help her. "Sure. Have you seen a woman who looks like me?"

He blinked. That was obviously not what he was expecting her to ask. "I'm not sure."

He almost sounded like Jess had asked him a trick question.

"I mean a lot like me. We could be sisters. Twins."

"No. Sorry." He still seemed confused. "I haven't."

"I know it sounds bizarre, but there is a woman in this store who looks just like me. Well, not just like me. She's not a clone." Jess gave him a light laugh, trying not to sound crazy. "Anyway, she's been stalking my family, and I just want to talk to her."

"I'm sorry to hear that." He clearly had no idea what else to say.

"Thanks. It's been rough. She's also trying to steal my baby."

"She took your baby?" He sounded worried. "This woman who looks like you? And she's here in the store?"

"No. No." Jess shook her head. This conversation wasn't going anywhere. "The baby is at home."

"I'm sorry, ma'am." He looked confused, rubbing his hands on that stupid red apron like he might find something else to say in one of the pockets. "I'm not sure what you're asking me."

"Forget it," Jess said, walking past him. "I'll find her myself."

"Should I get the police?"

"Fuck off."

She walked fast down another two empty aisles before rounding the corner and nearly crashing into a shopper in aisle number three. The man had leveled up when it came to casual dress. He wore shorts that looked like boxers, a tank top that might have been last washed three seasons of *Survivor* ago, and flip-flops that looked like they had been dragged across the beach by wild dogs. He had a reusable bag slung over his shoulder, his hair pulled back into a ponytail.

"Excuse me," Jess said.

The man turned to her. He looked stoned. "Yup?"

"Have you seen a woman who looks just like me?"

He looked Jess up and down, then gave her the wrong kind of smile. "I've seen a lot of women like you."

She glared at him. "Fuck you."

"Any time!"

She ran down the aisle and emerged at the front of the store near the registers. The employee she had cursed at was talking to a heavyset woman that Jess was certain was the Provisions manager. She caught sight of Jess and her mouth flattened into concern.

And Jess spotted Amber paying for her items at the self-checkout station.

She ran after her.

Amber exited the store.

Jess got caught behind a woman with a cart. "Hurry."

She startled the woman, who stepped aside. Jess hustled outside. But she didn't see Amber anywhere. Not to her left, or her right, or anywhere in the parking lot. The silver BMW looked lonely all by itself.

Then she spotted Amber rounding the corner toward the bakery. A man was walking toward her. Jess pointed. "Someone stop that woman!"

A few people turned to look at her. Staring at Jess like *she* was the crazy one.

She caught up to Amber in front of the bakery and grabbed her arm.

"Listen, bitch."

Amber gave a startled cry and spun around.

But it wasn't Amber.

And really, it wasn't even close.

The woman was blonde and slender, but the similarities ended there. And she might have been twice Amber's age.

"Where's Amber?" Jess asked, knowing how unreasonable she must sound.

"Amber?" The woman shook her head. "I have no idea who you're talking about."

Jess gestured to her. "She was wearing that hoodie."

The woman shook her head. "This is my hoodie."

"No. I saw her wearing it."

The woman squinted at her, as though really seeming to see her for the first time. "Are you okay?"

Jess ignored the question.

And then she saw Amber heading toward the BMW, her arms full of groceries. The hoodie was similar to the one this woman was wearing.

Fuck. She'd made a mistake.

251

Jess ran.

"Are you okay?" the woman asked.

Jess ignored her. Running across the parking lot. Amber had put the groceries in the trunk and was headed for the driver's door.

"Amber!"

She didn't respond.

"AMBER!"

Still nothing.

Dammit, Jess should have brought the gun.

Amber reached for the door handle just as Jess arrived. She grabbed her arm and yanked her around.

The woman screamed.

She had delicate features, big blue eyes, and a straight nose. And her small mouth was comically open wide in fear.

Definitely not Amber.

"What the hell is wrong with you?" the woman shrieked.

"I'm so sorry!" Jess said, stumbling back. "I thought you were someone else."

The woman didn't move. Her eyes were on a vehicle pulling up behind Jess. Maybe that was Amber?

She turned. But it was a police cruiser that stopped behind the BMW. Thank God. They could help her find Amber.

But then Mr. Red Apron, accompanied by his manager, walked out of the store toward the cop car.

The officer stepped out of the vehicle. "Everything okay here, folks?"

"She grabbed me," the woman said, jabbing her pointer finger at Jess. "Scared me half to death."

"It was a mistake." Christ, she sounded like David. "I thought she was someone else. I'm trying to find Amber."

"That's the woman you said is trying to steal your baby," said the manager.

Jess smiled. "That's right."

"There's a baby?" said the cop.

Jess nodded. "Yes."

The manager shook her head.

The cop narrowed his eyes. "Have you had anything to drink today, ma'am?"

"No!" Jess said. "Of course not!"

"Any drugs?"

"No! I haven't taken any drugs, and I haven't been drinking! Someone who looks like me has been stalking my family. She's using my name and trying to steal my baby, who she calls Gwen instead of Bella."

The manager and the officer traded a look. The owner of the BMW shuffled back a few steps but didn't stop watching. She appeared to be enjoying the show, probably memorizing it all for her story for later.

"I'm going to have to ask you to leave the premises, ma'am," said the officer.

Jess shook her head. "No. I'm not leaving until I find Amber."

The cop looked over at the manager. "You want her to leave?"

The manager nodded. "She's causing a disturbance."

Jess snorted. *Causing a disturbance.* That's what Amber had been arrested for the other night. "If you don't believe me, you can talk to Officer Carlson. She knows the whole story."

"I'm sure she does," the cop said.

"Aren't you going to call her?"

"I am not."

"Look, I know it sounds insane. But my life is spiraling

out of control because of a woman named Amber Brown."

The officer surveyed Jess with an unsettling mix of pity and skepticism, his hand resting lightly on his belt, where his handcuffs glinted in the morning light.

"Ma'am, I'll need you to calm down."

Jess felt a primal scream rising in her throat, strangled by disbelief and fury. "You're not listening to me!"

"Ma'am, if you can't leave on your own, I'll have to remove you from the premises."

"Fuck you."

The officer reached for his handcuffs.

Jess turned and walked off. But seconds later, she felt a hand on her arm. She pulled away. Or tried to. But seconds later, he'd handcuffed her wrists behind her back.

"I'm not doing anything wrong! I'm trying to protect my family!"

"You're disturbing the peace, ma'am."

Jess screamed, and she didn't stop.

Chapter Thirty-Three

Jessica got out of the car and studied it. Then she searched the interior. Every nook and cranny. Under the seats, glove compartment, beneath the floor mats. The trunk. The tool box. The spare tire.

Then she used her phone flashlight to look underneath the car. And there it was. An AirTag. So that's how he'd known she was at the motel.

She pulled out David's phone. And turned it on. It was paired to the tag.

"You fucking monster."

She got back in the car and opened the glove box, hurling the phone inside. Then shoved it closed.

She got back in the car, started the engine, and drove back to the motel, pulling into the parking lot.

But she didn't get out. She sat for the longest time, hugging the steering wheel, staring at her corner room, trying to convince herself to go back inside.

But she would rather charm a cobra than return to that room.

"Come on. You're a big girl. It won't be as bad as you

think." She reminded herself that once she did this, she would never have to think about it again.

Though, of course, she would be haunted with thoughts of it for the rest of her life. Who was she kidding?

But she sucked it up anyway.

When the coast was clear (although it wasn't like anyone was watching her in the crap motel's empty parking lot anyway), she got out of the car and took her bags back into her room.

She dropped them on the floor, then closed the door behind her. Through the worn-out peephole, she eyed the quiet stretch of parking lot.

She wasn't sure what she was waiting for. A squadron of police cars to roll up and arrest her?

She pulled the *DO NOT DISTURB* sign, opened the door, and added it to the outside door handle. Then she called for a cab, listening to the AC's rattling hum as she waited for her ride.

Except she had to pee.

Tough. She wasn't going back into that bathroom.

Except she was going to wet herself. The minutes stabbed at her bladder until finally she relented.

She ran into the bathroom, peeing as fast as she could with her eyes closed. Then she washed her hands and ran back out. Then she hesitated. And walked back in. Stood staring at Peter for a long time.

"Sorry about this."

She felt his coat pockets. The outer ones were empty. The inner one crinkled. She reached inside. Pulled out the envelope David had given to him. It was full of cash. Partially blood stained. Fuck.

She stashed the envelope in her own pocket. Then walked to the door.

When she looked outside this time, a cab swung into

the parking lot. She exited, the door closing behind her. She checked two, three, four times to ensure it was locked. And that the *DO NOT DISTURB* sign was in place.

Unlike the last cab, this one was beat to absolute shit, and looked as worn and weary as her. She climbed into the back seat.

A middle-aged man with a bushy mustache sat in the driver's seat. He shot her a sympathetic glance in his rearview mirror.

"Are you up early, or out late?" He sounded friendly enough.

But Jessica was not in the mood.

"Just trying to get some things done." She tried to smile, but it didn't work.

He pulled out of the parking lot and onto the road. "Where to?"

She gave him the address of the impound lot.

"Some of the best conversations happen around this time of the morning. And I say that as a driver who's worked all hours."

Jessica nodded. It was the best he was going to get. She ignored him, staring out the window.

It didn't take long before the impound lot came into view.

It was still locked up tight. The sign said that they weren't open until five in the morning, but she could see someone inside, a shadow moving behind the office window. Probably Monica.

"Thanks for the ride," she said to the driver, overtipping him with David's money. "I'm sorry for being a bitch. It isn't you."

He smiled, seeming more delighted by her apology than the tip.

"No problem, ma'am." He tipped his head. "I hope your day or night gets better."

Jessica gave him a nod, then turned around and walked up the steps of the cinderblock building. She knocked.

There was no response.

She pounded on it.

Monica looked out the glass window. "Son of a—"

Jessica did need to be a lip reader to understand what she said.

Monica unlocked the door and flung it open. She looked beyond irritated.

"Let me guess, you want something from your vehicle?"

"I actually just need the vehicle."

"We're not open. Signs says five a.m."

"I understand that." Jessica pulled out a thousand dollars and waved it at Monica.

She sighed. "Come in."

Jess scurried over to the Formica counter and laid the bills out. Monica glanced at them. Some were speckled in blood. "You okay, honey?"

"I'm good." Jessica nodded. Fuck her to pieces if she lost her shit and started crying. "I just need to get my U-Haul back."

Monica looked at her, then nodded. She woke her computer. Punched in some data. "It'll be $730."

Jessica nodded and paid. "Keys?"

Monica placed her change on the counter, then went and got the keys. Jessica grabbed them as soon as Monica held them out.

Then she ran across the office.

"Your change!" Monica said.

"Keep it!"

Then Jessica was out the door. She had the U-Haul

warmed up in no time. She drove it to the entry of the lot, waiting impatiently for Monica to open the gate so she could leave.

Soon as it was open, she floored it, bouncing over the security grate.

The motel parking lot was still just as desolate as it had been when Jessica had left it. She parked, backing the beast up so the big box faced her room. Then she opened the back, kicking the boxes aside, and lowered the ramp, *almost* to the door of room #17.

She unlocked the door and entered. Closed it and went to the bathroom.

She parted the shower curtain, half expecting Peter to be gone. But of course he was still there.

The blood in the tub was still wet, but it had dried into a crust on his clothes.

She returned to the bedroom and yanked a faded sheet off the bed, laying the stained polyester out on the bathroom floor.

Then she got to work, hoisting, hauling, shoving Peter's body out of the cold enamel tub and plopping him onto the sheet.

Each contact with his clammy skin sent a repellent chill down Jessica's spine. But finally she had wrangled him out of the bathtub. She wrapped him in the sheet, like it was some kind of cocoon.

Like that could ever help.

No way was he going to emerge from this one.

Then she grabbed the sheet and dragged him out of the bathroom, pulling him across the carpet. Then she wrapped the comforter around him. Extra padding, she supposed. Though he didn't need it.

She peered outside.

Still quiet.

She pulled up her hood and exited, closing the door partly behind her. Now or never. And then the door next to hers opened. A man stepped out.

For a moment, it looked like he might walk right past her, but then he paused and glanced from the U-Haul over to Jessica.

"Moving day?" He didn't care about her answer. "You're smart to start early. It's gonna be a hot one day."

"Yeah," she said in a monotone, her head still down and her hoodie still up, refusing to make eye contact with the guy.

"Well, then." He was definitely less friendly now. "Good luck with your move."

The man walked away.

Jessica watched him get in his car and drive away.

She stood with her back to the door for another minute, making sure she was still alone. Then she flung open the motel door, grabbed the comforter in both hands, and darted up the ramp.

Dragging Peter behind her.

The comforter snagged on the edge of the ramp.

She panicked, pulling instead of letting go.

The fabric tore and she lost her grip, falling flat on her ass in the back of the truck.

She scrambled to her feet, darting down the ramp, yanking the comforter free. Then she raced back up, pulling the body behind her, dragging it inside, adjusting the boxes to hide the body.

Then she ran out and yanked down the door. Locked the back and slid the ramp away.

Her heart was pounding.

She kept waiting for someone to point at her. Scream. Accuse her. *Murderer!* But no matter how many times she looked around the parking lot, the place was still empty.

She might actually get away with this.

She made sure the *DO NOT DISTURB* sign was still stuck in place.

Then she got into the U-Haul and reminded herself that everything was going according to plan, even if it was a plan that she should not ever have had to make.

Jessica parked several blocks away, then locked up the truck and got out. She walked back to the motel.

Perfect timing, as housecleaning had just arrived to clean the early riser's room.

"Excuse me?" Jessica said, catching the woman just as she headed inside.

The cleaner turned around and looked at Jessica, suspicious, as if she was about to solicit her for something.

"Yes?" the woman said.

"I was sick." Jessica put a hand over her stomach and nodded to her room. "In there."

The woman looked like she might want to spit on Jessica. "I'll get to it as soon as I can."

"No. I'm sorry." Jessica shook her head. "I would never ask you to clean that up for me." Jessica pressed her stomach harder and more performative against her stomach. "I'm happy to do it."

The woman looked shocked. "You want to clean your own mess?"

Jessica nodded. "I just need some bleach and a sponge."

"Are you sure?" The woman looked grateful. But clearly wanted to still check that Jessica was serious. "You wouldn't believe the things I've seen in this place."

"Yes, I'd prefer to at least try to make it right."

The woman gave her an appreciative smile. "I must say, this is a first." She grabbed a sponge and bleach from her cart, then handed them over.

Jessica returned to her room and instantly caught the bitter, metallic scent of blood.

Then she pulled her hair into a ponytail and rolled up her sleeves, getting to work. She got down on her hands and knees, scrubbing the tub with more ferocity than had been used on it in a decade. She ignored the bleach making her eyes water and the fire it started in her throat.

She scrubbed every inch of the bathroom, removing years of filth.

By the time she finished, the bathroom was far more spotless than it had any right to be in a dump like this.

Then she wiped down the rest of the room. Light switch. Desk. Chair. Any hard surface she might have touched. Then she collected the bloody towels and the sponge. And chucked them into the bag she had stolen from Replacement Jessica.

She grabbed both bags, then hesitated, went back into the bathroom and grabbed the bottle of bleach.

Then she took the whole lot outside. She left the door to the room open so it could air out.

She ran-walked back to the U-Haul, loaded the bags and bleach inside and drove away, wondering if she had really just gotten away with a murder she didn't even commit.

Chapter Thirty-Four

JESS STARED up at the hospital from the back seat of the police cruiser.

It was a modern building with large windows and clean lines, surrounded by lush greenery and trim landscaping. Probably hell inside.

The officer seemed to have softened now that Jess was no longer screaming at him. He opened the car door without talking, but he had a kind expression on his face as he waited for to emerge.

As soon as she was out, he placed a hand on her wrists and guided her into the hospital.

The lobby was filled with comfy furniture, calming artwork, and a soothing atmosphere. It almost looked like something other than a place for crazy people like her.

"I want to call my husband."

"I already told you, this isn't the police station and you're not under arrest, so I don't owe you a call."

"That's bullshit," Jess said.

He ignored her, collected his handcuffs, then handed

her over to the staff. Then he signed some paperwork. "Try to get some rest."

And then he was gone.

She was taken through to another reception room, where she was told to sit.

There was a nice-looking lady sitting at a desk.

Jess got up and walked over to her. "Can I please call my husband?"

She glanced at Jess, then pointed to the chair she had vacated. "Sit down."

"I just want to call me husband."

"Please understand, Mrs. Clarke, that it's our policy to limit external communication until after your initial evaluation. We appreciate your cooperation."

We. How patronizing.

"I didn't agree to cooperate with that," Jess said.

"The chair, Mrs. Clarke."

Jess glared at her. "How long is this going to take?"

The woman didn't answer.

Jess sighed and returned to her chair. Behind the reception desk, the hospital was abuzz with activity. People talking, phones ringing, nurses bustling back and forth with supplies. It was driving Jess out of her mind.

She got up and walked to the door. Tried it. Locked, of course.

"This is a secure ward," the receptionist said.

"I need to get home to my daughter."

"I'm sure your husband is taking good care of her."

Jess curled her lip. How did she know that? Had she talked to David? And if she had, how come Jess couldn't? She returned to her seat and started hugging her legs, resting her forehead against her knees.

Jess knew why she couldn't talk to him.

Because she had been here before. Sat in this same

exact room. Maybe even in this same goddamn chair. But Jess had been too fucked up at the time to remember much, though it was definitely a different officer of the law who had dragged her into this place.

The officer who bought her tonight was still much better than the last guy who had put her in the back of a cop car. He'd been rough and unkind, treating her need for treatment almost like a sport.

That had been the worst time of her life. Three miscarriages, off of her meds because she couldn't stand how much they made her feel like a robot. Trying to quit cold turkey right and then finding out that David was having an affair.

There were so many lies once she started digging. It broke her into pieces. At the time, she didn't know that she'd ever be whole again.

But David had begged and pleaded for forgiveness and she'd finally relented because she'd believed him when he said he could see how much he had hurt her and he never wanted to see that expression on her face again.

She'd always thought he had been the steadfast one, the anchor in their universe of two. But that facade crumbled the night he came clean. The lines on David's face had been a map of guilt and regret. The stoic man she married was gone, and in his place, she met a vulnerable stranger.

"Jess." He had barely been able to talk. His voice was thin and reedy, then clogged as he cried. "I made a mistake, a terrible, unforgivable mistake. But believe me when I say that I know how much I fucked up, and that I'm truly, deeply sorry. I will never, *ever* hurt you like that again."

She had still been too furious to answer. And he broke down then, with the most wretched sounding sobs she had ever heard from a human being. A pitiful, broken sound, full of sorrow and despair. His entire body had shaken with anguish. Tears had streamed down his face.

"It's okay," Jess had assured him, feeling a need to comfort him. For some reason, she couldn't stand to see him like this.

Her rock had shattered to pieces. His gut-wrenching apology was raw and real. At least she had thought it was.

And then, struggling with his emotions, he had pledged his love. "I can't take back what I've done. But I will spend the rest of my life making it up to you. I'm so sorry, Jess."

She had believed him in that moment. And had continued to believe him. For years. Working on herself.

Nearly making it to the other side of her dependence on the meds, but then the bad news came back from the first adoption company, followed by a series of similar emails. *Not suitable.*

All of them stating variations of the same theme until they had a pile of rejection letters. And Jess fell into the deepest depths of despair.

A vast abyss, dark and unending.

Each rejection added a new crack in her heart, making her feel smaller, lonelier, and increasingly insignificant. Unworthy to be a mother.

Of course she goddamn relapsed. Who wouldn't?

When Jess opened her mouth, the drugs kissed her back.

She went from an existential knife in her brain to floating in an ethereal dream, the sharp edges of reality smoothed out enough for her to breathe again.

Each pill had been a feathery cloud, carrying her further along the road to oblivion, a blessed reprieve from the torturous pangs of reality.

But that was not what was happening now. She lifted her head, blinking in the fluorescent light.

The receptionist looked over at her. "Doctor will be here shortly."

"Thanks."

She wasn't going to let this be like last time. She was stronger now. She was better. She was Jessica Fucking Clarke. She took a breath and began running through her gratitudes.

Grateful for Bella. Her home. For Clare. For even goddamn Muriel. Grateful for her creativity, for the sun, for the soil under her feet.

She wasn't the same person she had been before when she was here. She wasn't the same. She just wasn't.

Everything was different now.

Unlike the last Jess, this one had her baby girl waiting for her at home.

Chapter Thirty-Five

JESSICA DROVE until she arrived in long desolated expanses of sparse vegetation and sand. Then she finally stopped the U-Haul.

She looked up her location on the GPS. There didn't seem to be anything around.

She got out and went to the back, unlocking the truck, lifting the latch, throwing the door up. Then she hoisted herself up into the back. She kicked the boxes aside. Then grabbed the comforter and pulled Peter's body out of the truck.

It was much easier than getting him in.

She dragged him over to a ditch and rolled him in.

Then she jumped in beside him. An angry desert wind kicked up out of nowhere, whisking warm grains of sand across her face as she stripped the comforter and sheet from his body.

He lay there like a broken puppet without any strings.

She searched his pockets again. No phone. But she found his ID. *PETER FOSTER.* So he'd been telling her the truth about his name.

She pocketed the ID.

Hopefully, a coyote or some other scavenger would find him.

She continued to stare down at him. Wondering if anyone would miss him. She couldn't imagine a man like him having a family. But then, if she'd only met the version of David she'd seen last night, she would have said the same thing about him.

"Adios, asshole." She kicked some dirt onto the body, then turned around and headed back to the U-Haul.

She got into the back of the truck, flattening the cardboard boxes. Then she pulled out the knife and dumped it into the bottle of bleach, swirling it around.

She left it inside, returning to the cab and getting back into the driver's seat.

She drove until the neighborhood felt right. By no means nice, but not exactly dangerous. Definitely not a place where one was as likely to take special note of their fellow shoppers.

The Big D Savings Center was a small and rundown market at the corner of a neglected intersection. The parking lot was filled with potholes, and the store exterior was thirsty for paint.

Jess walked around the back of the building and emptied out the bleach bottle into a dumpster. She shook it until the knife fell out. Then she discarded the bleach bottle next to a mountain of rotting lettuce.

She walked over to a neighboring dumpster and tossed the knife.

Stinking of bleach, she went inside the Savings Center. The linoleum floor was more scuffed and scratched than the walls of her hotel room. She bought herself a box of black garbage bags, plus two magazines and a pack of gum along with a soda that she didn't even really want.

Then she found a gas station. Not a nice modern one with bright fluorescent lights, but an old, dimly lit one with two clusters of ancient pumps.

She filled the U-Haul with gas, then drove to a laundromat on the other side of the city.

Jessica stuffed the sheet, comforter, and her hoodie into a garbage bag. Then she carried them inside.

It was rundown and unkempt enough for her to recognize that the owner of the place had stopped giving a shit about the place long ago. Surely, he or she still raided the place for quarters, but it had been years since anyone cared enough to give it a fresh coat of paint. And the two cracks in the windows up front certainly didn't look new.

The walls were yellow from age, not choice. Small empty boxes of detergent lay strewn across the cracked linoleum floor amid a scattering of candy wrappers. Most of the machines were dented, fellow refugees from a life without maintenance.

She walked over to a washing machine and dumped the bedding and hoodie inside, then scraped the bottom of her purse for quarters.

She ran them through the hot cycle twice.

It didn't get out all the bloodstains. The hoodie still had a dark brownish blemish that was plenty obvious. But it could be mistaken for chocolate.

She dried the comforter, sheet, and hoodie on hot, though Jess was also sure that hot in this place probably had all the searing intensity of lukewarm tea.

She pulled a fresh black bag from the box and put the already used bag in the bottom. She stuffed the comforter into it and tied it up. Put the hoodie in a second bag, the sheet in a third, and tossed them both into the cabin of her U-Haul.

She started driving, turning corners and passing

through deserted alleyways, making her way to a series of random stopping points, each one decided by a bizarre formula of how deserted the location was balanced against how she felt in her gut.

After getting rid of the three bags in three separate locations, Jess drove to yet another shopping center.

She made her way around to a recycling bin behind the California Pizza Kitchen and parked. Then she opened up the back of the U-Haul, collected all the cardboard boxes, and tossed them inside the bin.

Then she drove off, making her way to something called the Lone Star Galleria. It looked like a grocery store. She sure as shit hoped it was one.

It was.

She dropped two gallons of bleach and a stack of dish rags into a cart, scanning the checkout aisles for the least attentive cashier until she spotted a young boy with tired eyes.

"You on cleanup duty, huh?"

"Something like that," Jessica said as he rang up her items.

She went back to the U-Haul, then drove a mile away and pulled into an empty parking lot. She drank the cola for energy, downing it with one long swallow. Then she got right to work, scrubbing every surface of the truck until the box shone.

The cabin came next.

Then Jess punched the U-Haul depot into the GPS and followed the instructions. Before she knew it, she had arrived.

She cracked the windows to help with the bleach smell, then collected her bags and got out, leaving the keys in the ignition. She patted the hood of the truck as though to say farewell. And then stopped.

Staring at the mural of Montana.

When she had rented it last week, she had the promise of a brand-new life ahead of her. She'd been happy. In love. A new mother. And it had all gone to shit. She had nothing. Not even her grandmother's quilt.

David had stripped everything away from her as surely as he would peel an orange.

Her stomach grumbled. She needed food.

She wanted to find her own way to the Griddle & Grits without driving. But when she looked it up on the GPS, it was too far. She called a cab. And was delivered there in minutes.

She entered the restaurant, pleased to see Bernice. The waitress gave her a nod and a smile.

Jessica sat at the counter again, but this time because she wanted to.

"Well, look who's back. Shake?"

"Just a black coffee, please."

"You got it."

Tomorrow, Jessica would buy a bus ticket and return to New York. Where she always belonged and never should have left. It meant leaving without Gwen. But she had begun to realize that was going to be inevitable.

She could never win the battle for her daughter. She couldn't even prove who she was. She had nothing. Just a ridiculous story about being married to a man who already had a wife and child and claimed not to know her.

Bernice walked over with a coffee cup. Steam poured out of the top. It smelled like heaven.

"Here's your coffee, hon." Bernice set the mug in front of her. "Just let me know when you want a refill and I'll top you off."

"Thank you." Jessica gestured to the payphone. "Do those still work?"

"Last I checked."

Jessica nodded, sipping her coffee as slowly as she could.

She even had Bernice top it off twice more before she finally got to her feet and walked over to the phones. She picked up the handset, plugged a quarter, and dialed the one number Jessica had sworn she would never dial again.

No matter what.

The phone rang.

A woman answered. "Yeah?"

"Hi, Mom," Jessica said.

Chapter Thirty-Six

"This way."

The receptionist gestured to the door.

Jess got up and walked over. The receptionist guided her through the door with an unexpectedly kind hand. Then she handed her off to a nurse. Who ushered her through yet another door, then down a hallway and into a private exam room.

The déjà vu felt surreal, along with the crippling paranoia. The two emotions were eating her alive.

"The doctor will be right with you," said the nurse, giving Jess a generous smile.

But it didn't matter. She still felt like she was going out of her goddamned mind.

The room was small and sterile. White walls, white ceiling, and bright white fluorescent lights. There was a bed with a monitor above it and a cabinet with various medical tools. A plastic human anatomy doll almost seemed like stage dressing for a nightmare.

She only waited for seconds before the door opened and a woman entered. Late thirties with light brown hair that curled at the ends. Deep brown eyes and a gentle smile. Confident posture, but also relaxed. Her name tag read *Dr. Clark* and Jess thought that either the woman or the universe was fucking with her.

"Your first name isn't Jessica, is it?" Jess asked.

"No." The doctor smiled. "Marianne. Why?"

Jess shook her head. "No reason. Am I being sectioned?"

"I don't know. Do you want to be?"

Jess blinked. This was a different kind of doctor than the one she had the last time she got dragged to this place.

"No." She shook her head. "Definitely not."

"Then how about we just chat. Does that sound good to you?"

"It does." Jess nodded, wanting to believe that this kindly doctor really did want to help her.

"How about you have a seat?" She gestured to the bed.

Jess eyed it. "Do you want me to lie down?"

"Only if you want."

"I'd like to sit."

"Excellent." She pulled up a chair and sat next to the bed, so that Jess was looking down at her. She appeared completely non-threatening.

"I'd like to start by asking you a few questions about what's been going on in your life lately. Will that be okay?"

Jess nodded again. "What would you like to know?"

"I read through your file."

"Oh."

"The last time you were in here. You'd been through some real shit, hey?"

Jess found herself wanting to smile. "Yeah, I went through some shit."

"I don't need you to rehash any of that, but I was

275

hoping that you could tell me some of what has been going on since then."

"I'm not sure that's such a good idea."

"And why not?"

"Because it will sound crazy." She swallowed. "You'll think that I'm crazy."

Dr. Clark gave her a reassuring smile. "Crazy isn't a word I like to use, and I would love to hear your story if you're willing to tell it."

Fuck. She had to trust somebody. So Jess took a chance.

"A few nights ago, this woman showed up on my front porch out of nowhere. And she looks like me, I mean, *just like me*, like more than my sister. Like she's my twin. And then she said that she *was* me, like she used my literal name. Jessica Clarke. And said that was married to my husband, David. You probably know him from my file."

She gave a bitter laugh. Dr. Clark said nothing, but gave a slow nod, so Jessica continued.

"The next morning, she broke into our house. Our fucking house! I was scared, you know. Because of Bella. My daughter. She talked like she knew her, too. Only she called her Gwen. I made David get a security system installed, but even after that, she came back and tried to take my baby. I thought I saw her at Provisions, so I went inside but then I couldn't find her and when I saw her going back out to the parking lot, I followed her and I didn't mean to crash into her like I did but that's when the officer—"

"It's okay." Dr. Clark raised a pacifying hand. "Take a breath."

Jess nodded.

Dr. Clark gave her a moment to get regulated. Once

Jess was back to taking regular breaths, she said, "There you go. How is David supporting you through this?"

"He isn't."

"And you stay home with the baby while he works a full-time job?"

"Yes, ma'am."

"Marianne." Smile. "David travels a lot?"

"Yes. Like two weeks of every month."

"It sounds like a lot of pressure, taking care of a baby."

"It just started, but yes, it is." Jess nodded. "I mean, I've been dreaming about it forever, and now I can't stop having nightmares of it all being taken away from me. I feel like I'm going out of my mind. So am I crazy?"

Marianne laughed. "No, you're not crazy. But I do have something I want you to do for me."

"What is it?"

"It's going to be a tricky one," said the doctor.

"I'm ready."

"Get some rest."

Jess blinked. "What?"

"Rest. Sleep. It makes all the difference when your household has been disrupted. And right now, it is clear that you're running on fumes."

"It's more than that."

"But is it?"

Jess stopped.

"Because it seems to me you've had a rather traumatic few years. During which you had three miscarriages, found out your husband was having an affair, went to marriage counseling, got yourself off drugs, adopted a baby, and had a disrupting force arrive on your front porch, upsetting your family. Did I miss anything?"

Jess thought for a moment. "David bought a gun."

Marianne made a note in the file. "You didn't want one?"

She shook her head. "I don't like guns. But he insisted."

"That's a lot for anyone to handle, Jess. Let alone someone who is a recovering addict."

Jess blinked back tears. Maybe Marianne was right. Everything seemed so much worse than it was because she was just flat out exhausted.

"So you think maybe you can get some rest?" Marianne asked.

"Maybe."

"Do you have a friend who can watch Bella for a few hours so you can get some rest?"

"Clare can watch Bella." Jess felt the need to say both of their names out loud.

Any bit of evidence to prove her reality.

"And Clare is?"

"My best friend."

Marianne made a note. "How is she as a support system?"

Jess smiled, her heart filling with love. "She's my rock. She'd do anything for me." Her voice caught. "I'm so grateful to have her."

"Then get Clare to watch Bella, so you can get some much-needed sleep. I can promise that you'll feel worlds better afterward."

"And what do I do about Amber Brown?"

"That the woman who came to your house?"

Jess nodded.

"You talk to the police about a restraining order. And if you feel that this woman is in any way a threat to you or the baby, or even your healthy state of mind, you stay somewhere else for a few days. It'll help take the edge off of what you're feeling. Do you think you can stay with Clare?"

Jess slowly nodded. "I can do that."

Marianne leaned forward and squeezed her hand. "I know you can. Everything will be good again, Jessica."

"Jess."

"Jess."

"So I'm not crazy?"

"You already asked me that."

"Guess I just want to make sure," Jess said.

Marianne laughed. "You would be shocked by the amount of times I've seen this exact kind of overwhelm among women with babies. The reality of motherhood isn't quite what we dream about. At the very least, it's a hell of a lot more exhausting."

Jess nodded. But she couldn't help thinking there was more to it than exhaustion.

"Stop overthinking it," Marianne said. "You need sleep."

Jess smiled. "Okay."

"Great. Now, there are some forms to fill out at the front desk on your way out. Otherwise, you're free to go."

Jess blinked. "I can go? You're not keeping me here?"

"Do you want to hurt yourself or anyone else?"

"No. Of course not. Well, maybe Amber Brown, but if that's an official question, then I totally didn't mean that."

The doctor smiled. "I'd like for you to check in with your family doctor in a few days. Or come back here to the hospital if you feel that you need immediate support. But otherwise, yes, absolutely, you are free to go. Assuming you keep your promise to sleep."

"Girl Scout's Honor!" Jess raised her hand.

"Were you ever a Girl Scout?"

Jess lowered her hand while shaking her head. "No."

"I believe you anyway." Dr. Clarke laughed. "Remember the forms on your way out." She gestured to a phone in the corner. "Would you like for me to call you a ride?"

Jess shook her head. "No thanks. I'll get a cab."

"Take care of yourself."

"I will."

Marianne patted her knee, then left the room.

Jess sat in silence. She could go. No, she was *free to go*. Free. That word had never sounded so good.

She got up and retraced her steps back to the receptionist. When she saw Jess, she buzzed the door open. She walked into the waiting room and around to the counter. "Dr — Marianne said I had to sign some paperwork."

The receptionist placed a few forms on the counter. Jess didn't even bother to read them. Just signed where the receptionist indicated.

Then she walked to the door and was buzzed out.

She exited the hospital near tears.

Not because she was sad, or even angry. She was proud. Proud of the person she no longer was.

And even prouder that she had just proved it.

Chapter Thirty-Seven

"Hɪ, Mᴏᴍ."

There was no response, but Jess could hear someone breathing.

"Are you there?" she said.

"I'm here." Mary sniffed. "I was just making a bet with myself, wondering whether you were calling because you wanted some money."

"I don't want your money."

"Of course, you want money. David finally knock you up? You need money for formula?"

"No." She wasn't going to cry. "I just need some help."

"Why? What did you do?"

"I didn't do anything!"

"Then ask David for help."

"I can't."

"Oh." Mary laughed. "You lose him already? I knew you'd never be able to keep a man like that. He's two classes ahead of you in rank. And a whole football field ahead of you in smarts."

"Mom. Please." Her voice cracked.

"Well, if you don't want money, what do you want?"

"I need a place to stay."

"You coming back to New York?"

"Yes."

"Bringing the baby?"

Jessica leaned her forehead against the wall. "No."

"No? You abandoning her? Jesus. You're shittier than your father."

"I'm not abandoning her. David — David—" She couldn't say it. She couldn't even think what to say.

"Oh. I see," Mary said. "You caught your Prince Charming fucking another woman, so now you wanna come home. Congratulations, now you know what it was like being married to your father. At least you don't have seventeen years invested with the man. You should probably thank your lucky stars you're getting the divorce over with ahead of schedule."

Jessica stared at her feet. Why had she called? Had she honestly thought her mother would help her?

"Well, you can have your room back. But you'll need to pay rent. Although if you're coming back, you better keep your legs closed. I'm not having you parade a bunch of unwashed assholes through my apartment at all hours."

Jessica hung up.

She blinked back tears.

Then walked to the counter and returned to her stool.

It was her own stupid fault for calling.

Why did she think that a woman who had never been able to show her an ounce of empathy would be there for her now?

Bernice walked over with the coffee urn and refilled her cup.

"Thanks."

The strong aroma made Jessica feel ever so slightly

better. Even more so when she wrapped her hands around the hot mug and felt it lightly burning her skin.

Bernice returned a few minutes later and set a donut on a dessert plate before her. "You look like you can use one."

And then she cried. It shocked her. But she couldn't stop. She clapped her hands over her mouth, trying to control herself.

But Bernice shook her head. "You let it out, young lady. Nothing good ever came from repressing feelings."

Jessica laughed. And cried. And it sounded like a half snort. "I'm an idiot."

"Oh, I doubt that very much," Bernice said.

Jessica shook her head. "It's true. I've never been smart."

"Bullshit. You came back here, didn't you?"

Jessica laughed again.

"Now tell me why you think you're an idiot."

Jessica wiped her nose with a napkin. "Because I called my mom. Why the hell did I do that? She's never not been terrible."

"Mine too. But you called her because you needed to believe that she loved you." She leaned in close. "And it's super fucked up to realize that sometimes they don't. But looking that truth in the eye allows you to live without it hurting so much."

"Am I crazy if that makes me feel better?"

"You're crazy if you don't start eating that donut. Gustavo just finished making them. And they always taste better fresh." She shook her head in seeming awe. "You have no idea what you're in for."

Jess looked down at the golden-brown donut, glistening with grease, slightly puffed-up, drizzled with still-wet chocolate. "It does look delicious."

"Might want to use a fork," Bernice said.

So she picked up her fork and dug in. And God, it was the best donut that Jess had ever put in her mouth. The dough was soft, with a light crunch from the caramelization. Sugar, cinnamon, nutmeg (maybe?), and vanilla (for sure), all mixing with the chocolate.

Another customer walked in, and Bernice disappeared, returning just as Jess was finishing up the final bite.

"That didn't take you long." Bernice looked down at her plate, empty except for a few drizzles of chocolate. If she hadn't returned, Jess would have scooped them up with her finger.

"That was amazing. Thank you."

Bernice nodded, then leaned in closer to Jess. "Can I offer you a word of advice?"

"If it's advising me to eat another donut, then I'm going to have to say no. Because then I'll just eat that one and want another one, and eventually someone is going to have to wheel me out of here."

Jessica stopped talking, because Bernice looked suddenly very serious.

She gestured to the array of small cuts on Jessica's face. "No man is worth that." She shook her head. "Understand?"

Jessica nodded, getting teary.

Bernice pointed at her coffee and donut. "That's on the house. And I have another one up at the register in a bag for you. It's the Mama's Birthday Cake. You're going to love it." She nodded at the empty plate. "That was just the Chocolate Drizzle. She's our starter. That Mama's Birthday Cake will level you up for sure."

Jess laughed again. Trying so hard not to cry because it had been too long since someone had shown her kindness.

"Thank you. For everything."

Bernice smiled. "I sat in that same seat once. Not here in this place, but wherever you are right now up here" — she tapped her head — "and I remember wishing from the top of my heart down to the tips of my toes that someone would reach out a hand and help me. And no one did. It's an awful long climb up when you have to do it yourself."

Bernice refilled her coffee, then headed out to the floor, attending to other customers.

Jessica sipped her coffee. Bernice was right. No man was worth this.

She returned to the pay phone, dropped another quarter, and dialed David's number. He answered on the second ring.

"Hello?"

"Hello, David," she said.

Silence. A very hostile one.

She let him have until the count of three.

"Surprised to hear from me? Maybe you thought Peter finished the job?"

"I told you not to call me again."

"How about you—"

"Goodbye, Jessica. If you—"

"Jessica? The name is Amber." She laughed. "*Oopsie.* You made a mistake, David."

Silence.

But he was still there ... breathing. And finally he spoke.

"You mean saying your name just now? That's not a mistake. You're the crazy bitch who has been running around Dallas using that name."

"No, David. You made another mistake. A few of them, actually."

"Get to the point or I'm hanging up."

"You won't hang up because you have no idea where I

am or what I have or how many ways I can destroy your life for good."

"What do you have?" *You fucking bitch*, he surely wanted to add.

"I have the envelope."

"What envelope?"

"The one you gave our good friend Peter."

"I don't know any Peter. And if I happen to know someone by that name, I definitely didn't give him any envelope."

"Oh, David…" She laughed again. "It has your fingerprints all over it. And I also have a photo of you handing the envelope to him. So keep the lies coming, asshole."

"What do you want?"

"To watch you get dragged behind a U-Haul for a dozen city blocks, but since I can't have that, I'll settle for the cops finding Peter's body in your car."

Silence.

"Unless you can get there first. I left it somewhere special for you to find."

More silence. A lot of it.

"Don't you want to know where it is, David?"

Heavy breathing, the sound of an emotional engine revving to murder.

"Last chance?" she said.

"You have twelve hours to leave Dallas, or it'll be you the cops find in the fucking bathtub, Jessica."

"Fuck you, David." A beat. "I love it when you say my name."

Then she hung up on him.

And replayed the recording she made on her phone.

It wasn't loud, but every word was still audible.

Got you, asshole.

The payphone started to ring.

Jessica smiled on her way back to the counter.

She took a final sip of lukewarm coffee, then left the remainder of the money she had stolen from the shoebox, just shy of $500 dollars, on the counter for Bernice as a tip.

Jess stopped at the register and collected her donut.

Bernice glanced over at her and waved.

"Thank you for your kindness," said Jess.

And then she was gone.

Chapter Thirty-Eight

JESS GOT out of the cab and strode up to the front door. Wondering how long it would take for her and David to be at each other's throats.

Because she was not in the mood to take so much as a molecule of his shit right now.

When she opened the door, David was pacing the living room, his brow furrowed, his lips pursed in frustration. He turned to her, surprised. Relaxing his clenched jaw.

"I take it you know where I've been?"

He nodded. "The cops called."

"And you didn't think to come and see me?"

He gestured upstairs. "I was looking after Bella."

"That's true. You certainly couldn't have gotten Clare or Mason over to sit while you came."

"Jess, I didn't know how long you would be there. The last time—"

"Was necessary. I was in a bad way and needed help. This time was bullshit. I wasn't sectioned, because I'm not fucking crazy."

"I never said you were crazy."

"You implied it hard enough to ink a tattoo." She relaxed her fists, not wanting to give him the satisfaction of her anger.

"Jess."

"*Don't.* I'm going to take a shower."

He opened his mouth but didn't bother to use it. She headed upstairs and took another shower. The tank had refilled. Once again, she let the water scald her skin, massaging her scalp with shampoo and then conditioner. Though it felt like her soul needed cleansing more than her skin.

She got dressed in yoga pants and a cami. Put her hair up in a ponytail.

David was sitting on the bed when she exited the shower. "I canceled my trip to New York. Grant was annoyed, but I think with all that's been going on here that I should stay."

"Go to New York."

"What?"

"I said go to New York."

"Jess. I already cancelled."

"Rebook it. I'll be fine. And besides, the doctor said that it might be good for the two of us to take some time apart."

"Take some time apart?"

She nodded. "That is word for word what I just said."

"Why would we need time apart?"

"Are you happy right now, David? Because you don't seem to be, and I sure as hell am not."

"Where is this coming from?"

"Are you serious?"

He didn't answer.

"You don't support me."

"How don't I support you? I did everything possible to get Bella."

"This isn't about Bella. It's about me. You make me feel like I'm crazy. And I'm sick of it."

"You're mad."

"Yeah. And I want some time apart. Go on your trip. Get back in Grant's good graces. Do a great job like always."

"Are you sure?" He still seemed uncertain.

"Jesus, how many times to I have to say it? I'm sure. Go."

"I don't want this to be one of those things that I'm misreading where you say you're really okay with me going when you actually want me to stay home."

"I know how to say what I mean, David. Go. Now where's Bella?"

"In her crib."

"Do you need help packing?"

"No." David shook his head. "I've got it."

He still looked uncertain as she left the room, but that was on him.

"I'm going to start packing!" he called to her.

She ignored him, closing the door. Then she went to the linen cupboard. And quiet as possible, she pushed aside the towels and opened the safe. Thank God, David had put the gun back.

She got it out, closed the closet door, then took it downstairs and put it in her purse.

Then she went back upstairs to check on Bella, creeping into the room just in case she really was asleep. She could never be sure with David, because she only needed to yawn and he'd be rushing upstairs to put her down in the crib.

But this time she was gurgling and snoring and looking about as adorable as a baby could be.

Jess smiled. Then went to the window, parted the curtains, and peeked outside onto the street just as a car was passing by.

A silver BMW, just like David's.

Jess started thinking, rewinding the days like a film in her mind, playing them back. Returning to recent scenes and revisiting them out of order. Abrading away some obfuscations of truth like the top layer of a scratch and sniff sticker.

She left the nursery and went down into the living room.

She looked out the window again. No BMW.

Then she pulled out her phone and called Clare.

"Are we playing Scooby Doo?" Clare asked.

"No. But I was wondering if I could drop Bella off for a few hours."

"Are you playing Scooby Doo without me?" She sounded disappointed.

"I'm taking David to the airport."

"Is that a sexual position?"

Jess laughed. "What?"

"Well, I hope it is, because that's infinitely more exciting and he can take an Uber to DFW."

"Of course he could take an Uber, but I need to do this."

"You don't have to explain, Jess. I'm just messing with you. Of course you can bring Bella over. When were you thinking?"

"Like right now, as long as David doesn't need to book a new flight."

"I'll be waiting. Bring me your progeny." She gave a malevolent laugh.

"You're nuts, you know that."

"It's why we love each other," Clare said. And hung up.

Jess tucked her phone away and went back upstairs to the bedroom. David had his overnight bag on his shoulder.

"I can take you to the airport."

"No need for that." He shook his head. "I can get a cab."

"It's no problem. Clare's going to watch Bella."

"She's sleeping."

"You're right." She shrugged. "It's not ideal. But I'm driving you."

"Okay." David did his best to hide that he didn't like the idea.

Jess walked down the hall and entered the nursery, easing Bella out of her crib, careful to not disturb her slumber. She managed to get Bella out of the house without waking her. Bella stirred when she got strapped into the car seat. Then she spotted Jess. The corner of her mouth twitched in a tiny smile.

Jess pressed a kiss on her forehead.

Bella closed her eyes again.

Then Jess texted Clare: *Big favor Bella is sleeping can you meet us in the driveway when we get there?*

Clare sent her a thumbs-up emoji.

David locked the door and headed toward the car with his overnight bag and laptop. He opened the trunk and stowed his gear. Then he got into the passenger seat. Jess pressed a finger to his lips when he opened his mouth.

He looked like he still wanted to say something.

Jess gave him a look: *It's a couple of minutes until we're at Clare's.*

Asshole.

Clare was waiting in her driveway.

The handoff was fast. Jess unhooked the whole car seat

and gave Bella to Clare. She was still sleeping like the "batteries included" baby that Clare had always claimed her to be. Clare gave her a hug, then Jess and David were on their way to the airport.

Whatever David had wanted to say, he didn't, staying quiet the remainder of the journey.

When she pulled up to the terminal, he tried to give her a kiss.

But Jess turned her cheek.

He got out, closed his car door, and unlatched the trunk, slamming it once he'd retrieved his luggage.

Then he turned and walked into the airport without looking back.

And Jess drove away.

Chapter Thirty-Nine

JESSICA HAD every intention of following the Volvo.

But then she spotted David emerging from the airport's glass doors.

The asshole barely even waited a minute. He was either getting brazen, or he had been getting away with his lies for so long that he truly believed no one would ever catch him.

And, oh, Jessica couldn't wait to catch him.

And destroy his life like he had destroyed hers.

No, like he *would have* done, if she had been stupid enough to let him. But she hadn't. Despite everything, she was still standing. And she still would be. Even after David was gone.

She let several cars in front of her, waving them forward, keeping an eye on David.

Meanwhile, the Volvo was still visible amid a cluster of cars ahead but would soon be out of sight.

She had to choose which one of them to follow.

David climbed into a cab.

Fuck it.

She had nothing left to say to David.

But she was absolutely dying for a conversation with Jessica.

She gunned it, peeling past the cab, following the Volvo.

Wherever David's cab was headed, she hoped it was straight to Hell.

Chapter Forty

DAVID STOOD by a ticket kiosk inside the airport, staring out the glass doors, waiting for the green Volvo to drift out of sight.

Fucking Jess.

What the hell was up with her?

And that stupid bitch, Jessica. This was all her goddamn fault. All of it.

He stretched his shoulders. Or his fault. But only because he let the cunt slip through the cracks a few times now.

He had been sloppy. And if he had paid more attention to the details instead of outsourcing to Peter, he wouldn't be in this mess right now.

Once David started thinking about it, he could pinpoint several things he could have done better. Such as, it had been foolish to involve anyone else, especially after executing everything so flawlessly while working solo.

But how was he supposed to be in two places at the same time? No matter how many times he'd run through the scenario, he couldn't figure that part out. So he had Peter drive the semi.

And it had worked.

Only the asshole got the wrong truck.

What did he really expect?

Everyone always fucked everything up.

The Volvo was nearing the end of this section of the terminal. So he headed out of the air-conditioning and into the Dallas heat.

He spotted a taxi and trotted over, waving.

The cabbie shook his head — David knew he wasn't supposed to get in there, taxis were supposed to pick up passengers only in designated places — but he opened the door and climbed in anyway.

"Thank you for making an exception," David said.

"Where are we going?" The cabbie didn't seem that upset about getting an unexpected fare.

"My gym." David gave him the address.

Working out at All Star Fitness made David feel like a boss. The place leaked more testosterone from its sleek metal panels and wide glass walls than most gyms rats had running through their veins. The entrance was framed with two large red columns and the front windows were emblazoned with the words *WELCOME TO ALL-STAR FITNESS*. Then under that: *You belong here.*

Fuck yeah, he did.

But David wouldn't be working out today.

He entered the gym, then called for another cab. Once confirmed, he walked past an open area populated by state-of-the-art exercise machines and a refrigerated juice bar and made his way into the locker room.

He dumped his suitcase and laptop bag into the locker, and changed into jogging pants, a dry fit T-shirt, and a hoodie.

He searched the top shelf of the locker and fumbled around until he felt the gun, then pulled the weapon into his hands. He checked the chamber. But he always kept it loaded.

Then he stuffed it into his gym bag and left All-Star Fitness behind, getting into the cab that was already outside and waiting for him.

"Where to?" asked the cabbie.

David gave him the address of the Sunset Plains, that shit heap motel where Jessica had been staying.

He slid a hand into his gym bag, fingering the weapon. Jess didn't know about this one. He'd bought it years ago when the company had started working with that goddamn charity. *Rehabilitating convicts, my ass.* Once a felon, always a felon. At least if Peter was anything to go by.

He got dropped a few blocks away from the motel and walked the rest of the way.

He studied the parking lot from across the street, and then again when he walked over to it.

No silver BMW. No U-Haul. And no bitch.

But he did see one of chambermaids, or the only chambermaid, considering how much of a dump the place was.

She was four doors down from Jessica's room.

He watched her work her way down the row of rooms. Coming up with more schemes. Maybe he should have given her a slow-acting poison that would have hit her a day on the road.

Two more doors.

Even an "overdose" the night before he left would have been an idea. Why had he even let her leave New York? Because he hadn't wanted her dead there. He'd spent three years investing in her. Someone was bound to notice.

But in Dallas? In Dallas, no one knew they were connected.

He'd taken her wallet.

Gotten rid of his phone.

Changed his name to Whiskerface.

He'd been meticulous.

Peter fucked up.

The housecleaner unlocked Jessica's room.

David ran up to the door and knocked. Then entered without waiting for a response.

"Excuse me," he said.

She turned, startled. Narrowing her eyes at the sight of him. She clearly didn't like that a strange man had followed her into the room.

She gripped a key in her hand. "Yes?"

"I'm so sorry to bother you." David's face was a sculpture of apology. "But my wife left her hair dryer in the bathroom. Would you mind if I checked? I promise I'll be fast. In and out."

The soothing sound of David's voice was the audible version of what he had done with his face.

The woman stepped back, giving him a tentative nod, then gestured to the bathroom.

He stalked inside.

The shower curtain was pulled back. Peter was gone. Not a single drop of blood.

The room reeked of bleach.

The bitch really hadn't been bluffing.

And now David needed to know where in the fuck that body was.

He stepped out of the bathroom, holding his smile.

"No hair dryer?" she asked.

"No." He shook his head. "Must have left it somewhere else."

"Must have," she said.

He had a feeling that she didn't believe him. But he didn't have time for that now.

David exited the room.

If the motel wall hadn't been made of stucco, he might have thrown his fist into it.

Instead, he called for a cab.

And got the same taxi that had just dropped him off a half hour ago.

"How about a day rate, buddy?" the cabbie said.

"How about fuck off?" David replied.

"You always an asshole?"

"Only when people force me to be."

"That's like the asshole mantra," the driver said, pulling out of the parking lot. "Where are we headed, Mr. Sunshine?"

"The impound lot." David gave him the address.

He hopped out of the cab soon as they pulled to the curb, tossing a twenty into the front seat. Then he ran up the cement stairs and entered the building like he owned the place.

The woman working behind the glass panel looked like a hippopotamus wearing a wig. She didn't seem to like the look of him, either.

"Hey Monica. I'm here about my wife's vehicle."

"Your wife got a name? Your vehicle got a plate?"

He parted his teeth. God, she was funny. "It was a U-Haul." He pulled his ID and passed it through the window. "She was in an accident, and I'm here to pick up her things."

"David Clarke?"

"Yeah."

"You wouldn't be Jessica's husband?"

"That'd be me." His voice sounded more uncertain than he wanted it to.

"She was in an accident?"

"Yeah."

"Funny, she looked healthy when she was here earlier today."

He froze. "She was here?"

"Sure was. Picking up *her* truck."

"Fuck." He rubbed his jaw. "She say where she was going?"

"Far away from you."

He glared at her. "She didn't say that."

"Didn't have to. She drove out of here with purpose."

"Thanks for your help." *Bitch.*

He walked out, not turning around. He had no doubt she wore a patronizing expression. The sour look only found his own face once he was on the other side of the door and calling for yet another cab.

If she'd used the fucking U-Haul to move Peter's body, they could be anywhere. And if she'd used the BMW, well, that opened a whole other kettle of fish that he didn't want to think about.

FUCK.

His phone rang.

He looked at the screen and saw a strange number.

Jessica maybe? She'd called from a payphone once before.

"What do you want, bitch?"

Silence, and then, "Mr. Clarke? Of Prairie Corporation?"

He donned his professional voice. "I'm sorry. I've been getting harassing phone calls all morning. And I just assumed. My deepest apologies. How may I help you?"

"This is Linda Foster. I received a call from your receptionist this morning, confirming Peter's appointment with you this afternoon."

"Appointment?" David hated what his stomach was doing.

"Yeah. Your receptionist said you were due to meet at two. But I haven't been able to reach him all night. Would you happen to know where he is?"

"I have no idea." And that was the God's honest truth. "And I've never even heard of the guy." He repeated the name with notes of incredulity. "Peter Foster?"

"Yes, Peter Foster." Now she sounded irritated. "And of course you know him. You sat at the same table as we did at the charity benefit last year."

Again: *FUCK*.

"Oh, that's right!" David poured a liter of pleasantries into his voice. "Yes. Of course, now I remember. Peter Foster. But I haven't talked to Peter since the benefit."

"That's strange," Linda said.

"And why is that?" David swallowed.

"Peter told me he was doing some work for you."

"Then Peter must be mistaken." David tried to keep the condescension out of his voice; he had been accused of having that tone more than a few times, and he was well aware that it diluted his results. Particularly when it came to sales.

And right now he had to sell Linda on the idea that he had not seen her husband.

He lowered his voice and added tones of under-standing and sympathy. "I'm really sorry, but I don't know why he would say he was working for me. Prairie Corporation isn't hiring and—"

"It wasn't for the company. It was personal."

"Personal?"

"That's what Peter said."

Jesus Christ. If Peter wasn't already dead, David would track him down and cut out his tongue.

"Well, are you sure you have the right David Clarke?"

"I don't imagine there are two of you at Prairie Corporation with the same name?"

"Indeed, there aren't." He forced himself to smile. "I'm one of a kind."

She didn't so much as offer a laugh. "Well, when you see him this afternoon, please let him know to call me."

"I would if we had a meeting. But I assure you we don't."

"Then why did your receptionist call and confirm?"

"She didn't. This must be some kind of prank. Now I really must go. If there's anything I can do to help…"

"I think you've helped enough, Mr. Clarke."

She hung up before he could. Which irritated him. So he blocked her number, because fuck Linda Foster in her sagging face.

It took ten more minutes for his cab to arrive. Fuck. It was the same guy.

"You again," the cabbie said, grinning, as David got inside, treating it like good news instead of the irritant that it was. "Where to this time?"

"A hotel."

"Which one?"

"Surprise me," David said.

"That kind of day, huh?"

"That kind of day," he agreed.

And maybe this time a little light conversation might not be such a bad idea.

Especially once the cabbie agreed that some women, not all of them mind you, could definitely be bitches.

He dropped David off at a Holiday Inn Express.

Or at least he tried to.

"Nope." David shook his head as he pulled into the lot. "I want some place with a bar."

"I could just take you to a liquor store," the cabbie said.

"I want a bar." After all, he might want to look for a little company. Depending on how drunk he got.

The cabbie dropped him at the Ramada.

David rented a room, then walked from the check-in counter directly to the elevator and took it to the skylight bar and lounge. He picked a table by the window, then set his gym bag on the chair next to him.

Then he sat, ordering a whisky on the rocks. When it arrived, he sipped his drink, staring out over the Dallas skyline. *Jessica was out there somewhere.*

But she wouldn't be for long.

And no one would ever find her once she was gone.

Chapter Forty-One

JESS FIXED her gaze on the rearview mirror, glancing back at traffic again whenever she felt like she absolutely needed to, but otherwise watching Amber following her Volvo in David's BMW.

At first, she wasn't sure that Amber had taken the bait. So she'd slowed. Until the asshole behind her had honked.

She was just beginning to think it hadn't worked when she caught sight of the BMW tearing around a cab, closing the distance between the two of them.

She reached over to the passenger seat and lay a hand on the purse. She couldn't feel the gun, but knowing it was inside gave her a strange sense of calm.

She continued driving, then pulled off, heading down one of the service roads that accessed the more industrial areas of the airport.

Jess tried to drive "normally," whatever that was. Surely, Amber had to be wondering what Jess was up to. Why she'd be driving toward the massive hangars with machinery and mechanics, where it reeked of fuel and exhaust.

But the wondering didn't stop her. She kept following Jess.

When this was all over, she was definitely getting rid of that silver BMW. She never wanted to see it again.

A lot like how she felt about David at the moment as well.

She drove past the warehouses, past FedEx and DHL, then behind a nondescript building that didn't even look like it was in operation. Every one of the cars in the quarter-filled parking lot could have been overflow from the packed lot next door.

It was still too busy, so Jess kept driving. But soon she was going to run out of road. But she needn't have worried. At the very end was a warehouse that was clearly not in use.

The window glass was broken. Birds flew in and out of the place, obviously using the building for a nest.

The parking lot — if that's what it was — was full of discarded machinery from the airport. Old luggage racks, half cannibalized baggage carts and old conveyer belts and sections of escalator.

She pulled through the lot, circumventing machinery as though she were making her way through a maze.

There was a kind of nook next to the building and she pulled in there.

Watching.

Waiting.

Her heart pounding in her chest.

And then the BMW rounded the bend.

Jess grabbed her purse and pulled out the gun, clenching it in her hand. She was already sweating. She transferred the weapon to her right hand, then rubbed her palm on her jeans.

Then she grabbed it again, keeping it out of sight.

She watched the BMW maneuver through the maze as she had. And then the vehicle came to a stop. She could see Amber looking around for her. And then she turned in her direction.

They locked eyes.

Jess tucked the gun in the back of her jeans and then got out of the car. Making sure that both her hands were visible.

She walked around and stood in front of the Volvo, folding her arms across her chest and waiting.

Amber still hadn't shut the BMW off. Or got out.

Instead, she drove closer.

Jess stood with her back to the Volvo, trying not to imagine Amber flooring the gas and turning Jess into the meat in a Northern European luxury car sandwich.

But then Amber stopped. The lights flashed, and she turned the car off. And then she got out.

The two of them stood, staring at one another.

It was impossible to not imagine Amber as her reflection.

Jesus, they really did look like one another.

Amber raised her hands. "I just want to talk."

"So talk," Jess said, leaning back against the Volvo. She shouldn't have done that. The gun slipped from her waistband and clattered to the ground.

They both looked at it.

Then they looked at each other.

Amber took a step back.

Jess lunged for the gun, grabbing it.

Amber dove for the car.

Jess shot.

The sound echoed in the abandoned lot. Birds erupted from the empty building in a tornado of feathers.

The bullet struck the car.

Amber yelped as she ran among the rusting machinery.

Jess scrambled to her feet and gave chase. Running past the broken vehicles that were scattered across the tarmac like some giant's discarded toys. All she could hear was her own breath. And the sound of Amber running. Or was that her?

She rounded an abandoned set of aircraft stairs and spotted Amber cowering behind a conveyer belt.

"I JUST WANT TO TALK!"

Jess ran toward her.

Amber ran around the side of the building. Jess followed. Big mistake. Amber was waiting.

She had a metal pole. She slammed it into Jess' arm.

Pain flashed up her arm.

She screamed.

Dropped the gun.

Amber kicked the weapon away. "I want to talk!"

"I don't!" Jess clutched her arm, barreling into Amber, knocking her off her feet.

Amber dropped the pole and grabbed her.

They both went tumbling to the ground.

Jess pushed the other woman away, lunging for the gun.

Amber grabbed her hair.

Jess whirled, kicking Amber in the shin. But Amber deflected the kick and landed a solid punch to her shoulder.

Now they were rolling on the ground, like some kind of stupid wrestling match. They went at each other, punching and kicking.

Jess bit Amber's hand.

Amber punched Jess in the belly.

They rolled. And the gun was right there. Jess grabbed for it. And got it.

But Amber grabbed her wrist, keeping the gun aimed into the sky.

Jess grunted, tearing at Amber's fingers. Drying to dislodge her grip. She knew only one thing. If Amber got the gun, then Jess would be dead.

She kicked. Catching Amber in the breast.

She recoiled, then fell forward.

The gun went off.

Chapter Forty-Two

David woke hungover.

He usually didn't drink a lot, given how much he'd had to juggle over the last three years. Wouldn't do to call Amber Jess, or Jess Amber. Which was part of the reason he made Amber change her name. At least if he slipped up with her, he had an easy excuse.

It would have been harder to explain if he made the same mistake with Jess.

But he never had.

He slid out of bed and walked into the bathroom, flicking on the lights. He winced. What was with hotels and their movie set lighting? So goddamn bright.

He looked in the mirror, staring at his reflection. He almost didn't recognize himself. His eyes were heavy and bloodshot, outlined in dark circles. His pale skin was reddish, his hair completely disheveled.

The pounding headache, sour taste in his mouth, and overall sense of malaise would have been bad enough. But the alcohol made him feel clumsy and slow.

His phone pinged.

He walked back to the bed and sat, staring at his phone. Probably Jess. Hopefully it would be an apology for acting like a shit.

Nope, not a notification at all.

An AirTag had been activated.

He checked the location: *FUCK*.

What the hell was she doing at Prairie Corporation? Well, whatever it was, it wouldn't be good.

David grabbed yesterday's clothes and got dressed in record time.

Then he rang the front desk and asked for a cab. He was told one would be waiting.

He didn't wait to see if the hotel room door had closed behind him as he ran down the hall to the elevator. It took too goddamn long to arrive. But just as he was heading for the stairs, it dinged open.

He snarled at the elderly couple already inside. No doubt they had held it up. They shuffled to the back corner. Though he could feel their disapproval radiating toward him.

When he got to the front drive, there was no cab. And he'd had to wait five minutes. By the time it arrived, David wanted to rip the driver's head from his stupid fucking shoulders.

He gave the address for Prairie Corporation and sat back. He should have rented a vehicle. This guy was too fucking slow.

But eventually they arrived. David gave him cash. Asked for the change. And didn't leave a tip.

The cab peeled away from the curb with a sharp squeal.

It was Saturday, so there were only a handful of cars.

He checked the AirTag again. She was inside the building.

He ran to the front entrance and pushed through the glass doors. His footsteps echoed in the silence of the empty lobby.

"David."

He froze. Then turned around and found himself looking at Grant.

His boss looked confused. "Aren't you supposed to be in New York?"

David didn't answer. And this was why he didn't drink. Despite this being exactly the kind of situation he was born to shine in (high pressure to convert the sale), his mind was sluggish. And failing to provide an escape route in the seconds Grant had given him to reply.

"You have the Henderson meeting in, oh, two hours," Grant said. Then more insulting: "Stan Henderson. Remember him?"

"I had a family emergency." Wasn't that the truth and then some?

"Is it Jess?" Now Grant suddenly looked worried.

"She's fine." But only one of them would be.

"Bella?"

"Never been better."

"Are you drunk, David?"

"Of course I'm not drunk." He rubbed his jaw. God, his breath stunk of alcohol.

"No?"

David paused. He was walking on hot coals. He actually didn't want to lie to his boss and give Grant the idea that he could be obscuring the truth about a few other things as well. He dropped his shoulders.

"Jess and I had a fight last night. She kicked me out." He watched his boss. Trying to leverage some sympathy. But Grant's face remained stoic.

"I suggest a few days off, David."

Jesus. Since when did Grant start acting like his goddamn father? "I'm fine."

"To reflect on your position here at Prairie Corp."

"That's the second time you've used my name."

Grant raised his brows. "I'm sorry?"

"That's what you do when you're asserting yourself with someone. I've seen you do in the room before. Always with subordinates."

"That's not the case here. I'm speaking to you as my peer."

"You mean your employee. You planning on firing me because I missed one meeting, Grant?"

"Calm down."

"I am calm." And he was. This was David being "yeti in a freezer" cool. "I'm just trying to understand what the fuck 'reflect on your position here' means."

"You seem to be going through some family issues." Grant touched his arm. "I merely meant perhaps the workload is too much for you now that you have a baby."

"Bullshit. You're trying to suggest I quit."

Grant's face tightened. "I suggested nothing of the sort."

"I've always been a rainmaker with Prairie. No one can top my sales."

"Yes, you have. But there is something clearly going on at home."

"I'm fixing that. We're fixing that."

"I hope so," Grant said. "Take the weekend to reflect on what I said. And I'll see you Monday."

"Yeah."

Asshole.

He watched Grant leave through the glass doors, then pulled out his phone. Jessica was on the third floor.

He made his way up. And into the conference room. It was empty. Except for a cleaning cart.

He walked out of the room.

Nope, it was saying Jessica was there.

He went back in. And spotted the Air Tag, affixed to the handle of the cart.

He grabbed it. Clenching it in his palm.

"Fucking bitch."

He heard a sound behind him and turned.

A cleaning lady stood there, face pale. He'd obviously heard her. He had no interest in addressing her low self-esteem.

"I'm looking for my wife. Jessica Clarke. She was supposed to meet me here."

The cleaning lady shook her head. "The only person I've seen today is Mr. Miller."

Fuck.

He stalked out, then called for yet another cab. He really should have rented a car. By the time he got back to the Ramada, he was itching to use the phone.

He dialed as soon as he entered his room.

She answered the phone but said nothing.

"What's the point of answering if you're not gonna say anything?" David asked.

She stayed quiet.

"Listen, bitch. I'm gonna make things much fucking worse for you than I ever did for Peter."

She disconnected.

He wanted to chuck the phone against the wall. But he still needed it. He took a breath. Then dialed her again.

This time, she didn't answer. Bringing her much closer to a death by David's own hand.

Which he should have handled himself. From the very

beginning. He went to the bathroom, flicked on the light, and stared at his reflection.

Shit. He looked worse than he thought.

He ran the hot water. Then got a cloth and soaked it. Scrubbed his skin. He still looked like shit, but at least he felt better.

He needed a plan. He was great with plans. It had made him the top earner in the company.

And right now — he only had one plan. And two days in which to do it.

And that was: kill Jessica.

Then, and only then, could he work on repairing the damage she had caused to his family.

He had no doubt that he could bring Jess back into the fold. She was angry at him, sure. But she still loved him. And he could use Bella as a bargaining chip if necessary.

He hated to do that to his kid, but at least she'd be too young to remember.

David exhaled, feeling better.

By this time tomorrow night, everything would be better. Jessica would be dead. And he'd be home with Jess and Bella.

He could see it in his mind. And that was the first step in manifesting what you wanted. Visualize it. And the universe would provide.

And then, when it provided Jessica, the rest would be up to him. But he could handle it.

After all, David had a reputation for always doing what he said he was going to do.

A reputation that Grant had profited from for years.

Even all of those bonus checks added together were a mere pittance compared to what David had brought to the company.

He took another breath.

If Peter had only done his job right, then David wouldn't be in this mess.

Something he took great pride in telling Peter when that whiny asshole threatened his baby.

Nobody threatened Bella. Or his life with Jess.

Not Peter.

Not Jessica.

They were both idiots. Neither as smart as David. It was why he picked them.

Peter thought because he was a big tattooed felon that he was scary. David viewed him as a simple cog in a machine. Something he took great delight in telling Peter.

And when the goon tried to attack him, he simply stabbed him in the heart. With Jessica's knife. That Peter willingly handed him.

The bitch stabbed me with this.

David didn't spend all that time in the gym for nothing. He might look like a nerd. Or a businessman. But he was strong. And lean.

No one threatened his family.

He'd thought he'd gotten rid of the pair with one stone. Kill Peter with Jessica's knife, leave his body in her hotel room.

He never expected her to clean it up. David did have to give her credit for that. She may have outsmarted him there. He imagined she would panic and flee. The maid would find the body. And then it would be twenty-five to life.

Because who would ever believe her batshit story?

But no, Jessica had fucked up his plans.

She should know what was coming to her.

He walked back to the bed, pulling the AirTag out and looking at it. *Bitch.*

He smashed it under his heel.

Then he walked to the mini fridge and gathered every bottle from inside. Dropping them onto the table. Then he sat, unscrewing the lids.

He'd been a heavy drinker when he met Jess. And he could tell she wasn't interested in that type of guy. So he had stopped cold turkey.

Jess had been astounded by his commitment.

But he'd told her that was the kind of guy he was. When he gave his word to something, he always kept it.

He'd seen the flash of interest in her eyes. And he knew that was the secret to unlocking her heart.

So he was giving his word to this: *Jessica would die.*

The only thing was, he had no fucking idea where she was. He called her number. It went straight to voice mail. Which meant that she had blocked him. Fuck. He hung up. Then called her again.

"We need to talk," was all the message said.

He needed her to call back. He had no doubt that he could convince her to meet. Somewhere public.

He'd even kill her then. He could make it look like an accident. A push into traffic. A nudge down some stairs. Whatever the universe gave him, he could make work. But first, she needed to call him back.

He waited.

She didn't call.

He continued to drink. All day and into the night. Ordering more when he ran out. Until his face crashed onto the table.

Chapter Forty-Three

When David climbed into the back of the claustrophobic cab on Sunday night, he was still hungover.

And Jessica had never called.

He's spent much of today wondering what she was up to. Hopefully, nothing. Hopefully, she'd turned tail and run all the way back to New York City.

But he imagined she hadn't.

He imagined she had spent the weekend plotting against him, as much as he had been plotting against her.

He'd killed her twenty times over the past few days. Every way possible, from chainsaw to strangulation. And the bloodier it was, the more she screamed. But of course, it was all in his mind.

He'd returned to the gym a disheveled man with a jigsaw puzzle of stubble and bloodshot eyes that were red enough to inspire fear in small children. He had only one regret: that he'd let things get out of hand. But at the same time, he felt full of resilience.

Inside the gym, he changed back into his work clothes. He thought about taking another shower, but the last one had gone on so long it was like David was trying to use enough hot water to justify the cost of his room.

Maybe he didn't need another shower, but he sure as shit needed a shave.

Because he looked every bit as hungover as he felt.

But then David thought, *fuck it*, and left the gym.

He got back in the cab, which actually waited for him as requested. It was only when they neared Longhorn that he straightened himself out. Trying to look halfway decent. He had no idea how Jess was going to react when she saw him.

But he already had an excuse.

One that had worked before.

He was sorry. He'd do anything … and then he would cry.

His phone pinged with another text. He knew it was Jess.

He looked at the screen, and of course he was right: *where r u?*

He glanced up to see that they were a block away.

Any second now, he texted.

The driver pulled onto Longhorn, slowing before 2097. He didn't even have the back door open before the door flung open. Light flooded out onto the porch and Jess stood in the doorway, staring out at him.

He paid the cabbie, added a substantial tip, then retrieved his overnight bag and laptop from the trunk.

Jess stepped aside to let him in the house.

And he was surprised to see she looked as shit as she did. Eyes tired, hair messy. Stains on her shirt.

The light was too bright inside. He winced. Jess closed the door behind him. But she didn't lock it. That was odd.

But he was tired. He made his way to the stairs. "David."

"Can we talk upstairs? Preferably when I'm horizontal?" He made his way up. Dropping his bags on the floor. Emptying his 'dirty work clothes' into the hamper. He could have just hung them in the closet to use next week and she probably wouldn't have noticed. But he couldn't be bothered.

Jess entered the bedroom. "Have you been drinking?"

"Yeah. I had a shit trip."

She blinked. "Oh."

Something was off. Her hands were flapping about like trapped birds. "What's wrong? You've been texting me since I landed."

Jess tried to talk, but nothing came out. She appeared to be choking on her words.

"Jesus, calm down," David said.

And finally she spoke. "*I killed her*."

He froze. "Killed who?" A lightning strike of panic hit the back of his skull. "Bella?"

"Jesus Christ. No, not Bella."

"Then who?" But David knew.

That's why Jessica hadn't picked it up the phone after that initial call. It wasn't because she was avoiding him. It was because *she* was dead.

Jess had already taken care of the problem he'd spent the whole weekend trying to solve.

He walked over to her, grabbed her by the shoulders, and kissed her. She looked shocked.

"What happened?"

"I didn't mean to, I swear, David. I just wanted to talk to her. But soon as I saw her, I got so mad. And then we started fighting, and she tried to get the—"

She broke off.

"Come on. You're in shock." He gently took her by the

arm and led her out of the room and down the hallway. She hesitated. "We don't want to wake Bella."

She nodded. "Right."

David led her to the kitchen and sat her down at the table.

Then he got out the whisky and a glass. She eyed it with suspicion. He said, "No honey or sleeping pills this time, I swear. Just the straight stuff." He uncapped the bottle and held it over the glass.

He saw hesitation in her eyes, but then she nodded. He poured the drink and slid it over to her. "Tell me what happened."

"It was self-defense."

"I'm sure it was." He got another glass, then sat opposite her and poured a drink for himself.

"Sort of self-defense," she clarified.

"Let's stick with self-defense. Keep going."

She shrugged, wiped her cheeks. "We fought. Struggled for the gun. It went off."

"Jesus, Jess. You could have been killed."

"But I wasn't." She swallowed the whisky. "And I need your help to bury the body."

"There's a body?" So this was definitely real. "What the fuck?"

"I told you I killed her!" she hissed. "How could there not be a body? Did you think she dissolved the moment I shot her?"

"Of course not. Stupid question."

Jess fiddled with her glass. "But that's the part I think I fucked up."

"Why?"

"She's in the trunk."

David froze. "What?"

"Amber is in the trunk."

"What the actual fuck, Jess?"

"What was I supposed to do, David? It's not like I could just leave her there. What if someone found her?"

"What if someone found her in the car?"

"That's a lot less likely. No one saw me kill her. And no one saw me put her in the car."

"That you know of."

"Don't you think if they did, I'd be in jail right now?"

He nodded. She had a point. "But you shouldn't have brought her here."

"I know that. I wasn't thinking straight. Did you miss the part about I KILLED A WOMAN?"

"*Shh.*" David waved a hand at her. "What if Patsy's listening? She's always snooping around."

"You think I don't know that? So what are we going to do?"

"Jesus Christ."

"You said that already," she told him.

He'd thought of a thousand possibilities for disposing of Jessica. Not this one. Not Jess killing her. But it was the best option.

If her body was found, all paths would lead to Jess. She'd had a breakdown before. She could have another. If it came to that.

He held his hand out. "Give me keys to the Volvo."

Jess complied. Then they got up and headed out the backdoor to the garage. He flicked the lights on and was surprised that the Volvo looked so ordinary. Not that he knew what he was expecting.

A large red *X* across the trunk? Blood dripping onto the concrete floor?

Jess closed the door behind them, and they walked to the trunk.

Then David popped it open.

And looked inside.

It was empty.

"Where'd you put the body, Jess?"

She looked at him in confusion. "What are you talking about?" She pointed toward the trunk, her gesture almost violent. "She's right there!"

This was some kind of fucking joke. She was getting him back for the other night. The only thing is, she actually looked terrified.

"There's no body."

"Please don't do this to me again, David." Tears filled her eyes. "Please tell me you see her."

He looked back into the trunk. "Jess."

She walked over and looked down, paling even further. "What?"

"Maybe you didn't kill her?"

"She was dead. I checked."

"Then—"

There was a knock on the side door.

David broke off.

A second later, Patsy peered in.

"I saw the lights go on and thought it might be that woman again."

"It's not," David said. "Just me and Jess."

She glanced from one to the other. Obviously noting Jess's tears. "I heard screaming."

"You heard raised voices," David told her. "We were having a discussion."

"Seemed more like another argument."

"Last time I checked," David said, "your name wasn't on the deed to 2097 Longhorn Drive, so get the fuck off our property."

Patsy's face reformed into an expression of indignity. "I wasn't aware it was inconsiderate to care about one's neighbors."

"Yeah, except you don't care. You only want the gossip. Jess and I are tired of being the number one names on your tongue. So fuck off."

Patsy paled.

"*Yeah*," Jess said, her voice shaking. "Fuck off, Patsy."

The woman sniffed, then retreated. Her footsteps slapping against the ground as she made her way back across the property line.

Then he looked back at Jess. She clapped her hands over her mouth. "Oh, fuck."

"What?"

"I fucked up big time, David."

"Tell me."

"No, you'll hate me."

"I won't hate you, Jess. But I can't help you if you don't tell me what's wrong."

"I must have put her in the—"

"Put her in the what?"

"The BMW."

He stared at her. "WHAT?"

"I was scared. I panicked. All I could think about was getting her in the trunk and getting rid of the car. It's the only thing that makes sense." She grabbed her stomach. "I think I'm gonna be sick."

He grabbed her arm. "You're not gonna be sick. Because I need you to fucking think right now."

She nodded.

"Can you find the car again?"

She shook her head. "No, wait. I can. I remember seeing the Dallas sign — that funny one with the bullet holes that we laugh about."

He nodded. "Okay. Here's what we're going to do."

He stopped, glancing over at the door. Not that he'd heard Patsy return. But he honestly didn't trust that bitch.

"What?" Jess asked.

"Not here. In the house."

He led the way back into the kitchen. Closing the door.

Then he poked his head into the hallway, just to make sure the front door was closed. It was.

He went and sat at the table, and she joined him. "Alright, here's what we're going to do. In a couple of hours—"

"A couple of hours!"

He glared at her. "You want to get caught?"

She shook her head.

"Then in a couple of hours, we'll head out to where you dropped the BMW. And God willing, it's still there, and we'll find a remote spot and bury Amber. Then we'll torch the BMW under the highway with the keys in the ignition. If there's anything left of the car, which I'm damn sure there won't be, there'll be more DNA on it than Dallas PD can process in seven lifetimes. Got it?"

She nodded. Seemed to be taking it all in. Or maybe she was just in shock.

"Then what?" asked Jess.

"Well, come back home and forget that Amber Brown ever happened."

"What if her body is found?"

"It won't be."

"But what if it is?"

"It won't be. Because I won't allow it to be."

"Okay. I'm sorry." She teared up again. "This is all my fault."

David leaned across the table and took her hand. "You were just protecting your family, Jess."

She nodded.

"Try to get some rest before we go."

"What are you going to do?"

"Get organized. We'll need shovels. Bleach. Maybe a saw."

Jess paled.

"Go on. I'll be up shortly."

She sniffed. Got up and headed for the door. Then hesitated. "I'm so sorry, David."

He sighed. "Not your fault. I shouldn't have gone to New York."

"And I shouldn't have screamed at you like that."

He got up, walked over, and kissed her. "It's all right. We'll figure this out together. Now go get some rest. It's gonna be a late night."

She nodded, and a few minutes later, he heard her feet on the stairs.

Then he went back out to the garage. Got shovels. A tarp. Bleach. And axe. Chucked the whole lot into the trunk.

Then he locked the car. Spotted Patsy watching him from her kitchen window. He gave her the finger. She retreated.

A moment later, the light went out.

He went back inside, locking the house. God, he wanted to go now. But no way in hell was he giving Patsy the satisfaction of being a witness in court if he and Jess were caught.

Scratch that, if Jess were caught.

Her body, her trial.

He went upstairs and found her standing next to his hamper, his back to her.

She turned around, holding the gun he kept at the gym.

Shit.

"What's this?" she asked.

"It's a gun."

"It's not my gun."

"Of course it's not your gun. Jesus. I went back to the store and got another one. Just in case."

She looked at him, nodding. "Good idea."

And then it struck him. "Where is your gun?"

"I—" She broke off, looking sick again.

"Jesus, Jess. Don't tell me you left it in the BMW."

"I didn't know what to do with it. It's not like I kill people all the time, David!" Her voice was high and reedy. He heard Bella fuss.

He held up his hands to pacify her. "You're right, you're right. We just need to remember to get it from the car, okay? Otherwise, it can be traced back to you."

"To you," she said.

"What?"

"To you," Jess sniffed. "It's your name on the paper-work at the store."

Christ, she was right. He took the gun from her hand and tucked it into his waistband. "Yeah. So let's not allow that to happen."

Chapter Forty-Four

DAVID WATCHED Jess buckle Bella into the backseat of the Volvo. They'd argued about bringing her.

Jess had wanted to leave her with Clare. Or have Clare come and sit. Until David asked what they were going to tell her. *Can you watch our kid while we go bury a body?*

Best to have no witnesses.

And Jess had agreed.

But how the hell had she mixed up the cars? Unless — she was using again. It wasn't a question. It was a statement. She did seem — altered. Usually, when Jess got thrown, she got snippy.

Not panicky.

Unless she was coming off her high.

Jesus, had she spent the weekend with Bella high?

But he couldn't think about that now.

Jess glanced at him. "Ready?"

He nodded. Hitting the switch on the garage door. Then they both climbed in and got buckled. He reversed the car out of the garage, backing into the alley.

"Where am I going?"

Jess gave him directions. He knew the spot. At least she'd picked a good one. He knew it would be deserted.

David stared into the darkness, his hands gripping the steering wheel tighter than they had in some time.

Jess didn't talk. But her hands were electric. Forming fists, picking at her jeans, itching her face.

"Explain what happened," he said.

"I already did."

"Explain it again. This time with details. I need a little more info than self-defense."

She clenched her teeth. "I'm not going to discuss it with my daughter in the car."

"She's less than a month old."

"I don't care. I'm not doing it."

Fair enough. He tried another tactic. "Where was Bella during all of this?"

"At Clare's."

"How did you get home?"

"I hitched a ride back."

"You hitched a ride? Jesus. You could have been kidnapped."

"Well, I wasn't. I met a very nice pastor and his kids. They gave me a lift to the library. I walked back to the Volvo from there."

"And what'd you tell them?"

"That I shot a woman and was disposing of her car."

"Jesus, Jess."

"What do you think I told him? Date gone bad."

"And Clare didn't wonder where you were all that time?"

She looked him straight in the eye. "I told her I was consulting a divorce lawyer."

"And she bought it? You look a mess."

"I looked just fine. Don't be insulting. I know how to compose myself."

"And you're sure that Amber is dead?"

Jess looked over at David like he was crazy. "I shot her in the head, David. So yes, I'm sure there is no other state she could possibly be in. *Of course she's fucking dead.*" She turned to look at Bella in the back seat. "Sorry about that."

"Where are your clothes?"

"I got rid of them. Dumped them around town."

They continued the rest of the ride in silence. Until she finally gestured to a road. "Down there."

They spend another fifteen minutes on the road, bouncing over potholes and ruts.

"Slow down."

He drove on. Slower. "Well?"

"It's dark. Everything looks different."

The headlights flashed across what looked like an abandoned road. "Stop. Down there."

He turned, driving.

And then the headlights caught a flash of silver. He grinned. The BMW.

"There it is." Jess sounded relieved.

But not as relieved as he felt.

She got out of the car. Walked around and raised the trunk.

He killed the engine and sat for a moment. What if this was all some kind of setup? But for what? What possible reason would Jess have to drag him out here at this time of night?

He glanced into the back seat. And with Bella.

Jess slammed the trunk, carting the shovels toward the BMW.

He got out.

"Get the body," she said.

He nodded and headed for the BMW.

The trunk was already unlatched. That had been smart of her. It would have made it easier for predators to get at the body. Or maybe it wasn't smart. And it was a stupid mistake on her part.

He raised the trunk. And caught the whiff of decay. Christ, she was right. She did kill Amber.

He pulled out his phone and lit it up.

But it wasn't Amber.

Peter stared up at him.

David stumbled back.

Heard the sound of an engine starting.

Jess was behind the wheel, driving off.

He chased after her, raising his hands and waving.

"STOP!"

He opened his mouth to bellow again, not that she could hear him with her window rolled up and the engine roaring.

And then he stopped. Another car was barreling up the road toward them.

What the actual fuck?

Chapter Forty-Five

THE VEHICLE SCREECHED TO A STOP, throwing up gravel.

The headlights were blinding. David threw up an arm to shield his eyes. His heart pounded. He felt sick. Maybe it was the alcohol. Maybe it was something else.

The Volvo came to a halt next to the other car.

A figure emerged and walked toward him. He squinted. Jessica. And she had his gun. No, not his gun. Another one. Peter's maybe?

His blood ran cold. "What the fuck is this?"

Jessica didn't answer, holding her arm steady as Jess climbed out of the Volvo. And now she was holding her weapon.

Both muzzles were trained on him.

David raised his arms. "What the fuck is this?"

"We thought we'd give you an opportunity to have both your wives in the same room at the same time."

"This is hardly a room," David said.

She smiled at him. It was cold. Not a hint of affection. "So you don't deny it."

"Obviously you've talked."

"We have."

"So you never shot her," David said. "It was all a lie."

"Oh, I tried to shoot her," Jess corrected him.

Jessica nodded. "She really did."

Maybe if he could keep them talking, he could get to one of the cars.

He took a step. Jessica fired at his feet. He froze.

The sound of the shot echoed around him.

"Don't move," she said.

He kept his face neutral.

He would not show them he was afraid.

"But soon as it went off, we stared at each other for a long time, David. And I was so relieved it didn't hit her. And I just started crying."

Jessica placed a soft hand on Jess' shoulder.

David curled his lip. Didn't want her touching his wife.

"And so did she. And then we started talking. Or actually, Jessica did."

"Amber," he said.

Jess laughed. It sounded like metal scraping together. "And then *Jessica* started rattling off all kinds of interesting things that only someone you were intimate with would know."

"Intimate for three years," Jessica added.

Jess nodded. "Like how you always hum the opening bars to 'Seven Nation Army' when you're cooking. The scar on your left foot is from stepping on a rusty nail when you were twelve. Your incessant need to align all your books by height."

"Or how you need a glass of warm milk every night before going to bed because of that stupid article you read like ten years ago," Jessica said.

Jess cut in. "Your childhood crush on Gillian Anderson, and how it translates to the bedroom." He flinched. "But the stories I was most interested in were the ones about your life in New York City."

"For three years," Jessica said again.

"For three years." The words sounded different coming out of Jess's mouth. Less angry, more bitter. "Three years spent isolating Jessica from her friends and family, making her quit her job so she could stay at home with the baby. And you know what? It sounded so goddamn familiar. Because it was what you did to me."

"For you," David said, sensing a hook he could cling to. "You always said that you would feel like the luckiest woman in the world if you could stay home with a baby."

"I think you said that *for* me," Jess said.

"Yeah, and I did this all for you. Because I love you."

"Bullshit," the women said in unison.

Jess said, "You know, the only thing we couldn't figure out at first was how you knew Jessica was staying at the Sunset Plains. But then we figured you spotted me following you and probably set up that little bullshit moment with your new employee. While Jessica was inside watching you, Peter was outside tagging the car."

"Are we right?" Jessica asked.

"Jesus." David rolled his eyes, turning to Jess. "You aren't seriously buying any of this, are you?"

"Really, David? That's how you want to play this?" Jess narrowed her eyes at him. "You killed a man. You framed Jessica for it. You were willing to help me cover up her murder. And you know what's worse of all? You played us. For three goddamn years."

"I'm not saying it isn't true." Not anymore, he wasn't. "I'm saying that I need you to understand that I did this all for you. I meant what I said after the affair."

"You said a lot of things after that," said Jess.

"He does love to hear himself talk."

"Shut up, Jessica!"

It was a bad move he shouldn't have made. He saw Jess' eyes get angrier. He held up his hands again. He started conjuring his tears.

"After *we* wouldn't adopt—"

Jess glared at him. "I think you need to shut up now, David."

"I can't." He shook his head. "You need to know how hard I worked for us. The only reason I got with Jessica was so that the three of us — you, me, Bella — could be together. You're the reason we couldn't adopt, Jess. But Jessica could. I just needed to get the hard part done and bring the baby home to you."

Jessica tightened her grip on the gun. "YOU'RE SUCH A FUCKING ASSHOLE!"

"Jessica may have adopted Bella—"

"Her name is Gwen!" Jessica said.

"—but you're her mother. I always intended to bring her home to the woman I really love."

"So you're the hero here because you stole her baby?" Jess stared at David in disbelief.

"Our baby."

"And what about Jessica?" Jess looked over at her. "I still, for the life of me, can't understand how you ever thought that this possibly could work."

"It almost did work," David said.

Jess and Jessica traded another glance.

"She wasn't ever supposed to make it here."

"What does that mean, David?" asked Jess.

He studied her face. What the hell. He had one shot at pulling this off.

"We're waiting," Jessica said.

He kept his eyes on Jess. "Peter was supposed to stop her on the highway."

"What do you mean, stop her?" Jess asked.

He didn't answer.

"The accident!" Jessica said, shuffling back. "That was supposed to be me!"

"What accident?" Jess asked.

"The U-Haul. Only I stopped for a potty break and some coffee."

"You tried to kill her?" Jess sounded horrified.

"Not me. Peter."

She snorted. "Under your authority."

"You can act all high and mighty now, Jess, but if the plan had worked, if Peter hadn't fucked it up, you wouldn't know about any of this. We would be happy right now, happier than we ever have been before. I've loved you since the day that we met, Jess, and I will never love anyone else. We were born for each other. And you know that, same as me. You also know that we can still make this work. If we want to. And I do. I've never wanted anything more in my life. And no one has ever proved their love to their wife more than me. I killed for you. I got a baby for you. I may be guilty of directing my undying love for you in the wrong direction, but that's it. And if I can learn from that experience, I will, but you need to understand—"

"Oh my God," Jess said. "Did he talk this much in New York?"

"Constantly. Sometimes I felt like I was listening to a podcast."

David clenched his jaw. He was done. Jess had chosen the wrong side, and that was on her.

He pulled the gun out from under his shirt and took a step back, toggling his aim in between them.

Jess froze.

"You shouldn't have given it to me," he said, then turned his aim on Jessica.

She paled, whimpering.

Jess stepped in front of her, keeping her gun trained on him. "You're not killing Jessica."

Now they were two gunslingers standing just steps apart.

"Alright then," David said. "We can move on from this in two ways. Jessica can shut the fuck up and disappear, leaving us alone. Or I'll make her disappear. And I like that option better."

"You don't seem to understand that we shared everything," said Jess. "Did you really think I'd let you hurt either one of us?"

David was confused.

"The bullets, David," Jessica said.

He shook his head.

She gestured to the gun.

He looked down at it. Then back at her. Then he pulled the trigger.

Empty. Empty. Empty.

David screamed and lunged at her.

Jessica stepped to the side, and then she and Jess pulled their triggers in unison.

Chapter Forty-Six

GUNSHOTS ECHOED AROUND THEM.

Jess drew a deep breath of cool night air.

Jessica ran over to David. And crouched down. She looked back at Jess, then walked over. "Well?"

She shook her head.

Jess crouched and felt for a pulse. None.

They looked at one another.

"What do we do?" Jess asked. "This is my first murder."

Jessica laughed. It was half hysterical. She clapped her hands over her mouth. Jess placed a hand on her shoulder until she finally stopped.

Then Jessica took a breath. "Clean up. I know how to do that."

Jess nodded. She walked down and got the Volvo, reversing it up the dirt road until she reached the BMW.

Jessica wiped down Peter's gun, then tossed it into the trunk with him.

Then the two of them lifted David into the driver's seat of the BMW. They left the door open. Jessica cleaned her prints off and the gun and added Peter's. Tossing that one into the trunk with him as well.

Then Jessica got out her knife. Cleaned the handle. Then set it in David's hand.

They kept the third gun, the one David had pulled on them.

Then Jess got Bella from the back seat of the Volvo. She looked bright eyed and clearly interested in her adventure.

"Shall we?" she asked.

Jessica nodded, staring at Bella.

"Here," Jess said. "Why don't you hold her on the drive."

Jessica sucked back air and nodded. She handed the baby over, not even feeling a twinge of fear.

Jessica smiled. And Bella cooed. Then they walked back to Jessica's rental car. There was no car seat, but Jessica held tight to Bella. And Jess was careful to drive slowly.

They drove away, leaving the two bodies and cars to either be found or slowly rust away in the desert. Neither woman cared.

The taillights on the Volvo looked like the eyes of a vengeful desert beast, glowing in the murky darkness as they pulled away. Then they disappeared.

The silence was thick, and for a long time neither woman spoke.

"I wonder which one of us has slept worse," Jess said.

Jessica laughed. "Not Bella."

Jess glanced over. Their baby was asleep. "No, not Bella."

It seemed to take less time to return home than drive out. Which was impossible. But Jess felt strangely light.

Like she had a hundred pounds of horror show in her head.

She pulled into the garage and they both got out.

Jess led the way to the back door and unlocked it. Then punched in the security code. Holding the door wide. "Come on in."

And Jessica did. "I'm sorry about breaking in."

"Don't worry about. Though I would like my driver's license back. It's eighty bucks to replace it."

Jessica laughed. "You got it."

They stood for a moment in awkward silence.

"Can I put her to bed?" Jessica asked.

"Of course. You do that. I'll call the cops."

"Do you want to rehearse again?"

"Ugh. No." Jess shook her head. "If I do it one more time, I'll feel over-rehearsed."

"Me too!" Jessica laughed. But she didn't leave right away.

Instead, she waited, watching from the door as though to make sure Jess didn't need her help.

"I'd like to report a missing person," Jess said into the phone.

Jessica smiled and made her way upstairs. That was odd. Not showing a stranger where the nursery was. Breaking in had given her the lay of the land.

Jess rubbed her head. Crazy to think how much had changed in so little time.

She got the whisky out, then sat at the kitchen table. But she couldn't drink what reminded her of David.

The doorbell rang.

She got up and peered into the hall. Saw lights flashing.

Jessica appeared at the top of the stairs and nodded. "I got this."

Jess nodded back and withdrew into the kitchen, listening at the door.

Jessica answered. And invited the cop inside.

She took him to the living room.

Jess couldn't hear what she was saying, but she knew if Jessica needed her help, she'd excuse herself and come and get a glass of water.

The cop was there for about an hour before finally leaving.

Jessica came into the kitchen and pointed to the whisky. "Is that for me?"

"Help yourself."

"He's going to write up a warrant for his arrest." She pointed to her bruised face. "For the domestic violence."

"And you let him know about the gun."

She nodded.

"And this." Jessica hit play on her voice notes.

Listen, you bitch. I'm gonna make things much fucking worse for you than I ever did for Peter.

"Did he ask about Peter?" Jess asked.

Jessica nodded. "I said I think he worked at David's company. And David had recently accused him of stealing his BMW. But I wasn't really sure."

"Did we miss anything?" Jessica asked?

Jess shook her head. "I can't think of anything. Can you?"

Jessica bit her lip. She couldn't. Who knew what would happen when the bodies were discovered? Hopefully, enough days would pass that any DNA they might have left behind would be compromised.

They looked at one another.

Jessica broke first.

Then Jess.

And then they held each other and sobbed with relief.

Chapter Forty-Seven

Jessica started laughing as she swung the U-Haul into the driveway. "You know I never wanted to drive one of these again, right?"

"Suck it up, bitch. That was a year ago."

Jessica mock punched her arm. And then they got serious. Staring out the front windshield at the house.

It had been another three-day drive across the country, this time from Texas to Florida, but Jessica hadn't been alone. She and Jess split the driving duties right down the middle, same as they had been doing with everything else since they killed David.

And neither of them minded the long drive, if it meant getting the hell out of Dallas. The SOLD sign hadn't even been taken down before they left. Patsy hadn't even come out to say goodbye.

"We're here!" Jessica said.

"We're here!" Jess repeated. "I can't believe it."

Bella Gwen started laughing in the backseat.

A fresh start was what they meant to say.

They climbed out and stretched. Then Jessica got Bella

Gwen out of her car seat just as Jess's phone started to ring.

She glanced at the screen. "Detective Cooper." The detective in charge of her case.

Or rather, *their* case, though of course the detective had no idea.

Jessica froze, cradling Bella Gwen.

"Hey Sarah. Good to hear from you. Uh huh. Uh huh." Jess walked off, taking the call that made Jessica too anxious.

She walked up to the front door, but no way was she entering without Jess.

Jess finally ended the call and came over to Jessica with a smile.

"What?" Jessica asked.

"It's over."

"*Over* over? Or just over?"

"*Over* over. They've concluded that Peter was trying to find a hitman to off me, but the deal went south during one of their desert meetings."

"Fuck."

"Yeah."

"And what about the money?"

"They got it to Peter's widow."

"Good."

"Yeah."

They rested their foreheads together for a moment in silence. This was it. A brand-new life.

Then they pulled back, and each kissed Bella Gwen.

"Shall we?" Jess asked.

"I feel like we're newlyweds," Jessica said.

"Ha!"

"Hello there!"

They both turned.

A woman, their age, walked across the grass that separated their house from hers. "Welcome to Locust Run. And yes, we all agree the name is bizarre." She stopped cold. "My gosh, you're the spitting image of one another."

Jess glanced at Jessica.

"We're twins," they said together.

The End

What to read next...

Her perfect life is a lie, but who's the liar?

After being the driver in a car accident that claimed the lives of her sister and her unborn nephew, Denise Grady is ravaged by survivor's guilt. She finds solace in the arms of the only person as shattered as she is: her sister's widowed husband.

They try to pick up the pieces and build a perfect life together, but something is deeply, dangerously wrong.

Pick up your copy of In Her Place today!

About The Authors

Nolon King writes fast-paced psychological thrillers set in the glitzy world of entertainment's power players with a bold, insightful voice. He's not afraid to explore the darker side of human nature through stories featuring families torn apart by secrets and lies.

Nolon loves to write about big questions and moral quandaries. How far would you go to cover up an honest mistake? Would you destroy your career to protect your family? How much of your soul would you sell to get the life of your dreams? Would you cheat on your husband to keep your children safe? Would you give in to a stalker's demands to save your marriage?

Lauren Street has always loved a mystery. As a kid growing up in bible belt country she devoured every whodunit book she could get her sticky little hands on and secretly investigated all of her (seemingly) normal boring neighbors. Sometimes their pets and farm animals too. All grown up now and living in the UK with her thoroughly unsuspicious (and often unsuspecting) husband, she writes domestic psychological thrillers about families torn apart by secrets and lies. And she sometimes still peers over garden walls to check up on the neighbors.

Also By Nolon King

Replaced

Replaced

Cold Vengeance

Cold Vengeance

Cold Reckoning

Cold Retribution

Hidden Justice

Hidden Justice

Hidden Honor

Hidden Shame

Hidden Virtue

No Justice

No Justice

No Escape

No Hope

No Return

No Stopping

No Fear

Once Upon A Crime

Once Upon A Crime

Twice Upon A Lie

Three Times a Murder

Dead For Good

Dead For Good

Left For Dead

Dead Of Night

Wake The Dead

Dead For Life

Stand Alone Novels

Pretty Killer

12

Blown

Miserable Lies

The Target

Secrets We Keep

Close To Home

Heat To Obsession

A Simple Kill

Tell Me No Lies

Red Carpet Black

Fade To Black

Victim

Also By Lauren Street

The Bishop Smoky Mountain Thrillers

Hide Me Away

Fuel To The Flame

Closer By The Hour

A Gamble Either Way

Calling My Children Home

Replaced with Nolon King

Replaced

www.ingramcontent.com/pod-product-compliance
Lightning Source LLC
Chambersburg PA
CBHW010526100726
47903CB00011B/2917